CONTEMPORARY SHORT STORIES

Representative Selections

Volume II

The American Heritage Series
OSKAR PIEST, FOUNDER

The American Heritage Series

CONTEMPORARY SHORT STORIES

Representative Selections

VOLUME II

Edited, with an introduction, by

MAURICE BAUDIN, JR.

Assistant Professor of English, New York University

The American Heritage Series

published by

 THE **BOBBS-MERRILL** COMPANY, INC.
A SUBSIDIARY OF HOWARD W. SAMS & CO., INC.
Publishers • INDIANAPOLIS • NEW YORK

ACKNOWLEDGMENTS

For permission to reprint the stories in the present volume, acknowledgment is made to the following authors, publishers, and agents:

Brandt & Brandt for "The Tuxedos." Copyright, 1939, by Jerome Weidman.

Doubleday & Company, Inc., for "Young Man Axelbrod," from *Selected Short Stories*, by Sinclair Lewis. Copyright, 1917, by Sinclair Lewis; reprinted by permission of Doubleday & Company, Inc.

Edna Ferber for "Old Man Minick," by Edna Ferber; reprinted by permission of the author.

Harcourt, Brace and Company, Inc., for "Send in Your Answer," from *Trial Balance*, copyright, 1945, by William March. Reprinted by permission of Harcourt, Brace and Company, Inc.

J. B. Lippincott Company for "Blood Pressure," from *Guys and Dolls*, by Damon Runyon. Copyright, 1929, 1930, 1931, by Damon Runyon, published by J. B. Lippincott Company.

David Lloyd for "The Old Demon," from *Today and Forever*. Copyright, 1933, 1941, by Pearl S. Buck, published by The John Day Company, Inc. Reprinted by permission of the author's agent David Lloyd, New York, N. Y.

Harold Matson for "Blue Murder." Copyright, 1925, 1953, by Wilbur Daniel Steele; reprinted by permission of Harold Matson.

Harold Ober Associates for "Nice Girl," by Sherwood Anderson. Copyright, 1936, by The New Yorker Magazine, Inc.; reprinted by permission of Harold Ober Associates.

Charles Scribner's Sons for "Babylon Revisited"; reprinted from *Taps at Reveille*, by F. Scott Fitzgerald. Copyright, 1935, by Charles Scribner's Sons; used by permission of the publishers.

For "The Undefeated"; reprinted from *Men Without Women*, by Ernest Hemingway. Copyright, 1926, 1927, by Charles Scribner's Sons; used by permission of the publishers.

The Viking Press, Inc., for "The Leader of the People," from *The Portable Steinbeck*. Copyright, 1938, 1943, by John Steinbeck; reprinted by permission of The Viking Press, Inc., New York.

Thyra Samter Winslow for "City Folks"; reprinted from *Picture Frames*, by Thyra Samter Winslow. Copyright, 1923, by Alfred A. Knopf, Inc.; used by permission of the author.

CONTENTS
·················

CONTEMPORARY SHORT STORIES II

INTRODUCTION

Technique, which in the short story consists of the methods of procedure by which material is presented to most significant effect, is not in itself enough to make a story memorable. The story that offers technical skill without the unique outlook, the individual commentary which is the writer's own, will be little more than a mechanical exercise. It may divert the reader for the time it takes him to finish it, but its lasting appeal will be negligible. The story in which the writer has worked on technique for its own sake, rather than as a concentration upon the most effective methods of conveying certain intellectual and emotional meanings, must stand or fall largely upon its success as epigram; and when it stands, it does not stand very high. Of one of the most famous technical-trick stories of recent time, Frank R. Stockton's "The Lady or the Tiger?," in which the author creates a situation that is dramatic and suspenseful in the extreme, and then modestly declines to solve it, few readers remember for long the question of the conflict which has torn the proud and imperious princess. They recall with amused irritation that the question of whether a lady or a tiger emerged from the door of the lover's choice is forever unanswered; and they forget the more fascinating problem of the quality of the young princess' love for the beset hero, the question of whether jealousy or unselfishness triumphs in her makeup. The story that is primarily a technical experiment (or, as with the Stockton piece, a technical joke) is remembered, if at all, for some device or other.

The inadequacy of mere technique is apparent when one considers the hollowness of certain writers' technical imitations of certain other writers. Many young writers, for instance, have been able to turn out copies of Ernest Hemingway which, when only superficially examined, were quite acceptable. The terse statements, the repetitive rhythms, the understatements in reporting feeling and violence: these traits have become a borrowable currency, the trademark no longer of an individual but of a school. The quality that cannot be borrowed from Hemingway—and it is this that has saved him from successful counterfeit, although it must be said that the copies do somewhat lessen the validity of the original—is the writer's own way of looking at things and reporting them: his individual temperament. The imitators, then, are adopting the devices that Hemingway has found effective for what *he* has to say, and superimposing those devices upon what *they* have to say (frequently very little); and the interest of such technical finagling is primarily statistical: How many Hemingway stories were written last year by writers other than Hemingway? Any original writer possessed of what appear to be borrowable characteristics must expect to be raided by copyists. But a story by Hemingway is easily discernible from, and superior to, a story written under the Hemingway influence. Chekhov remains Chekhov no matter how many Chekhovian insights enlighten his imitators; Katherine Mansfield remains Katherine Mansfield no matter what brilliant flashes dazzle hers.

But what does make a story memorable? The answer is, the material and the writer's attitude toward and feeling about that material as these are communicated (preferably, with the aid of advantageous technique) to the reader. Somerset Maugham has stated, perhaps somewhat confusingly, that the purpose of fiction is not to educate but to entertain. It is true that a short story, even a highly didactic short story, can only exemplify and not formulate; and the things it exemplifies are usually known, in some way, to the reader.

The reader knows, for instance, that people may survive by many years the most meaningful adventures of their lives. Nonetheless, when he reads in Steinbeck's "The Leader of the People" of the grandfather who in his prime led a wagon train across the western plains to the coast, sees the old man's own view of himself impinged upon by his sudden awareness that to some of the younger generation he is a comic bore, with his oft-repeated stories, and to others a pitiable figure, the sensitive reader responds with warmth and understanding to this exemplification of a principle which, baldly stated, would leave him unmoved. And so with Edna Ferber's "Old Man Minick." Nearly everyone, nowadays, can cite statistics and opinions as to juvenile delinquency, the plight of the white-collar worker, the care of the aged. But the glibbest, most persuasive of geriatric aphorisms is meaningless beside Miss Ferber's poignant dramatization of the thesis that dignity and serenity are impossible to an old man who has no rightful place in the world. Or, to take another example, consider William March's "Send in Your Answer." Many people have questioned the decency of the radio or television program on which people parade their emotions out of some consideration of personal gain. But when they read Mr. March's synthesis of the bathetic awfulness of this sort of entertainment, they are experiencing a viewpoint probably sharper and more ruthless than their own as it gives the clinical once-over to utter vulgarity.

Thus, through the exemplification, the specific instance of a human condition, if it has behind it the force of a distinctive, creative personality, the reader may find his sense of identification exercised and his sympathies quickened. This new and fuller understanding of what before was only abstraction, is at once his best reason for reading fiction and fiction's best reason for being. To be unaware of this is of necessity to take a low view of the function of entertainment.

What, then, is a story about? It is about a person or a group functioning believably in a recognizable (not necessarily familiar) situation of representational value. One has only to set a statement of the surface events beside a statement of the meaning of the story to see that the real signification often lies beneath the apparent conflict. For if a story has anything to it, it represents expression on several levels. First, and immediately apparent to the reader, is the narrative level of character and event: Who, engaged in what conflict, does what? Beneath this will be the emotional level (what is the nature of the emotional experience being expressed?) ; the interpretive level (what is the writer's comment? What is he saying about what occurs in the story? What, then, is the theme?) ; and the cultural level (what generalizes the events of the story and makes them applicable to the world of reality? What relates the story to its abstraction?).

It is true of much fiction that apart from its narrative it has little to offer except appeals to the familiar and commonplace. It lends itself, then, to synopsis, but isn't worth synopsizing. It has been remarked of Katherine Mansfield, on the other hand, that what a story of hers says can be adequately conveyed only by the story itself. If it is unfair to synopsize a good and meaningful story, it is equally unfair to give it a surface reading. Tolstoy unwittingly provided a rare example of this sort of injustice when in his pamphlet on Shakespeare (who, his thesis went, far from being a genius was not even average) he made an exposition of the action of *King Lear*, finding it inane, tiresome, incredible and unintelligible. Bent upon demolishing Shakespeare via the surface reading, he chose to discover none of the meanings of the play. And so the reader, bent upon following the surface action, not concerning himself with the other, usually more rewarding levels of meaning, will accept the easiest interpretation, no interpretation at all, and miss the actual meanings, miss what Faulkner calls "the old universal truths lacking which any story is ephemeral and doomed—love and honor and pity and pride and compassion and sacrifice."

SHERWOOD ANDERSON

(1876-1941)

To Sherwood Anderson, along with Ernest Hemingway, belongs much of the credit for the improvement in the short story that was so notable in the 1920's. The product of little formal schooling but much experience through working at odd jobs, serving in the Spanish-American war, managing a paint factory, writing advertising copy, Anderson revolted against the conventionalized plot story which had dominated the field since the days of O. Henry. He rejected as invalid the mechanized plot, which, he felt, resulted in characters trimmed to fit its demands. ". . . the imagination," he wrote (in his *Notebooks*), "must constantly feed upon reality or starve." The belief of Sigmund Freud that most people suffer from an unfulfilled need for self-expression and for more meaningful relations with their fellow beings struck a responsive note in Anderson, whose typical stories are of the feeling of isolation, of the secret dreams and unhappinesses of lonely people. In "Nice Girl," Anderson writes of a character turned malignant through loneliness and frustration. Among Anderson's best books are the story collections *Winesburg, Ohio, The Triumph of the Egg* and *Death in the Woods,* and the reminiscences, *A Story Teller's Story,* and Sherwood Anderson's *Memoirs.*

NICE GIRL

No one saw Agnes come down the stairs. She had a way of going about unnoticed. It made her father and her brother Harry furious. Her father mentioned it sometimes but Harry didn't, which might have been because Agnes knew too much about him. Sometimes Harry just stood and looked at her. "Oh, Lord, help us," he said. Occasionally, when she came into a room where the others were, her father looked

1

up from his book or his paper. "Well," he said in amazement, "how'd you get in here?"

"Why I just came in," Agnes said.

She didn't like such remarks. "Just because I don't go around making a racket," she thought.

She came down the stairs from her own room and heard voices in her mother's room. So there was something in the wind. Her father was scolding. (Agnes was a slender one. She walked softly.) There was a telephone stand in the big hall near the door to her mother's room. The door was closed at the moment. It was called the "big hall" not because it was particularly magnificent but to differentiate it from the upstairs hall. That one was called the "up hall." "I left my glasses on the window ledge in the up hall." It was convenient. Most of the rooms in the house were named, often rather fantastically: "the paint room," "the cider room," "Papa's coat room." The last was from Agnes's grandfather, on her mother's side. Agnes had heard an explanation. "Oh, he always came in and threw his overcoat on the bed in there."

Agnes stopped by the telephone stand, near the door to her mother's room, and picked up the telephone book. If either her father or her mother came suddenly out there, she would be in a quite innocent-seeming position, not eavesdropping on her father and mother, just looking for a number in the book.

She stood, her eyes shining. "So, that's it." Her sister Miriam's husband, Tom Haller, wanted to get a divorce. Agnes was thrilled, even joyous. Of course, not because Miriam was in trouble. "So, she didn't tell me that *that's* why she came home from Chicago," she thought. "Tom's chucking her, eh?" and then right away her thoughts went back to Miriam. "The sly little cat—not saying a word to me." They were always thinking in the family that Miriam was open and aboveboard. "They accuse me of being sly. What about *her?*" And now both her father and her mother knew about Tom and Miriam. If it turned out that Harry also knew and that Agnes herself was the only one left out, she would be good and sore. If she had any sympathy for Miriam, it would go fast enough if she found *that* out.

Her father was furious and was tramping up and down in her mother's room. "If he comes here, I'll show him!" he shouted. Tom Haller wanted a divorce and he didn't want to pay Miriam alimony.

"By God, I'll make him pay to the last cent. I'll take his skin off inch by inch."

It would be funny to see her father trying to take Tom Haller's skin off. Alfred Wilson, the father, was a rather small man and Tom was big. As for Harry, he was a physical weakling. Harry was older than either Miriam or Agnes, and had been in the World War. He had been gassed, and there was something wrong with his lungs and he got drunk. He got drunk oftener than anyone, except Agnes, in the family knew. She knew where he kept his bottle of whiskey hidden in the house. Harry knew that she was on to a lot no one else knew. It made him a little afraid of her.

Her father kept tramping up and down in her mother's room. All the others in the house thought that Agnes was away for the afternoon. She had told them all she was going driving with Mary Culbertson and had left the house just after lunch. Then she had changed her mind and had come back. She had phoned Mary from the drugstore and had come silently into the house and had gone up to her own room. Had she been playing a hunch? She hadn't known why she suddenly decided not to go with Mary. Her father's shoes made a queer creaking noise on the floor of her mother's room.

"Alfred, where did you get those shoes?" her mother said, and "Oh, damn shoes!" her father shouted. There was talk about her father's speaking too loud. "Kate will hear you, Alfred," her mother said. Kate was the new maid, a tall red-haired country woman. She had been working in the Wilson family only two weeks. It wouldn't do to let Kate find out too much about the family too rapidly. It was no good letting a maid become too familiar, almost impertinent, the way the last one was allowed to do.

Agnes stood now by the door of her mother's room listening, the telephone book in her hand, and then her father came to the door. She saw the knob turn, but he didn't come out at once. He just stood by the door talking big. So Agnes put down the telephone book and went, softly as usual, out to the front porch. She sat there a moment and then went to the side porch. She decided she would wait there. Presently her father would go off downtown to his law office and she would go to her mother's room. She would find out if her mother wanted to go on keeping everything a secret. Miriam had left the house just before Agnes came downstairs, and Agnes knew that Miriam would go downtown and find Harry. The two would go somewhere in Harry's car. "I bet they drink together," Agnes thought. She thought that it didn't look just right, a brother and sister being so thick. Before Miriam had married Tom Haller, she and Harry were always together during the years Miriam was going away to school and coming home for summer vacations. Agnes knew at that time that Miriam used to put up with, and even encourage, Harry's drinking. Before repeal, Harry had got his liquor from a man at the filling station out on the Mud Creek Highway. Agnes had known about it. She even knew that Miriam sometimes drove out there with Harry and waited in the car while he went in. Agnes had got the filling-station man arrested and sent to jail. No one knew about it. She had written a letter to the sheriff and signed a made-up name, and it worked. The sheriff raided the place and sure enough found a lot of whiskey, and the man was tried and sent to jail, but of course Harry just began getting whiskey somewhere else.

What had most aroused Agnes the day she heard her father and mother discussing Miriam's divorce was something that happened after she went down to meet Mary Culbertson and changed her mind. She had come back into the house unnoticed and had gone to her own room, off the "up hall." Then the telegraph boy arrived on his bicycle and she saw him through the window. He rang the bell and Kate, the maid, answered it. Her father was already in her mother's room with the door closed, but he wasn't talking loud then. The new maid was such a big, red-haired, red-armed thing and she had such a harsh, untrained voice, thought Agnes. And what a nerve, too, for she came to the foot of the stairs and called. "Miriam! Miriam! Here's a telegram for you," she called. Miriam should have reprimanded her. "Such management of things to let a maid call you by your first name!" Kate often called that way to Agnes, too, but Agnes couldn't protest, because if she did, if she were the only one in the house who did, she would only make the maid sore and then she couldn't get a thing done for her. If she wanted a dress pressed in a hurry, for instance, Kate could put it off, or even get purposely careless and burn it.

After she heard Kate call, Agnes had just stayed in her room, watching and listening. The door into the hall was closed, but Agnes went and opened it a crack. Miriam came quickly out of her own room, on the other side of the hall, and went part way down the stairs. If that new maid, Kate, were well trained, as she should be, if she had been told plainly by the mother how to do things when she had first come into the house, of course she would have come quietly up the stairs to the door of Miriam's room and knocked quietly. Agnes stood inside the door of her room and, through the crack, watched Miriam going part way down the stairs to the landing where the stairs turned, and Kate coming part way up.

"I signed for it," Kate said, handing the telegram to Miriam. "I got something boiling on the stove," she said, but she stood and waited until Miriam read it. That was because she was so curious. The nerve of her, calling out Miriam's name like that, actually screaming it, "Miriam! Miriam!"

Miriam wasn't slender like Agnes and she wasn't pretty. Her mouth was too big. It was like her mother's mouth. Miriam was an intellectual and she had gone away to school, to the University of Chicago, and Agnes hadn't. Just when Agnes, who was four years older than Miriam, got out of high school, her father went and speculated, like a fool, and lost a lot of money. He got back on his feet again after three or four years, and then he offered to send Agnes away to school, but she wouldn't go. She wasn't going to be in classes where she was the oldest one.

Agnes thought she was prettier than Miriam. She knew she was. She thought it was foolish, wasting your time with books. Men didn't like bookish women. She had a mass of shining, reddish-brown hair and nice, interesting, grayish-green eyes. She spent a lot of time keeping herself looking nice. It paid. Sometimes Harry tried to kid her about it, but she knew how to tell Harry where to get off, for, once, she had seen something happen. It was with the maid, the married one, they'd had just before Kate came. Her name was Mrs. Henry and her husband had got arrested for hitting a man with a billiard cue in a tough poolroom. She was good-looking, a tall blonde, and Agnes had heard things about her. Agnes wouldn't go so far as to say there was actually something between her and Harry, but one day Harry was in the kitchen, where he never should have been, right in the middle of the afternoon. Agnes thought he was a little lit up. He was trying to get a piece of fried chicken out of the refrigerator and Mrs. Henry didn't want him to have it. Agnes had come to the kitchen door and stood looking. Mrs. Henry said that if Harry took any of the chicken there wouldn't be enough for dinner. The woman's first name was Alice. "Ah, what the hell, Alice?" Harry said, and then she started to push him away from the icebox; they were both laughing, and Harry gave her a quick push and turned her right around and slapped her on the place where a person sits down. It was a sign of something.

On the stairs that day, Kate, the new maid, was burning with curiosity. She didn't really care if something did boil over in the kitchen. If you get a telegram in a family and have a maid who is a country woman, just off the farm, she always thinks something dreadful must have happened. Country people, farmers, don't get telegrams except when someone dies. Miriam's hand trembled as she opened the envelope. She went to her room and put on her hat and coat and went downstairs and called her father out of her mother's room and said a few words to him Agnes couldn't hear, although she was in the "up hall" listening, and then Miriam went out. But afterward Agnes heard her father go back into his wife's room and heard him talking to her about the telegram. It said that Tom Haller was coming on Wednesday. It was only Monday now. He was coming to have it out with Miriam about a divorce. That was it. Agnes had got a good look at Miriam before she went out and saw how scared and upset she looked. "I'm glad she's in trouble," she thought. Then she was ashamed and thought, "No, I'm not."

She had thought something was up when Miriam first came home from Chicago, two months before. She and Mollie Wilson, her mother, were always having whispered conferences, and there was a queer strained look in Miriam's eyes. She didn't have interesting eyes like Agnes's—they were a faded kind of blue. "I'll bet she's pregnant," Agnes thought at first, but later, before she found out the truth, she had already changed her mind. (Miriam and Tom Haller had been married three years. Miriam had got him when she went to Chicago to school.) Agnes had noticed things about Miriam, and wondered why she always looked as though she had been crying and why she was letting herself get fat. But she found out that it wasn't what she thought at first. Still, it was funny that neither Miriam nor her mother told Agnes, even though the Wilsons had always been a secretive family. She thought that if it were herself—if she, rather than Miriam, had married Tom Haller—this couldn't have happened, because of the way she felt the first time she ever saw Tom, when he came to Carlsville to marry Miriam. She thought that, if it had been herself, she would have got pregnant right away, and decided that if she ever got married that would be the best way. "I'll bet I could, too," she thought.

She had a lot of thoughts, after Miriam got the telegram and before that, ever since Miriam had married Tom. Tom, who was tall and blond, had come from Chicago and had married Miriam in the Wilsons' house in Carlsville. Agnes had been bridesmaid. It was quite a wedding, because Alfred Wilson was in politics. He was in the State Senate, and of course he had to invite everyone. The joke was that two of the most important men in Carlsville to invite, for political reasons, he didn't invite at all. He thought he had invited them, but he had not. Agnes had mailed the invitations, had carried them to the post office after they were addressed, and she had taken the two invitations out of the pile and torn them up. The wives of those two politicians were rarely invited anywhere by the best people, yet even so, Agnes hardly knew why she did it. She just did.

She herself, she thought, had been quite nice at the wedding. Tom Haller had come bringing another man with him, to be best man—certainly not a very interesting-looking man. He was older than Tom, a young professor of English or something, and he wore glasses and was shy. Agnes didn't like him at all and, besides, he was poor and an intellectual and nearsighted. Agnes would even bet anything that Tom had loaned his best man the money to come down to Carlsville from Chicago. Although she didn't want to say anything against Miriam, she just couldn't see what Tom and Miriam saw in each other, whereas if Miriam had taken a fancy to that English professor—he and Miriam both being so bookish—it would have made more sense. Of course she didn't say anything of that sort. She liked Tom. Once, when she was coming downstairs, the evening before the wedding—she had been upstairs in her room trying on her bridesmaid's gown and was going down to show it to her mother—she met Tom on the stairs, and he suddenly took her into his arms and kissed her. He said it was a brotherly kiss, but it wasn't. She knew better than that.

Finally, that day, after she had found out what all the other Wilsons knew, none of them having bothered to tell her, Agnes went up into her own room and sat by a window. She had a very satisfactory hour sitting up there and thinking. So the family hadn't thought it wise to tell her. Tom Haller was coming to see Miriam to talk over with her the matter of getting a divorce. Anyway, Tom couldn't get married again until he got the divorce, but, in spite of her father, Miriam would let him have it. Very likely she wouldn't even ask for alimony. Miriam was a fool. Agnes remembered again that moment on the stairs with Tom, the night before his wedding. "They are all fools," Agnes thought, and decided that if the family wanted to go on keeping things from her, she would be justified in keeping secret her own plans. She sat for a time having her own thoughts, and then got up and looked at herself in the glass. Tom Haller was to arrive in two days. "I'll go and get me a permanent tomorrow," she thought.

DAMON RUNYON

(1884-1946)

Damon Runyon's typical character is someone from the fringe of the entertainment or the sports world, or someone whose livelihood is a sporadic series of quick pennies from some minor unlawful enterprise. Influenced very considerably by Ring Lardner and his experiments in American idiom, Runyon fashioned a style for his own stories, especially his first-person stories, that has become his trademark. He was an inveterate user of slang and wisecracks, and he used them in a context of simple statement, simple understatement and equally simple but preposterous overstatement. His narrator characters are never at a loss for words, even though they rarely find the right words; and it is in the ingenuity with which they manhandle English speech that they are most interesting, for the adventures in which they engage become fairly predictable after one has read a certain number of Runyon stories. Like any stylist whose chief characteristics are prominent and not too numerous, Runyon has been widely imitated by amateur writers. One of his best story collections is *Guys and Dolls*, in which "Blood Pressure" appears.

BLOOD PRESSURE

IT IS MAYBE ELEVEN-THIRTY of a Wednesday night, and I am standing at the corner of Forty-eighth Street and Seventh Avenue, thinking about my blood pressure, which is a proposition I never before think much about.

In fact, I never hear of my blood pressure before this Wednesday afternoon when I go around to see Doc Brennan about my stomach, and he puts a gag on my arm and tells me that my blood pressure is higher than a cat's back, and the idea is for me to be careful about what I eat, and to avoid excitement, or I may pop off all of a sudden when I am least expecting it.

"A nervous man such as you with a blood pressure away up in the paint cards must live quietly," Doc Brennan says. "Ten bucks, please," he says.

Well, I am standing there thinking it is not going to be so tough to avoid excitement the way things are around this town right now, and wishing I have my ten bucks back to bet it on Sun Beau in the fourth race at Pimlico the next day, when all of a sudden I look up, and who is in front of me but Rusty Charley.

Now if I have any idea Rusty Charley is coming my way, you can go and bet all the coffee in Java I will be somewhere else at once, for Rusty Charley is not a guy I wish to have any truck with whatever. In fact, I wish no part of him. Furthermore, nobody else in this town wishes to have any part of Rusty Charley, for he is a hard guy indeed. In fact, there is no harder guy anywhere in the world. He is a big wide guy with two large hard hands and a great deal of very bad disposition, and he thinks nothing of knocking people down and stepping on their kissers if he feels like it.

In fact, this Rusty Charley is what is called a gorill, because he is known to often carry a gun in his pants pocket, and sometimes to shoot people down as dead as door nails with it if he does not like the way they wear their hats—and Rusty Charley is very critical of hats. The chances are Rusty Charley shoots many a guy in this man's town, and those he does not shoot he sticks with his shiv—which is a knife—and the only reason he is not in jail is because he just gets out of it, and the law does not have time to think up something to put him back in again for.

Anyway, the first thing I know about Rusty Charley being in my neighborhood is when I hear him saying: "Well, well, well, here we are!"

Then he grabs me by the collar, so it is no use of me thinking of taking it on the lam away from there, although I greatly wish to do so.

"Hello, Rusty," I say, very pleasant. "What is the score?"

"Everything is about even," Rusty says. "I am glad to see you, because I am looking for company. I am over in Philadelphia for three days on business."

"I hope and trust that you do all right for yourself in Philly, Rusty," I say; but his news makes me very nervous, because I am a great hand for reading the papers and I have a pretty good idea what Rusty's business in Philly is. It is only the day before that I see a little item from Philly in the papers about how Gloomy Gus Smallwood, who is a very large operator in the alcohol business there, is guzzled right at his front door.

Of course I do not know that Rusty Charley is the party who guzzles Gloomy Gus Smallwood, but Rusty Charley is in Philly when Gus is guzzled, and I can put two and two together as well as anybody. It is the same thing as if there is a bank robbery in Cleveland, Ohio, and Rusty Charley is in Cleveland, Ohio, or near there. So I am very nervous, and I figure it is a sure thing my blood pressure is going up every second.

"How much dough do you have on you?" Rusty says. "I am plumb broke."

"I do not have more than a couple of bobs, Rusty," I say. "I pay a doctor ten bucks today to find out my blood pressure is very bad. But of course you are welcome to what I have."

"Well, a couple of bobs is no good to high-class guys like you and me," Rusty says. "Let us go to Nathan Detroit's crap game and win some money."

Now, of course, I do not wish to go to Nathan Detroit's crap game; and if I do wish to go there I do not wish to go with Rusty Charley, because a guy is sometimes judged by the company he keeps, especially around crap games, and Rusty Charley is apt to be considered bad company. Anyway, I do not have any dough to shoot craps with, and if I do have dough to shoot craps with, I will not shoot craps with it at all, but will bet it on Sun Beau, or maybe take it home and pay off some of the overhead around my joint, such as rent.

Furthermore, I remember what Doc Brennan tells me about avoiding excitement, and I know there is apt to be excitement around Nathan Detroit's crap game if Rusty Charley goes there, and maybe run my blood pressure up and cause me to pop off very unexpected. In fact, I already feel my blood jumping more than somewhat inside me, but naturally I am not going to give Rusty Charley any argument, so we go to Nathan Detroit's crap game.

This crap game is over a garage in Fifty-second Street this particular night, though sometimes it is over a restaurant in Forty-seventh Street, or in back of a cigar store in Forty-fourth Street. In fact, Nathan Detroit's crap game is apt to be anywhere, because it moves around every night, as there is no sense in a crap game staying in one spot until the coppers find out where it is.

So Nathan Detroit moves his crap game from spot to spot, and citizens wishing to do business with him have to ask where he is every night; and of course almost everybody on Broadway knows this, as Nathan Detroit has guys walking up and down, and around and about, telling the public his address, and giving out the password for the evening.

Well, Jack the Beefer is sitting in an automobile outside the garage in Fifty-second Street when Rusty Charley and I come along, and he says "Kansas City," very low, as we pass, this being the password for the evening; but we do not have to use any password whatever when we climb the stairs over the garage, because the minute Solid John, the doorman, peeks out through his peephole when we knock, and sees Rusty Charley with me, he opens up very quick indeed, and gives us a big castor-oil smile, for nobody in this town is keeping doors shut on Rusty Charley very long.

It is a very dirty room over the garage, and full of smoke, and the crap game is on an old pool table; and around the table and packed in so close you cannot get a knitting needle between any two guys with a mawl, are all the high shots in town, for there is plenty of money around at this time, and many citizens are very prosperous. Furthermore, I wish to say there are some very tough guys around the table, too, including guys who will shoot you in the head, or maybe the stomach, and think nothing whatever about the matter.

In fact, when I see such guys as Harry the Horse, from Brooklyn, and Sleepout Sam Levinsky, and Lone Louie, from Harlem, I know this is a bad place for my blood pressure, for these are very tough guys indeed, and are known as such to one and all in this town.

But there they are wedged up against the table with Nick the Greek, Big Nig, Gray John, Okay Okun, and many other high shots, and they all have big coarse G notes in their hands which they are tossing around back and forth as if these G notes are nothing but pieces of waste paper.

On the outside of the mob at the table are a lot of small operators who are trying to cram their fists in between the high shots now and then to get down a bet, and there are also guys present who are called Shylocks, because they will lend you dough when you go broke at the table, on watches or rings, or maybe cuff links, at very good interest.

Well, as I say, there is no room at the table for as many as one more very thin guy when we walk into the joint, but Rusty Charley lets out a big hello as we enter, and the guys all look around, and the next minute there is space at the table big enough not only for Rusty Charley but for me too. It really is quite magical the way there is suddenly room for us when there is no room whatever for anybody when we come in.

"Who is the gunner?" Rusty Charley asks, looking all around.

"Why, you are, Charley," Big Nig, the stick man in the game, says very quick, handing Charley a pair of dice, although afterward I hear that his pal is right in the middle of a roll trying to make nine when we step up to the table. Everybody is very quiet, just looking at Charley. Nobody pays any attention to me, because I am known to one and all as a guy who is just around, and nobody figures me in on any part of Charley, although Harry the Horse looks at me once in a way that I know is no good for my blood pressure, or for anybody else's blood pressure as far as this goes.

Well, Charley takes the dice and turns to a little guy in a derby hat who is standing next to him scrooching back so Charley will not notice him, and Charley lifts the derby hat off the little guy's head, and rattles the dice in his hand, and chucks them into the hat and goes "Hah!" like crap shooters always do when they are rolling the dice. Then Charley peeks into the hat and says "Ten," although he does not let anybody else look in the hat, not even me, so nobody knows if Charley throws a ten, or what.

But, of course, nobody around is going to up and doubt that Rusty Charley throws a ten, because Charley may figure it is the same thing as calling him a liar, and Charley is such a guy as is apt to hate being called a liar.

Now Nathan Detroit's crap game is what is called a head-and-head game, although some guys call it a fading game, because the guys bet against each other rather than against the bank, or house. It is just the same kind of game as when two guys get together and start shooting craps against each other, and Nathan Detroit does not have to bother with a regular crap table and a layout such as they have in gambling houses. In fact, about all Nathan Detroit has to do with the game is to find a spot, furnish the dice and take his percentage which is by no means bad.

In such a game as this there is no real action until a guy is out on a point, and then the guys around commence to bet he makes this point, or that he does not make this point, and the odds in any country in the world that a guy does not make a ten with a pair of dice before he rolls seven, is two to one.

Well, when Charley says he rolls ten in the derby hat nobody opens their trap, and Charley looks all around the table, and all of a sudden he sees Jew Louie at one end, although Jew Louie seems to be trying to shrink himself up when Charley's eyes light on him.

"I will take the odds for five C's," Charley says, "and Louie, you get it"—meaning he is letting Louie bet him $1000 to $500 that he does not make his ten.

Now Jew Louie is a small operator at all times and more

of a Shylock than he is a player, and the only reason he is up there against the table at all at this moment is because he moves up to lend Nick the Greek some dough; and ordinarily there is no more chance of Jew Louie betting a thousand to five hundred on any proposition whatever than there is of him giving his dough to the Salvation Army, which is no chance at all. It is a sure thing he will never think of betting a thousand to five hundred a guy will not make ten with the dice, and when Rusty Charley tells Louie he has such a bet, Louie starts trembling all over.

The others around the table do not say a word, and so Charley rattles the dice again in his duke, blows on them, and chucks them into the derby hat and says "Hah!" But, of course, nobody can see in the derby hat except Charley, and he peeks in at the dice and says "Five." He rattles the dice once more and chucks them into the derby and says "Hah!" and then after peeking into the hat at the dice he says "Eight." I am commencing to sweat for fear he may heave a seven in the hat and blow his bet, and I know Charley has no five C's to pay off with, although, of course, I also know Charley has no idea of paying off, no matter what he heaves.

On the next chuck, Charley yells "Money!"—meaning he finally makes his ten, although nobody sees it but him; and he reaches out his hand to Jew Louie, and Jew Louie hands him a big fat G note, very, very slow. In all my life I never see a sadder-looking guy than Louie when he is parting with his dough. If Louie has any idea of asking Charley to let him see the dice in the hat to make sure about the ten, he does not speak about the matter, and as Charley does not seem to wish to show the ten around, nobody else says anything either, probably figuring Rusty Charley is not a guy who is apt to let anybody question his word especially over such a small matter as a ten.

"Well," Charley says, putting Louie's G note in his pocket, "I think this is enough for me tonight," and he hands the derby hat back to the little guy who owns it and motions me to come on, which I am glad to do, as the silence in the joint is making my stomach go up and down inside me, and I know this is bad for my blood pressure. Nobody as much as opens his face from the time we go in until we start out, and you will be surprised how nervous it makes you to be in a big crowd with everybody dead still, especially when you figure it a spot that is liable to get hot any minute. It is only just as we get to the door that anybody speaks, and who is it but Jew Louie, who pipes up and says to Rusty Charley like this:

"Charley," he says, "do you make it the hard way?"

Well, everybody laughs, and we go on out, but I never hear myself whether Charley makes his ten with a six and a four, or with two fives—which is the hard way to make a ten with the dice—although I often wonder about the matter afterward.

I am hoping that I can now get away from Rusty Charley and go on home, because I can see he is the last guy in the world to have around a blood pressure, and, furthermore, that people may get the wrong idea of me if I stick around with him, but when I suggest going to Charley, he seems to be hurt.

"Why," Charley says, "you are a fine guy to be talking of quitting a pal just as we are starting out. You will certainly stay with me because I like company, and we will go down to Ikey the Pig's and play stuss. Ikey is an old friend of mine, and I owe him a complimentary play."

Now, of course, I do not wish to go to Ikey the Pig's, because it is a place away downtown, and I do not wish to play stuss, because this is a game which I am never able to figure out myself, and, furthermore, I remember Doc Brennan says I ought to get a little sleep now and then; but I see no use in hurting Charley's feelings, especially as he is apt to do something drastic to me if I do not go.

So he calls a taxi, and we start downtown for Ikey the Pig's, and the jockey who is driving the short goes so fast that it makes my blood pressure go up a foot to a foot and a half from the way I feel inside, although Rusty Charley pays no attention to the speed. Finally I stick my head out the window and ask the jockey to please take it a little easy, as I wish to get where I am going all in one piece, but the guy only keeps busting along.

We are at the corner of Nineteenth and Broadway when all of a sudden Rusty Charley yells at the jockey to pull up a minute, which the guy does. Then Charley steps out of the cab and says to the jockey like this:

"When a customer asks you to take it easy, why do you not be nice and take it easy? Now see what you get."

And Rusty Charley hauls off and clips the jockey a punch on the chin that knocks the poor guy right off the seat into the street, and then Charley climbs into the seat himself and away we go with Charley driving, leaving the guy stretched out as stiff as a board. Now Rusty Charley once drives a short for a living himself, until the coppers get an idea that he is not always delivering his customers to the right address, especially such as may happen to be drunk when he gets them, and he is a pretty fair driver, but he only looks one way, which is straight ahead.

Personally, I never wish to ride with Charley in a taxicab under any circumstances, especially if he is driving, because he certainly drives very fast. He pulls up a block from Ikey the Pig's, and says we will leave the short there until somebody finds it and turns it in, but just as we are walking away from the short up steps a copper in uniform and claims we cannot park the short in this spot without a driver.

Well, Rusty Charley just naturally hates to have coppers give him any advice, so what does he do but peek up and down the street to see if anybody is looking, and then haul off and clout the copper on the chin, knocking him bow-legged. I wish to say I never see a more accurate puncher than Rusty Charley, because he always connects with that old button. As the copper tumbles, Rusty Charley grabs me by the arm and starts me running up a side street, and after we go about a block we dodge into Ikey the Pig's.

It is what is called a stuss house, and many prominent citizens of the neighborhood are present playing stuss. Nobody seems any too glad to see Rusty Charley, although Ikey the

Pig lets on he is tickled half to death. This Ikey the Pig is a short fat-necked guy who will look very natural at New Year's, undressed, and with an apple in his mouth, but it seems he and Rusty Charley are really old-time friends, and think fairly well of each other in spots.

But I can see that Ikey the Pig is not so tickled when he finds Charley is there to gamble, although Charley flashes his G note at once, and says he does not mind losing a little dough to Ikey just for old time's sake. But I judge Ikey the Pig knows he is never going to handle Charley's G note, because Charley puts it back in his pocket and it never comes out again even though Charley gets off loser playing stuss right away.

Well, at five o'clock in the morning, Charley is stuck one hundred and thirty G's, which is plenty of money even when a guy is playing on his muscle, and of course Ikey the Pig knows there is no chance of getting one hundred and thirty cents off of Rusty Charley, let alone that many thousands. Everybody else is gone by this time and Ikey wishes to close up. He is willing to take Charley's marker for a million if necessary to get Charley out, but the trouble is in stuss a guy is entitled to get back a percentage of what he loses, and Ikey figures Charley is sure to wish this percentage even if he gives a marker, and the percentage will wreck Ikey's joint.

Furthermore, Rusty Charley says he will not quit loser under such circumstances because Ikey is his friend, so what happens Ikey finally sends out and hires a cheater by the name of Dopey Goldberg, who takes to dealing the game and in no time he has Rusty Charley even by cheating in Rusty Charley's favor.

Personally, I do not pay much attention to the play but grab myself a few winks of sleep in a chair in a corner, and the rest seems to help my blood pressure no little. In fact, I am not noticing my blood pressure at all when Rusty Charley and I get out of Ikey the Pig's, because I figure Charley will let me go home and I can go to bed. But although it is six o'clock, and coming on broad daylight when we leave Ikey's,

Charley is still full of zing, and nothing will do him but we must go to a joint that is called the Bohemian Club.

Well, this idea starts my blood pressure going again, because the Bohemian Club is nothing but a deadfall where guys and dolls go when there is positively no other place in town open, and it is run by a guy by the name of Knife O'Halloran, who comes from down around Greenwich Village and is considered a very bad character. It is well known to one and all that a guy is apt to lose his life in Knife O'Halloran's any night, even if he does nothing more than drink Knife O'Halloran's liquor.

But Rusty Charley insists on going there, so naturally I go with him; and at first everything is very quiet and peaceful, except that a lot of guys and dolls in evening clothes, who wind up there after being in the night clubs all night, are yelling in one corner of the joint. Rusty Charley and Knife O'Halloran are having a drink together out of a bottle which Knife carries in his pocket, so as not to get it mixed up with the liquor he sells his customers, and are cutting up old touches of the time when they run with the Hudson Dusters together, when all of a sudden in comes four coppers in plain clothes.

Now these coppers are off duty and are meaning no harm to anybody, and are only wishing to have a dram or two before going home, and the chances are they will pay no attention to Rusty Charley if he minds his own business, although of course they know who he is very well indeed and will take great pleasure in putting the old sleeve on him if they only have a few charges against him, which they do not. So they do not give him a tumble. But if there is one thing Rusty Charley hates it is a copper, and he starts eying them from the minute they sit down at a table, and by and by I hear him say to Knife O'Halloran like this:

"Knife," Charley says, "what is the most beautiful sight in the world?"

"I do not know, Charley," Knife says. "What is the most beautiful sight in the world?"

"Four dead coppers in a row," Charley says.

Well, at this I personally ease myself over toward the door, because I never wish to have any trouble with coppers, and especially with four coppers, so I do not see everything that comes off. All I see is Rusty Charley grabbing at the big foot which one of the coppers kicks at him, and then everybody seems to go into a huddle, and the guys and dolls in evening dress start squawking, and my blood pressure goes up to maybe a million.

I get outside the door, but I do not go away at once as anybody with any sense will do, but stand there listening to what is going on inside, which seems to be nothing more than a loud noise like ker-bump, ker-bump, ker-bump. I am not afraid there will be any shooting, because as far as Rusty Charley is concerned he is too smart to shoot any coppers, which is the worst thing a guy can do in this town, and the coppers are not likely to start any blasting because they will not wish it to come out that they are in a joint such as the Bohemian Club off duty. So I figure they will all just take it out in pulling and hauling.

Finally the noise inside dies down, and by and by the door opens and out comes Rusty Charley, dusting himself off here and there with his hands and looking very much pleased, indeed, and through the door before it flies shut again I catch a glimpse of a lot of guys stretched out on the floor. Furthermore, I can still hear guys and dolls hollering.

"Well, well," Rusty Charley says, "I am commencing to think you take the wind on me, and am just about to get mad at you, but here you are. Let us go away from this joint, because they are making so much noise inside you cannot hear yourself think. Let us go to my joint and make my old woman cook us up some breakfast, and then we can catch some sleep. A little ham and eggs will not be bad to take right now."

Well, naturally ham and eggs are appealing to me no little at this time, but I do not care to go to Rusty Charley's joint. As far as I am personally concerned, I have enough of Rusty Charley to do me a long, long time, and I do not care to enter into his home life to any extent whatever, although to tell the truth I am somewhat surprised to learn he has any such life. I believe I do once hear that Rusty Charley marries one of the neighbors' children, and that he lives somewhere over on Tenth Avenue in the Forties, but nobody really knows much about this, and everybody figures if it is true his wife must lead a terrible dog's life.

But while I do not wish to go to Charley's joint I cannot very well refuse a civil invitation to eat ham and eggs, especially as Charley is looking at me in a very much surprised way because I do not seem so glad and I can see that it is not everyone that he invites to his joint. So I thank him, and say there is nothing I will enjoy more than ham and eggs such as his old woman will cook for us, and by and by we are walking along Tenth Avenue up around Forty-fifth Street.

It is still fairly early in the morning, and business guys are opening up their joints for the day, and little children are skipping along the sidewalks going to school and laughing tee-hee, and old dolls are shaking bedclothes and one thing and another out of the windows of the tenement houses, but when they spot Rusty Charley and me everybody becomes very quiet, indeed, and I can see that Charley is greatly respected in his own neighborhood. The business guys hurry into their joints, and the little children stop skipping and tee-heeing and go tip-toeing along, and the old dolls yank in their noodles, and a great quiet comes to the street. In fact, about all you can hear is the heels of Rusty Charley and me hitting on the sidewalk.

There is an ice wagon with a couple of horses hitched to it standing in front of a store, and when he sees the horses Rusty Charley seems to get a big idea. He stops and looks the horses over very carefully, although as far as I can see they are nothing but horses, and big and fat, and sleepy-looking horses, at that. Finally Rusty Charles says to me like this:

"When I am a young guy," he says, "I am a very good puncher with my right hand, and often I hit a horse on the skull with my fist and knock it down. I wonder," he says, "if I lose my punch. The last copper I hit back there gets up twice on me."

Then he steps up to one of the ice-wagon horses and hauls off and biffs it right between the eyes with a right-hand smack that does not travel more than four inches, and down goes old Mister Horse to his knees looking very much surprised, indeed. I see many a hard puncher in my day, including Dempsey when he really can punch, but I never see a harder punch than Rusty Charley gives this horse.

Well, the ice-wagon driver comes busting out of the store all heated up over what happens to his horse, but he cools out the minute he sees Rusty Charley, and goes on back into the store leaving the horse still taking a count, while Rusty Charley and I keep walking. Finally we come to the entrance of a tenement house that Rusty Charley says is where he lives, and in front of this house is a wop with a push cart loaded with fruit and vegetables and one thing and another, which Rusty Charley tips over as we go into the house, leaving the wop yelling very loud, and maybe cussing us in wop for all I know. I am very glad, personally, we finally get somewhere, because I can feel that my blood pressure is getting worse every minute I am with Rusty Charley.

We climb two flights of stairs, and then Charley opens a door and we step into a room where there is a pretty little red-headed doll about knee high to a flivver, who looks as if she may just get out of the hay, because her red hair is flying around every which way on her head, and her eyes seem still gummed up with sleep. At first I think she is a very cute sight, indeed, and then I see something in her eyes that tells me this doll, whoever she is, is feeling very hostile to one and all.

"Hello, tootsie," Rusty Charley says. "How about some ham and eggs for me and my pal here? We are all tired out going around and about."

Well, the little red-headed doll just looks at him without saying a word. She is standing in the middle of the floor with one hand behind her, and all of a sudden she brings this hand around, and what does she have in it but a young baseball bat, such as kids play ball with, and which cost maybe two bits; and the next thing I know I hear something go ker-bap, and I can see she smacks Rusty Charley on the side of the noggin with the bat.

Naturally I am greatly horrified at this business, and figure Rusty Charley will kill her at once, and then I will be in a jam for witnessing the murder and will be held in jail several years like all witnesses to anything in this man's town; but Rusty Charley only falls into a big rocking-chair in a corner of the room and sits there with one hand to his head, saying, "Now hold on, tootsie," and "Wait a minute there, honey." I recollect hearing him say, "We have company for breakfast," and then the little red-headed doll turns on me and gives me a look such as I will always remember, although I smile at her very pleasant and mention it is a nice morning.

Finally she says to me like this:

"So you are the trambo who keeps my husband out all night, are you, you trambo?" she says, and with this she starts for me, and I start for the door; and by this time my blood pressure is all out of whack, because I can see that Mrs. Rusty Charley is excited more than somewhat. I get my hand on the knob and just then something hits me alongside the noggin, which I afterward figure must be the baseball bat, although I remember having a sneaking idea the roof caves in on me.

How I get the door open I do not know, because I am very dizzy in the head and my legs are wobbling, but when I think back over the situation I remember going down a lot of steps very fast, and by and by the fresh air strikes me, and I figure I am in the clear. But all of a sudden I feel another strange sensation back of my head and something goes plop against my noggin, and I figure at first that maybe my blood pressure runs up so high that it squirts out the top of my bean. Then I peek around over my shoulder just once to see that Mrs. Rusty Charley is standing beside the wop peddler's cart snatching fruit and vegetables of one kind and another off the cart and chucking them at me.

But what she hits me with back of the head is not an apple, or a peach, or a rutabaga, or a cabbage, or even a casaba melon, but a brickbat that the wop has on his cart to weight down the paper sacks in which he sells his goods. It is this brickbat which makes a lump on the back of my head so big that Doc Brennan thinks it is a tumor when I go to him the next day about my stomach, and I never tell him any different.

"But," Doc Brennan says, when he takes my blood pressure again, "your pressure is down below normal now, and as far as it is concerned you are in no danger whatever. It only goes to show what just a little bit of quiet living will do for a guy," Doc Brennan says. "Ten bucks, please," he says.

SINCLAIR LEWIS

(1885-1951)

Sinclair Lewis' great talent was his ability to portray qualities that both Americans and Europeans have enjoyed thinking of as the American average: provincialism and naïveté. Despite the fact that many of his books were written as attacks on prejudice, ignorance and provincialism, the supposed victims of those attacks, if they were readers, have enjoyed his work. A number of his characters, such as George F. Babbitt, Martin Arrowsmith, Carol Kennicott and Sam Dodsworth, became familiar symbols, and as a result Lewis has perhaps come to seem more a teller of reportorial truths than a creative novelist. In his heyday, which was the decade of the 1920's, he functioned as an exposer of familiar hypocrisies. He was primarily a novelist, but two of his short stories, "The Man Who Knew Coolidge" (later expanded to a novel of the same name) and "Young Man Axelbrod," have attained eminence. His best books are *Main Street, Babbitt, Arrowsmith*, and *Dodsworth*. In 1930 he was awarded the Nobel Prize in literature, the first American to be so honored.

YOUNG MAN AXELBROD

THE COTTONWOOD IS A TREE of a slovenly and plebeian habit. Its woolly wisps turn gray the lawns and engender neighborhood hostilities about our town. Yet it is a mighty tree, a refuge and an inspiration; the sun flickers in its towering foliage, whence the tattoo of locusts enlivens our dusty summer afternoons. From the wheat country out to the sagebrush plains between the buttes and the Yellowstone it is the cottonwood that keeps a little grateful shade for sweating homesteaders.

In Joralemon we call Knute Axelbrod "Old Cottonwood."
As a matter of fact, the name was derived not so much from
the quality of the man as from the wide grove about his gaunt
white house and red barn. He made a comely row of trees on
each side of the country road, so that a humble, daily sort of
a man, driving beneath them in his lumber wagon, might fancy
himself lord of a private avenue.

And at sixty-five Knute was like one of his own cottonwoods,
his roots deep in the soil, his trunk weathered by rain and
blizzard and baking August noons, his crown spread to the
wide horizon of day and the enormous sky of a prairie night.

This immigrant was an American even in speech. Save for
a weakness about his j's and w's, he spoke the twangy Yankee
English of the land. He was the more American because in his
native Scandinavia he had dreamed of America as a land of
light. Always through disillusion and weariness he beheld
America as the world's nursery for justice, for broad, fair
towns, and eager talk; and always he kept a young soul that
dared to desire beauty.

As a lad Knute Axelbrod had wished to be a famous scholar,
to learn the ease of foreign tongues, the romance of history, to
unfold in the graciousness of wise books. When he first came
to America he worked in a sawmill all day and studied all
evening. He mastered enough book-learning to teach district
school for two terms; then, when he was only eighteen, a great-
hearted pity for faded little Lena Wesselius moved him to
marry her. Gay enough, doubtless, was their hike by prairie
schooner to new farmlands, but Knute was promptly caught in
a net of poverty and family. From eighteen to fifty-eight he
was always snatching children away from death or the farm
away from mortgages.

He had to be content—and generously content he was—with
the second-hand glory of his children's success and, for himself, with pilfered hours of reading—that reading of big, thick,
dismal volumes of history and economics which the lone mature learner chooses. Without ever losing his desire for strange
cities and the dignity of towers he stuck to his farm. He

acquired a half-section, free from debt, fertile, well-stocked, adorned with a cement silo, a chicken-run, a new windmill. He became comfortable, secure, and then he was ready, it seemed, to die; for at sixty-three his work was done, and he was unneeded and alone.

His wife was dead. His sons had scattered afar, one a dentist in Fargo, another a farmer in the Golden Valley. He had turned over his farm to his daughter and son-in-law. They had begged him to live with them, but Knute refused.

"No," he said, "you must learn to stand on your own feet. I vill not give you the farm. You pay me four hundred dollars a year rent, and I live on that and vatch you from my hill."

On a rise beside the lone cottonwood which he loved best of all his trees Knute built a tar-paper shack, and here he "bached it"; cooked his meals, made his bed, sometimes sat in the sun, read many books from the Joralemon library, and began to feel that he was free of the yoke of citizenship which he had borne all his life.

For hours at a time he sat on a backless kitchen chair before the shack, a wide-shouldered man, white-bearded, motionless; a seer despite his grotesquely baggy trousers, his collarless shirt. He looked across the miles of stubble to the steeple of the Jackrabbit Forks church and meditated upon the uses of life. At first he could not break the rigidity of habit. He rose at five, found work in cleaning his cabin and cultivating his garden, had dinner exactly at twelve, and went to bed by afterglow. But little by little he discovered that he could be irregular without being arrested. He stayed abed till seven or even eight. He got a large, deliberate, tortoise-shell cat, and played games with it; let it lap milk upon the table, called it the Princess, and confided to it that he had a "sneaking idee" that men were fools to work so hard. Around this coatless old man, his stained waistcoat flapping about a huge torso, in a shanty of rumpled bed and pine table covered with sheets of food-daubed newspaper, hovered all the passionate aspiration of youth and the dreams of ancient beauty.

He began to take long walks by night. In his necessitous life night had ever been a period of heavy slumber in close rooms. Now he discovered the mystery of the dark; saw the prairies wide-flung and misty beneath the moon, heard the voices of grass and cottonwoods and drowsy birds. He tramped for miles. His boots were dew-soaked, but he did not heed. He stopped upon hillocks, shyly threw wide his arms, and stood worshipping the naked, slumbering land.

These excursions he tried to keep secret, but they were bruited abroad. Neighbors, good, decent fellows with no sense about walking in the dew at night, when they were returning late from town, drunk, lashing their horses and flinging whisky bottles from racing democrat wagons, saw him, and they spread the tidings that Old Cottonwood was "getting nutty since he give up his farm to that son-in-law of his and retired. Seen the old codger wandering around at midnight. Wish I had his chance to sleep. Wouldn't catch me out in the night air."

Any rural community from Todd Center to Seringapatam is resentful of any person who varies from its standard, and is morbidly fascinated by any hint of madness. The countryside began to spy on Knute Axelbrod, to ask him questions, and to stare from the road at his shack. He was sensitively aware of it, and inclined to be surly to inquisitive acquaintances. Doubtless that was the beginning of his great pilgrimage.

As a part of the general wild license of his new life— really, he once roared at that startled cat, the Princess: "By gollies! I ain't going to brush my teeth tonight. All my life I've brushed 'em, and always wanted to skip a time vunce"— Knute took considerable pleasure in degenerating in his taste in scholarship. He wilfully declined to finish *The Conquest of Mexico*, and began to read light novels borrowed from the Joralemon library. So he rediscovered the lands of dancing and light wines, which all his life he had desired. Some economics and history he did read, but every evening he would stretch out in his buffalo-horn chair, his feet on the cot and the Princess in his lap, and invade Zenda or fall in love with Trilby.

Among the novels he chanced upon a highly optimistic story

of Yale in which a worthy young man "earned his way through" college, stroked the crew, won Phi Beta Kappa, and had the most entertaining, yet moral, conversations on or adjacent to "the dear old fence."

As a result of this chronicle, at about three o'clock one morning, when Knute Axelbrod was sixty-four years of age, he decided that he would go to college. All his life he had wanted to. Why not do it?

When he awoke he was not so sure about it as when he had gone to sleep. He saw himself as ridiculous, a ponderous, oldish man among clean-limbed youths, like a dusty cottonwood among silver birches. But for months he wrestled and played with that idea of a great pilgrimage to the Mount of Muses; for he really supposed college to be that sort of place. He believed that all college students, except for the wealthy idlers, burned to acquire learning. He pictured Harvard and Yale and Princeton as ancient groves set with marble temples, before which large groups of Grecian youths talked gently about astronomy and good government. In his picture they never cut classes or ate.

With a longing for music and books and graciousness such as the most ambitious boy could never comprehend, this thick-faced farmer dedicated himself to beauty, and defied the unconquerable power of approaching old age. He sent for college catalogues and school books, and diligently began to prepare himself for college.

He found Latin irregular verbs and the whimsicalities of algebra fiendish. They had nothing to do with actual life as he had lived it. But he mastered them; he studied twelve hours a day, as once he had plodded through eighteen hours a day in the hayfield. With history and English literature he had comparatively little trouble; already he knew much of them from his recreative reading. From German neighbors he had picked up enough Plattdeutsch to make German easy. The trick of study began to come back to him from his small school teaching of forty-five years before. He began to believe that he could really put it through. He kept assuring himself that in college, with rare and sympathetic instructors to help him, there would not be this baffling search, this nervous strain.

But the unreality of the things he studied did disillusion him, and he tired of his new game. He kept it up chiefly because all his life he had kept up onerous labor without any taste for it. Toward the autumn of the second year of his eccentric life he no longer believed that he would ever go to college.

Then a busy little grocer stopped him on the street in Joralemon and quizzed him about his studies, to the delight of the informal club which always loafs at the corner of the hotel.

Knute was silent, but dangerously angry. He remembered just in time how he had once laid wrathful hands upon a hired man, and somehow the man's collar bone had been broken. He turned away and walked home, seven miles, still boiling. He picked up the Princess, and, with her mewing on his shoulder, tramped out again to enjoy the sunset.

He stopped at a reedy slough. He gazed at a hopping plover without seeing it. Suddenly he cried:

"I am going to college. It opens next veek. I t'ink that I can pass the examinations."

Two days later he had moved the Princess and his sticks of furniture to his son-in-law's house, had bought a new slouch hat, a celluloid collar and a solemn suit of black, had wrestled with God in prayer through all of a star-clad night, and had taken the train for Minneapolis, on the way to New Haven.

While he stared out of the car window Knute was warning himself that the millionaires' sons would make fun of him. Perhaps they would haze him. He bade himself avoid all these sons of Belial and cleave to his own people, those who "earned their way through."

At Chicago he was afraid with a great fear of the lightning flashes that the swift crowds made on his retina, the batteries of ranked motor cars that charged at him. He prayed, and ran for his train to New York. He came at last to New Haven.

Not with gibing rudeness, but with politely quizzical eye-

brows, Yale received him, led him through entrance examinations, which, after sweaty plowing with the pen, he barely
passed, and found for him a roommate. The roommate was a
large-browed soft white grub named Ray Gribble, who had
been teaching school in New England and seemed chiefly to
desire college training so that he might make more money as
a teacher. Ray Gribble was a hustler; he instantly got work
tutoring the awkward son of a steel man, and for board he
waited on table.

He was Knute's chief acquaintance. Knute tried to fool himself into thinking he liked the grub, but Ray couldn't keep his
damp hands off the old man's soul. He had the skill of a professional exhorter of young men in finding out Knute's motives,
and when he discovered that Knute had a hidden desire to sip
at gay, polite literature, Ray said in a shocked way:

"Strikes me a man like you, that's getting old, ought to be
thinking more about saving your soul than about all these
frills. You leave this poetry and stuff to these foreigners and
artists, and you stick to Latin and math. and the Bible. I tell
you, I've taught school, and I've learned by experience."

With Ray Gribble, Knute lived grubbily, an existence of
torn comforters and smelly lamp, of lexicons and logarithm
tables. No leisurely loafing by fireplaces was theirs. They
roomed in West Divinity, where gather the theologues, the
lesser sort of law students, a whimsical genius or two, and a
horde of unplaced freshmen and "scrub seniors."

Knute was shockingly disappointed, but he stuck to his
room because outside of it he was afraid. He was a grotesque
figure, and he knew it, a white-polled giant squeezed into a
small seat in a classroom, listening to instructors younger than
his own sons. Once he tried to sit on the fence. No one but
"ringers" sat on the fence any more, and at the sight of him
trying to look athletic and young, two upper-class men snick-
ered, and he sneaked away.

He came to hate Ray Gribble and his voluble companions
of the submerged tenth of the class, the hewers of tutorial wood.
It is doubtless safer to mock the flag than to question that

best-established tradition of our democracy—that those who "earn their way through" college are necessarily stronger, braver, and more assured of success than the weaklings who talk by the fire. Every college story presents such a moral. But tremblingly the historian submits that Knute discovered that waiting on table did not make lads more heroic than did football or happy loafing. Fine fellows, cheerful and fearless, were many of the boys who "earned their way," and able to talk to richer classmates without fawning; but just as many of them assumed an abject respectability as the most convenient pose. They were pickers up of unconsidered trifles; they toadied to the classmates whom they tutored; they wriggled before the faculty committee on scholarships; they looked pious at Dwight Hall prayermeetings to make an impression on the serious minded; and they drank one glass of beer at Jake's to show the light minded that they meant nothing offensive by their piety. In revenge for cringing to the insolent athletes whom they tutored, they would, when safe among their own kind, yammer about the "lack of democracy of college today." Not that they were so indiscreet as to do anything about it. They lacked the stuff of really rebellious souls. Knute listened to them and marveled. They sounded like young hired men talking behind his barn at harvest time.

This submerged tenth hated the dilettantes of the class even more than they hated the bloods. Against one Gilbert Washburn, a rich esthete with more manner than any freshman ought to have, they raged righteously. They spoke of seriousness and industry till Knute, who might once have desired to know lads like Washburn, felt ashamed of himself as a wicked, wasteful old man.

Humbly though he sought, he found no inspiration and no comradeship. He was the freak of the class, and aside from the submerged tenth, his classmates were afraid of being "queered" by being seen with him.

As he was still powerful, one who could take up a barrel of pork on his knees, he tried to find friendship among the athletes. He sat at Yale Field, watching the football tryouts, and tried to get acquainted with the candidates. They stared at him and answered his questions grudgingly—beefy youths who in their simple-hearted way showed that they considered him plain crazy.

The place itself began to lose the haze of magic through which he had first seen it. Earth is earth, whether one sees it in Camelot or Joralemon or on the Yale campus—or possibly even in the Harvard yard! The buildings ceased to be temples to Knute; they became structures of brick or stone, filled with young men who lounged at windows and watched him amusedly as he tried to slip by.

The Gargantuan hall of Commons became a tri-daily horror because at the table where he dined were two youths who, having uncommonly penetrating minds, discerned that Knute had a beard, and courageously told the world about it. One of them, named Atchison, was a superior person, very industrious and scholarly, glib in mathematics and manners. He despised Knute's lack of definite purpose in coming to college. The other was a play-boy, a wit and a stealer of street signs, who had a wonderful sense for a subtle jest; and his references to Knute's beard shook the table with jocund mirth three times a day. So these youths of gentle birth drove the shambling, wistful old man away from Commons, and thereafter he ate at the lunch counter at the Black Cat.

Lacking the stimulus of friendship, it was the harder for Knute to keep up the strain of studying the long assignments. What had been a week's pleasant reading in his shack was now thrown at him as a day's task. But he would not have minded the toil if he could have found one as young as himself. They were all so dreadfully old, the money-earners, the serious laborers at athletics, the instructors who worried over their life work of putting marks in class-record books.

Then, on a sore, bruised day, Knute did meet one who was young.

Knute had heard that the professor who was the idol of the college had berated the too-earnest lads in his Browning class, and insisted that they read *Alice in Wonderland*. Knute floundered dustily about in a second-hand bookshop till he found an "Alice," and he brought it home to read over his lunch of a hot-dog sandwich. Something in the grave absurdity of the book appealed to him, and he was chuckling over it when Ray Gribble came into the room and glanced at the reader.

"Huh!" said Mr. Gribble.

"That's a fine, funny book," said Knute.

"Huh! *Alice in Wonderland!* I've heard of it. Silly nonsense. Why don't you read something really fine, like Shakespeare or *Paradise Lost?*"

"Vell———" said Knute, all he could find to say.

With Ray Gribble's glassy eye on him, he could no longer roll and roar with the book. He wondered if indeed he ought not to be reading Milton's pompous anthropological misconceptions. He went unhappily out to an early history class, ably conducted by Blevins, Ph.D.

Knute admired Blevins, Ph.D. He was so tubbed and eyeglassed and terribly right. But most of Blevins' lambs did not like Blevins. They said he was a "crank." They read newspapers in his class and covertly kicked one another.

In the smug, plastered classroom, his arm leaning heavily on the broad tablet-arm of his chair, Knute tried not to miss one of Blevins' sardonic proofs that the correct date of the second marriage of Themistocles was two years and seven days later than the date assigned by that illiterate ass, Frutari of Padua. Knute admired young Blevins' performance, and he felt virtuous in application of these hard, unnonsensical facts.

He became aware that certain lewd fellows of the lesser sort were playing poker just behind him. His prairie-trained ear caught whispers of "Two to dole," and "Raise you two beans." Knute revolved, and frowned upon these mockers of sound learning. As he turned back he was aware that the offenders were chuckling, and continuing their game. He saw that Blevins, Ph.D., perceived that something was wrong; he frowned, but he said nothing. Knute sat in meditation. He saw Blevins as merely a boy. He was sorry for him. He would do the boy a good turn.

When class was over he hung about Blevins' desk till the other students had clattered out. He rumbled:

"Say, Professor, you're a fine fellow. I do something for you. If any of the boys make themselves a nuisance, you yust call on me, and I spank the son of a guns."

Blevins, Ph.D., spake in a manner of culture and nastiness:

"Thanks so much, Axelbrod, but I don't fancy that will ever be necessary. I am supposed to be a reasonably good disciplinarian. Good day. Oh, one moment. There's something I've been wishing to speak to you about. I do wish you wouldn't try quite so hard to show off whenever I call on you during quizzes. You answer at such needless length, and you smile as though there were something highly amusing about me. I'm quite willing to have you regard me as a humorous figure, privately, but there are certain classroom conventions, you know, certain little conventions."

"Why, Professor!" wailed Knute, "I never make fun of you! I didn't know I smile. If I do, I guess it's yust because I am so glad when my stupid old head gets the lesson good."

"Well, well, that's very gratifying, I'm sure. And if you will be a little more careful———"

Blevins, Ph.D., smiled a toothy, frozen smile, and trotted off to the Graduates' Club, to be witty about old Knute and his way of saying "yust," while in the deserted classroom Knute sat chill, an old man and doomed. Through the windows came the light of Indian summer; clean, boyish cries rose from the campus. But the lover of autumn smoothed his baggy sleeve, stared at the blackboard, and there saw only the gray of October stubble about his distant shack. As he pictured the college watching him, secretly making fun of him and his smile, he was now faint and ashamed, now bull-angry. He was lonely for his cat, his fine chair of buffalo horns, the sunny doorstep of his shack, and the understanding land. He had been in college for about one month.

Before he left the classroom he stepped behind the instructor's desk and looked at an imaginary class.

"I might have stood there as a prof if I could have come earlier," he said softly to himself.

Calmed by the liquid autumn gold that flowed through the streets, he walked out Whitney Avenue toward the butte-like hill of East Rock. He observed the caress of the light upon the scarped rock, heard the delicate music of leaves, breathed in air pregnant with tales of old New England. He exulted: " 'Could write poetry now if I yust—if I yust could write poetry!"

He climbed to the top of East Rock, whence he could see the Yale buildings like the towers of Oxford, and see Long Island Sound, and the white glare of Long Island beyond the water. He marveled that Axelbrod of the cottonwood country was looking across an arm of the Atlantic to New York state. He noticed a freshman on a bench at the edge of the rock, and he became irritated. The freshman was Gilbert Washburn, the snob, the dilettante, of whom Ray Gribble had once said: "That guy is the disgrace of the class. He doesn't go out for anything, high stand or Dwight Hall or anything else. Thinks he's so doggone much better than the rest of the fellows that he doesn't associate with anybody. Thinks he's literary, they say, and yet he doesn't even heel the 'Lit,' like the regular literary fellows! Got no time for a loafing, mooning snob like that."

As Knute stared at the unaware Gil, whose profile was fine in outline against the sky, he was terrifically public-spirited and disapproving and that sort of moral thing. Though Gil was much too well dressed, he seemed moodily discontented.

"What he needs is to vork in a threshing crew and sleep in the hay," grumbled Knute almost in the virtuous manner of Gribble. "Then he vould know when he vas vell off, and not look like he had the earache. Pff!" Gil Washburn rose, trailed toward Knute, glanced at him, sat down on Knute's bench.

"Great view!" he said. His smile was eager.

That smile symbolized to Knute all the art of life he had come to college to find. He tumbled out of his moral attitude with ludicrous haste, and every wrinkle of his weathered face creased deep as he answered:

"Yes: I t'ink the Acropolis must be like this here."

"Say, look here, Axelbrod; I've been thinking about you."

"Yas?"

"We ought to know each other. We two are the class scandal. We came here to dream, and these busy little goats like Atchison and Giblets, or whatever your roommate's name is, think we're fools not to go out for marks. You may not agree with me, but I've decided that you and I are precisely alike."

"What makes you t'ink I come here to dream?" bristled Knute.

"Oh, I used to sit near you at Commons and hear you try to quell old Atchison whenever he got busy discussing the reasons for coming to college. That old, motheaten topic! I wonder if Cain and Abel didn't discuss it at the Eden Agricultural College. You know, Abel the mark-grabber, very pious and high stand, and Cain wanting to read poetry."

"Yes," said Knute, "and I guess Prof. Adam say, 'Cain, don't you read this poetry; it von't help you in algebry.'"

"Of course. Say, wonder if you'd like to look at this volume of Musset I was sentimental enough to lug up here today. Picked it up when I was abroad last year."

From his pocket Gil drew such a book as Knute had never seen before, a slender volume, in a strange language, bound in hand-tooled crushed levant, an effeminate bibelot over which the prairie farmer gasped with luxurious pleasure. The book almost vanished in his big hands. With a timid forefinger he stroked the levant, ran through the leaves.

"I can't read it, but that's the kind of book I alvays t'ought there must be some like it," he sighed.

"Listen!" cried Gil. "Ysaye is playing up at Hartford tonight. Let's go hear him. We'll trolley up. Tried to get some of the fellows to come, but they thought I was a nut."

What an Ysaye was, Knute Axelbrod had no notion; but "Sure!" he boomed.

When they got to Hartford they found that between them they had just enough money to get dinner, hear Ysaye from gallery seats, and return only as far as Meriden. At Meriden Gil suggested:

"Let's walk back to New Haven, then. Can you make it?"

Knute had no knowledge as to whether it was four miles or forty back to the campus, but "Sure!" he said. For the last few months he had been noticing that, despite his bulk, he had to be careful, but tonight he could have flown.

In the music of Ysaye, the first real musician he had ever heard, Knute had found all the incredible things of which he had slowly been reading in William Morris and "Idylls of the King." Tall knights he had beheld, and slim princesses in white samite, the misty gates of forlorn towns, and the glory of the chivalry that never was.

They did walk, roaring down the road beneath the October moon, stopping to steal apples and to exclaim over silvered hills, taking a puerile and very natural joy in chasing a profane dog. It was Gil who talked, and Knute who listened, for the most part; but Knute was lured into tales of the pioneer days, of blizzards, of harvesting, and of the first flame of the green wheat. Regarding the Atchisons and Gribbles of the class both of them were youthfully bitter and supercilious. But they were not bitter long, for they were atavisms tonight. They were wandering minstrels, Gilbert the troubadour with his man-at-arms.

They reached the campus at about five in the morning. Fumbling for words that would express his feeling, Knute stammered:

"Vell, it vas fine. I go to bed now and I dream about——"

"Bed? Rats! Never believe in winding up a party when it's going strong. Too few good parties. Besides, it's only the shank of the evening. Besides, we're hungry. Besides—oh, besides! Wait here a second. I'm going up to my room to get some money, and we'll have some eats. Wait! Please do!"

Knute would have waited all night. He had lived almost seventy years and traveled fifteen hundred miles and endured Ray Gribble to find Gil Washburn.

Policemen wondered to see the celluloid-collared old man and the expensive-looking boy rolling arm in arm down Chapel Street in search of a restaurant suitable to poets. They were all closed.

"The Ghetto will be awake by now," said Gil. "We'll go buy some eats and take 'em up to my room. I've got some tea there."

Knute shouldered through dark streets beside him as naturally as though he had always been a nighthawk, with an aversion to anything as rustic as beds. Down on Oak Street, a place of low shops, smoky lights and alley mouths, they found the slum already astir. Gil contrived to purchase boxed biscuits, cream cheese, chicken-loaf, a bottle of cream. While Gil was chaffering, Knute stared out into the street milkily lighted by wavering gas and the first feebleness of coming day; he gazed upon Kosher signs and advertisements in Russian letters, shawled women and bearded rabbis; and as he looked he gathered contentment which he could never lose. He had traveled abroad tonight.

The room of Gil Washburn was all the useless, pleasant things Knute wanted it to be. There was more of Gil's Paris days in it than of his freshmanhood: Persian rugs, a silver tea service, etchings, and books. Knute Axelbrod of the tarpaper shack and piggy farmyards gazed in satisfaction. Vast bearded, sunk in an easy chair, he clucked amiably while Gil lighted a fire.

Over supper they spoke of great men and heroic ideals. It was good talk, and not unspiced with lively references to Gribble and Atchison and Blevins, all asleep now in their correct beds. Gil read snatches of Stevenson and Anatole France; then at last he read his own poetry.

It does not matter whether that poetry was good or bad. To Knute it was a miracle to find one who actually wrote it.

The talk grew slow, and they began to yawn. Knute was sensitive to the lowered key of their Indian-summer madness, and he hastily rose. As he said good-by he felt as though he had but to sleep a little while and return to this unending night of romance.

But he came out of the dormitory upon day. It was six-thirty of the morning, with a still, hard light upon red-brick walls.

"I can go to his room plenty times now; I find my friend," Knute said. He held tight the volume of Musset, which Gil had begged him to take.

As he started to walk the few steps to West Divinity Knute felt very tired. By daylight the adventure seemed more and more incredible.

As he entered the dormitory he sighed heavily:

"Age and youth, I guess they can't team together long." As he mounted the stairs he said: "If I saw the boy again, he vould get tired of me. I tell him all I got to say." And as he opened his door, he added: "This is what I come to college for—this one night. I go avay before I spoil it."

He wrote a note to Gil, and began to pack his telescope. He did not even wake Ray Gribble, sonorously sleeping in the stale air.

At five that afternoon, on the day coach of a westbound train, an old man sat smiling. A lasting content was in his eyes, and in his hands a small book in French.

WILBUR DANIEL STEELE

(1886-   )

Wilbur Daniel Steele writes what he calls the "constructed story," the story with a beginning, a middle, and an end. His stories are, then, a little out of fashion and were so even at the height of his productivity and their popularity, in the dozen years between 1919 and 1931. His work is closer to the "effect" stories of Bierce, for instance, than to the stories of such of his contemporaries as Porter and Hemingway. But where Bierce used his best effects principally to vent his spleen on his characters, Steele uses his last-minute twists to provide startling insight into the motives behind human behavior. A good story is none the less good for being told in an older than current fashion, and while the numerous prizes awarded to Steele in the 1920's do reflect the critics' unsureness of the more experimental stories, their easy preference for the tried and true, they also reflect Steele's genuine mastery of the carefully plotted story. His best collections are *The Man Who Saw Through Heaven, and Other Stories* (from which "Blue Murder" is taken), and *Tower of Sand, and Other Stories*.

BLUE MURDER

A T MILL CROSSING it was already past sunset. The rays, redder for what autumn leaves were left, still laid fire along the woods crowning the stony slopes of Jim Bluedge's pastures; but then the line of the dusk began and from that level it filled the valley, washing with transparent blue the buildings scattered about the bridge, Jim's house and horse sheds and hay barns, Frank's store, and Camden's blacksmith shop.

The mill had been gone fifty years, but the falls which had turned its wheel still poured in the bottom of the valley, and when the wind came from the Footstool way their mist wet the smithy, built of the old stone on the old foundations, and their pouring drowned the clink of Camden's hammer.

Just now they couldn't drown Camden's hammer, for he wasn't in the smithy; he was at his brother's farm. Standing inside the smaller of the horse paddocks behind the sheds he drove in stakes, one after another, cut green from saplings, and so disposed as to cover the more glaring of the weaknesses in the five-foot fence. From time to time, when one was done and another to do, he rested the head of his sledge in the pocket of his leather apron (he was never without it; it was as though it had grown on him, lumpy with odds and ends of his trade—bolts and nails and rusty pliers and old horseshoes) and, standing so, he mopped the sweat from his face and looked up at the mountain.

Of the three brothers he was the dumb one. He seldom had anything to say. It was providential (folks said) that of the three enterprises at the Crossing one was a smithy; for while he was a strong, big, hungry-muscled fellow, he never would have had the shrewdness to run the store or the farm. He was better at pounding—pounding while the fire reddened and the sparks flew, and thinking, and letting other people wonder what he was thinking of.

Blossom Bluedge, his brother's wife, sat perched on the top bar of the paddock gate, holding her skirts around her ankles with a trifle too much care to be quite unconscious, and watched him work. When he looked at the mountain he was looking at the mares, half a mile up the slope, grazing in a line as straight as soldiers, their heads all one way. But Blossom thought it was the receding light he was thinking of, and her own sense of misgiving returned and deepened.

"You'd have thought Jim would be home before this, wouldn't you, Cam?"

Her brother-in-law said nothing.

"Cam, look at me!"

It was nervousness, but it wasn't all nervousness—she was the prettiest girl in the valley; a small part of it was mingled coquetry and pique.

The smith began to drive another stake, swinging the hammer from high overhead, his muscles playing in fine big rhythmical convulsions under the skin of his arms and chest, covered with short blond down. Studying him cornerwise, Blossom muttered, "Well, *don't* look at me then!"

He was too dumb for any use. He was as dumb as this: when all three of the Bluedge boys were after her a year ago, Frank, the storekeeper, had brought her candy: chocolates wrapped in silver foil in a two-pound Boston box. Jim had laid before her the Bluedge farm and with it the dominance of the valley. And Camden! To the daughter of Earl Beck, the apple grower, Camden had brought a *box of apples!*— and been bewildered too, when, for all she could help it, she had had to clap a hand over her mouth and run into the house to have her giggle.

A little more than just bewildered, perhaps. Had she, or any of them, ever speculated about that? . . . He had been dumb enough before; but that was when he had started being as dumb as he was now.

Well, if he wanted to be dumb let him be dumb. Pouting her pretty lips and arching her fine brows, she forgot the unimaginative fellow and turned to the ridge again. And now, seeing the sun was quite gone, all the day's vague worries and dreads — held off by this and that — could not be held off longer. For weeks there had been so much talk, so much gossip and speculation and doubt.

"Camden," she reverted suddenly. "Tell me one thing; did you hear———"

She stopped there. Some people were coming into the kitchen yard, dark forms in the growing darkness. Most of them lingered at the porch, sitting on the steps and lighting their pipes. The one that came out was Frank, the second of her brothers-in-law. She was glad. Frank wasn't like Camden; he would talk. Turning and taking care of her skirts, she gave him a bright and sisterly smile.

"Well, Frankie, what's the crowd?"

Far from avoiding the smile, as Camden's habit was, the storekeeper returned it with a brotherly wink for good measure. "Oh, they're tired of waiting down the road, so they come up here to see the grand arrival." He was something of a man of the world; in his calling he had acquired a fine turn for skepticism. "Don't want to miss being on hand to see what flaws they can pick in 'Jim's five hundred dollars' wuth of expiriment.'"

"Frank, ain't you the least bit worried over Jim? So late?"

"Don't see why."

"All the same, I wish either you or Cam could've gone with him."

"Don't see why. Had all the men from Perry's stable there in Twinshead to help him get the animal off the freight, and he took an extra rope and the log chain and the heavy wagon, so I guess no matter how wild and woolly the devil is he'll scarcely be climbing in over the tailboard. Besides, them Western horses ain't such a big breed; even a stallion."

"All the same—(look the other way, Frankie)." Flipping her ankles over the rail, Blossom jumped down beside him. "Listen, Frank, tell me something; did you hear—did you hear the reason Jim's getting him cheap was because he killed a man out West there, what's-its-name, Wyoming?"

Frank was taking off his sleeve protectors, the pins in his mouth. It was Camden, at the bars, speaking in his sudden deep rough way, "Who the hell told you that?"

Frank got the pins out of his mouth. "I guess what it is, Blossie, what's mixed you up is his having that name, 'Blue Murder.'"

"No sir! I got some sense and some ears. You don't go fooling me."

Frank laughed indulgently and struck her shoulder with a light hand.

"Don't you worry. Between two horsemen like Jim and Cam——"

"Don't *Cam* me! He's none of my horse. I told Jim once ——" Breaking off, Camden hoisted his weight over the fence

and stood outside, his feet spread and his hammer in both
hands, an attitude that would have looked a little ludicrous
had anyone been watching him.

Jim had arrived. With a clatter of hoofs and a rattle of
wheels he was in the yard and come to a standstill, calling
aloud as he threw the lines over the team, "Well, friends, here
we are."

The curious began to edge around, closing a cautious circle.
The dusk had deepened so that it was hard to make anything
at any distance of Jim's "expiriment" but a blurry silhouette
anchored at the wagon's tail. The farmer put an end to it,
crying from his eminence, "Now, now, clear out and don't
worry him; give him some peace to-night, for Lord's sake!
Git!" He jumped to the ground and began to whack his arms,
chilled with driving, only to have them pinioned by Blossom's
without warning.

"Oh, Jim, I'm so glad you come. I been so worried; gi'
me a kiss!"

The farmer reddened, eying the cloud of witnesses. He felt
awkward and wished she could have waited. "Get along, didn't
I tell you fellows?" he cried with a trace of the Bluedge
temper. "Go wait in the kitchen then; I'll tell you all about
everything soon's I come in. . . . Well now—wife——"

"What's the matter?" she laughed, an eye over her shoulder.
"Nobody's looking that matters. I'm sure Frank don't mind.
And as for Camden——"

Camden wasn't looking at them. Still standing with his
hammer two-fisted and his legs spread, his chin down and his
thoughts to himself (the dumbhead) he was looking at Blue
Murder, staring at that other dumbhead, which, raised high
on the motionless column of the stallion's neck, seemed hearkening with an exile's doubt to the sounds of this new universe,
tasting with wide nostrils the taint in the wind of equine
strangers, and studying with eyes accustomed to far horizons
these dark pastures that went up in the air.

Whatever the smith's cogitations, presently he let the
hammer down and said aloud, "So you're him, eh?"

Jim had put Blossom aside, saying, "Got supper ready? I'm

hungry!" Excited by the act of kissing and sense of witnesses to it, she fussed her hair and started kitchenward as he turned to his brothers.

"Well, what do you make of him?"

"Five hundred dollars," said Frank. "However, it's your money."

Camden was shorter. "Better put him in."

"All right; let them bars down while I and Frank lead him around."

"No, thanks!" The storekeeper kept his hands in his pockets. "I just cleaned up, thanks. Cam's the boy for horses."

"He's none o' my horses!" Camden wet his lips, shook his shoulders, and scowled. "Be damned, no!" He never had the right words, and it made him mad. Hadn't he told Jim from the beginning that he washed his hands of this fool Agricultural College squandering, "and a man killer to the bargain"?

"Unless," Frank put in slyly, "unless Cam's scared."

"Oh, is Cam scared?"

"Scared?" And still, to the brothers' enduring wonder, the big dense fellow would rise to that boyhood bait. "Scared? The hell I'm scared of any horse ever wore a shoe! Come on, I'll show you! I'll show you!"

"Well, be gentle with him, boys; he may be brittle." As Frank sauntered off around the shed he whistled the latest tune.

In the warmth and light of the kitchen he began to fool with his pretty sister-in-law, feigning princely impatience and growling with a wink at the assembled neighbors, "When do we eat?"

But she protested, "Land, I had everything ready since five, ain't I? And now if it ain't you it's them to wait for. I declare for men!"

At last one of the gossips got in a word.

"What you make of Jim's purchase, Frank?"

"Well, it's Jim's money, Darred. If *I* had the running of this farm——" Frank began drawing up chairs noisily, leaving it at that.

Darred persisted. "Don't look to me much like an animal for women and children to handle, not yet awhile."

"Cowboys han'les 'em, pa." That was Darred's ten-year-old, big-eyed.

Blossom put the kettle back, protesting, "Leave off, or you'll get me worried to death; all your talk . . . I declare, where *are* those bad boys?" Opening the door she called into the dark, "Jim! Cam! Land's sake!"

Subdued by distance and the intervening sheds, she could hear them at their business—sounds muffled and fragmentary, soft thunder of hoofs, snorts, puffings, and the short words of men in action: "Aw, leave him be in the paddock to-night." . . . "With them mares there, you damn fool?" . . . "Damn fool, eh? Try getting him in at that door and see who's the damn fool!" . . . "Come on, don't be so scared." . . . "Scared, eh? Scared?" . . .

Why was it she always felt that curious tightening of all her powers of attention when Camden Bluedge spoke? Probably because he spoke so rarely, and then so roughly, as if his own thickness made him mad. Never mind.

"Last call for supper in the dining car, boys!" she called and closed the door. Turning back to the stove she was about to replace the tea water for the third time, when, straightening up, she said, "What's that?"

No one else had heard anything. They looked at one another.

"Frank, go—go see what—go tell the boys to come in."

Frank hesitated, feeling foolish, then went to the door.

Then everyone in the room was out of his chair.

There were three sounds. The first was human and incoherent. The second was incoherent too, but it wasn't human. The third was a crash, a ripping and splintering of wood.

When they got to the paddock they found Camden crawling from beneath the wreckage of the fence where a gap was opened on the pasture side. He must have received a blow on the head, for he seemed dazed. He didn't seem to know they were there. At a precarious balance—one hand at the back of his neck—he stood facing up the hill, gaping after the diminuendo of floundering hoofs, invisible above.

So seconds passed. Again the beast gave tongue, a high wild horning note, and on the back of the stony hill to the right of it a faint shower of sparks blew like fireflies where the herding mares wheeled. It seemed to awaken the dazed smith. He opened his mouth: *"Almighty God!"* Swinging, he flung his arms toward the shed. *"There! There!"*

At last someone brought a lantern. They found Jim Bluedge lying on his back in the corner of the paddock near the door to the shed. In the lantern light, and still better in the kitchen when they had carried him in, they read the record of the thing which Camden, dumb in good earnest now, seemed unable to tell them with anything but his strange unfocused stare.

The bloody offense to the skull would have been enough to kill the man, but it was the second, full on the chest above the heart, that told the tale. On the caved grating of the ribs, already turning blue under the yellowish down, the iron shoe had left its mark; and when, laying back the rag of shirt, they saw that the toe of the shoe was upward and the cutting calk-ends down they knew all they wanted to know of that swift, black, crushing episode.

No outlash here of heels in fright. Here was a forefoot. An attack aimed and frontal; an onslaught reared, erect; beast turned biped; red eyes mad to white eyes aghast. . . . And only afterward, when it was done, the blood-fright that serves the horse for conscience; the blind rush across the inclosure; the fence gone down. . . .

No one had much to say. No one seemed to know what to do.

As for Camden, he was no help. He simply stood propped on top of his logs of legs where someone had left him. From the instant when with his *"Almighty God!"* he had been brought back to memory, instead of easing its hold as the minutes passed, the event to which he remained the only living human witness seemed minute by minute to tighten its grip. It set its sweat-beaded stamp on his face, distorted his eyes, and tied his tongue. He was no good to anyone.

As for Blossom, even now—perhaps more than ever now—her dependence on physical touch was the thing that ruled her. Down on her knees beside the lamp they had set on the floor, she plucked at one of the dead man's shoes monotonously, and as it were idly, swaying the toe like an inverted pendulum from side to side. That was all. Not a word. And when Frank, the only one of the three with any sense, got her up finally and led her away to her room, she clung to *him*.

It was lucky that Frank was a man of affairs. His brother was dead, and frightfully dead, but there was to-morrow for grief. Just now there were many things to do. There were people to be gotten rid of. With short words and angry gestures he cleared them out, all but Darred and a man named White, and to these he said, "Now first thing, Jim can't stay here." He ran and got a blanket from a closet. "Give me a hand and we'll lay him in the ice house overnight. Don't sound good, but it's best, poor fellow. Cam, come along!"

He waited a moment, and as he studied the wooden fool the blood poured back into his face. "Wake up, Cam! You great big scared stiff, you!"

Camden brought his eyes out of nothingness and looked at his brother. A twinge passed over his face, convulsing the mouth muscles. "Scared?"

"Yes, you're scared!" Frank's lip lifted, showing the tips of his teeth. "And I'll warrant you something: if you wasn't the scared stiff you was, this hellish damn thing wouldn't have happened, maybe. Scared! You, a blacksmith! Scared of a horse!"

"*Horse!*" Again that convulsion of the mouth muscles, something between irony and an idiot craft. "Why don't you go catch 'im?"

"Hush it! Don't waste time by going loony now, for God's sake. Come!"

"My advice to anybody——" Camden looked crazier than ever, knotting his brows. "My advice to anybody is to let somebody else go catch that—that——" Opening the door he faced out into the night, his head sunk between his shoulders and the fingers working at the ends of his hanging arms; and before they knew it he began to swear. They could hardly hear because his teeth were locked and his breath soft. There were all the vile words he had ever heard in his life, curses and threats and abominations, vindictive, violent, obscene. He stopped only when at a sharp word from Frank he was made aware that Blossom had come back into the room. Even then he didn't seem to comprehend her return but stood blinking at her, and at the rifle she carried, with his distraught blood-shot eyes.

Frank comprehended. Hysteria had followed the girl's blankness. Stepping between her and the body on the floor, he spoke in a persuasive, unhurried way. "What you doing with that gun, Blossie? Now, now, you don't want that gun, you know you don't."

It worked. Her rigidity lessened appreciably. Confusion gained.

"Well, but—oh, Frank—well, but when we going to shoot him?"

"Yes, yes, Blossie—now, yes—only you best give me that gun; that's the girlie." When he had got the weapon he put an arm around her shoulders. "Yes, yes, course we're going to shoot him; what you think? Don't want an animal like that running round. Now first thing in the morning——"

Hysteria returned. With its strength she resisted his leading.

"No, now! *Now!* He's gone and killed Jim! Killed my husband! I won't have him left alive another minute! I won't! *Now!* No sir, I'm going myself, I am! Frank, I am! Cam!"

At his name, appealed to in that queer screeching way, the man in the doorway shivered all over, wet his lips, and walked out into the dark.

"There, you see?" Frank was quick to capitalize anything. "Cam's gone to do it. Cam's gone, Blossie! . . . Here, one of you—Darred, take this gun and run give it to Camden, that's the boy."

"You sure he'll kill him, Frank? You *sure?*"

"Sure as daylight. Now you come along back to your room like a good girl and get some rest. Come, I'll go with you."

When Frank returned to the kitchen ten minutes later, Darred was back.

"Well, now, let's get at it and carry out poor Jim; he can't lay here. . . . Where's Cam gone *now*, damn him!"

"Cam? Why, he's gone and went."

"Went where?"

"Up the pasture, like you said."

"Like I——" Frank went an odd color. He walked to the door. Between the light on the sill and the beginnings of the stars where the woods crowned the mountain was all one blackness. One stillness too. He turned on Darred. "But look, you never gave him that gun, even."

"He didn't want it."

"Lord's sake; what did he say?"

"Said nothing. He'd got the log chain out of the wagon and when I caught him he was up hunting his hammer in under that wreck at the fence. Once he found it he started off up. 'Cam,' says I, 'here's a gun; want it?' He seem not to. Just went on walking on up."

"How'd he look?"

"Look same's you seen him looking. Sick."

"The damned fool!" . . .

Poor dead Jim! Poor fool Camden! As the storekeeper went about his business and afterward when, the ice house door closed on its tragic tenant and White and Darred gone off home, he roamed the yard, driven here and there, soft-footed, waiting, hearkening—his mind was for a time not his own property but the plaything of thoughts diverse and wayward. Jim, his brother, so suddenly and so violently gone. The stallion. That beast that had kicked him to death. With anger and hate and pitiless impatience of time he thought of the morrow, when they would catch him and take their revenge with guns and clubs. Behind these speculations, covering the background of his consciousness and stringing his nerves to endless vigil, spread the wall of the mountain: silent from instant to instant but devising under its black silence (who-could-know-what instant to come) a neigh, a yell, a spark-line of iron hoofs on rolling flints, a groan. And still behind that and deeper into the borders of the unconscious, the storekeeper thought of the farm that had lost its master, the rich bottoms, the broad well-stocked pastures, the fat barns, and the comfortable house whose chimneys and gable ends fell into changing shapes of perspective against the stars as he wandered here and there. . . .

Jim gone. . . . And Camden, at any moment . . .

His face grew hot. An impulse carried him a dozen steps. "I ought to go up. Ought to take the gun and go up." But there shrewd sanity put on the brakes. "Where's the use? Couldn't find him in this dark. Besides, I oughtn't to leave Blossom here alone."

With that he went around toward the kitchen, thinking to go in. But the sight of the lantern, left burning out near the sheds, sent his ideas off on another course. At any rate it would give his muscles and nerves something to work on. Taking the lantern and entering the paddock, he fell to patching the gap into the pasture, using broken boards from the wreck. As he worked his eyes chanced to fall on footprints in the dung-mixed earth—Camden's footprints leading away beyond the little ring of light. And beside them, taking off from the landing place of that prodigious leap, he discerned the trail of the stallion. After a moment he got down on his knees where the earth was softest, holding the lantern so that its light fell full.

He gave over his fence building. Returning to the house his gait was no longer that of the roamer; his face, caught by the periodic flare of the swinging lantern, was the face of another man. In its expression there was a kind of fright and a kind of calculating eagerness. He looked at the clock on the kitchen shelf, shook it, and read it again. He went to the telephone and fumbled at the receiver. He waited till his hand quit shaking, then removed it from the hook.

"Listen, Darred," he said, when he had got the farmer at last, "get White and whatever others you can and come over first thing it's light. Come a-riding and bring your guns. No, Cam ain't back."

He heard Blossom calling. Outside her door he passed one

hand down over his face, as he might have passed a wash rag, to wipe off what was there. Then he went in.

"What's the matter with Blossie? Can't sleep?"

"No, I can't sleep. Can't think. Can't sleep. Oh, Frankie!"

He sat down beside the bed.

"Oh, Frankie, Frankie, *hold my hand!*"

She looked almost homely, her face bleached out and her hair in a mess on the pillow. But she would get over that. And the short sleeve of the nightgown on the arm he held was edged with pretty lace.

"Got your watch here?" he asked. She gave it to him from under the pillow. This too he shook as if he couldn't believe it was going.

Pretty Blossom Beck. Here for a wonder he sat in her bedroom and held her hand. One brother was dead and the other was on the mountain.

But little by little, as he sat and dreamed so, nightmare crept over his brain. He had to arouse and shake himself. He had to set his thoughts resolutely in other roads. . . . Perhaps there would be even the smithy. The smithy, the store, the farm. Complete. The farm, the farmhouse, the room in the farmhouse, the bed in the room, the wife in the bed. Complete beyond belief. If . . . Worth dodging horror for. If . . .

"Frank, has Cam come back?"

"Cam? Don't you worry about Cam. . . . Where's that watch again?" . . .

Far from rounding up their quarry in the early hours after dawn, it took the riders, five of them, till almost noon simply to make certain that he wasn't to be found—not in any of the pastures. Then when they discovered the hole in the fence far up in the woods beyond the crest where Blue Murder had led the mares in a break for the open country of hills and ravines to the south, they were only at the beginning.

The farmers had left their work undone at home and, as the afternoon lengthened and with it the shadows in the hollow places, they began to eye one another behind their leader's back. Yet they couldn't say it; there was something in the storekeeper's air to-day, something zealous and pitiless and fanatical, that shut them up and pulled them plodding on.

Frank did the trailing. Hopeless of getting anywhere before sundown in that unkempt wilderness of a hundred square miles of scrub, his companions slouched in their saddles and rode more and more mechanically, knee to knee, and it was he who made the casts to recover the lost trail and, dismounting to read the dust, cried back, "He's still with 'em," and with gestures of imperious excitement beckoned them on.

"Which you mean?" Darred asked him once. "Cam, or the horse?"

Frank wheeled his beast and spurred back at the speaker. It was extraordinary. "You don't know what you're talking about!" he cried, with a causelessness and a disordered vehemence which set them first staring, then speculating. "Come on, you dumbheads; don't talk—*ride!*"

By the following day, when it was being told in all the farmhouses, the story might vary in details and more and more as the tellings multiplied, but in its fundamentals it remained the same. In one thing they certainly all agreed: they used the same expression—"It was like Frank was drove. Drove in a race against something, and not sparing the whip."

They were a good six miles to the south of the fence. Already the road back home would have to be followed three parts in the dark.

Darred was the spokesman. "Frank, I'm going to call it a day."

The others reined up with him but the man ahead rode on. He didn't seem to hear. Darred lifted his voice. "Come on, call it a day, Frank. To-morrow, may be. But you see we've run it out and they're not here."

"Wait," said Frank over his shoulder, still riding on into the pocket.

White's mount—a mare—laid back her ears, shied, and stood trembling. After a moment she whinnied.

It was as if she had whinnied for a dozen. A crashing in the woods above them to the left and the avalanche came—down streaming, erupting, wheeling, wheeling away with volleying snorts, a dark rout.

Darred, reining his horse, began to shout, "Here they go this way, Frank!" But Frank was yelling, "Up here boys! This way, quick!"

It was the same note, excited, feverish, disordered, breaking like a child's. When they neared him they saw he was off his horse, rifle in hand, and down on his knees to study the ground where the woods began. By the time they reached his animal the impetuous fellow had started up into the cover, his voice trailing, "Come on; spread out and come on!"

One of the farmers got down. When he saw the other three keeping their saddles he swung up again.

White spoke this time. "Be darned if I do!" He lifted a protesting hail, "Come back here, Frank! You're crazy! It's getting dark!"

It was Frank's own fault. They told him plainly to come back and he wouldn't listen.

For a while they could hear his crackle in the mounting underbrush. Then that stopped, whether he had gone too far for their ears or whether he had come to a halt to give his own ears a chance. . . . Once, off to his right, a little higher up under the low ceiling of the trees that darkened moment by moment with the rush of night, they heard another movement, another restlessness of leaves and stones. Then that was still, and everything was still.

Darred ran a sleeve over his face and swung down. "God alive, boys!"

It was the silence. All agreed there—the silence and the deepening dusk.

The first they heard was the shot. No voice. Just the one report. Then after five breaths of another silence a crashing of growth, a charge in the darkness under the withered scrub, continuous and diminishing.

They shouted, "Frank!" No answer. They called, *"Frank Bluedge!"*

Now, since they had to, they did. Keeping contact by word, and guided partly by directional memory (and mostly in the end by luck), after a time they found the storekeeper in a brake of ferns, lying across his gun.

They got him down to the open, watching behind them all the while. Only then, by the flares of successive matches, under the noses of the snorting horses, did they look for the damage done.

They remembered the stillness and the gloom; it must have been quite black in there. The attack had come from behind —equine and pantherine at once, and planned and cunning. A deliberate lunge with a forefoot again: the shoe which had crushed the backbone between the shoulder blades was a foreshoe; that much they saw by the match flares in the red wreck.

They took no longer getting home than they had to, but it was longer than they would have wished. With Frank across his own saddle, walking their horses and with one or another ahead to pick the road (it was going to rain, and even the stars were lost), they made no more than a creeping speed.

None of them had much to say on the journey. Finding the break in the boundary fence and feeling through the last of the woods, the lights of their farms began to show in the pool of blackness below, and Darred uttered a part of what had lain in the minds of them all during the return:

"Well, that leaves Cam."

None followed it up. None cared to go any closer than he was to the real question. Something new, alien, menacing and pitiless had come into the valley of their lives with that beast they had never really seen; they felt its oppression, every one, and kept the real question back in their minds: "*Does* it leave Cam?"

It answered itself. Camden was at home when they got there.

He had come in a little before them, empty-handed. Empty-headed too. When Blossom, who had waited all day, part of the time with neighbor women who had come in and part of the time alone to the point of going mad—when she saw him coming down the pasture, his feet stumbling and his shoulders dejected, her first feeling was relief. Her first words, however, were, "Did you get him, Cam?" And all he would answer was, "Gi'me something to eat, can't you? Gi'me a few hours' sleep, can't you? Then wait!"

He looked as if he would need more than a few hours' sleep. Propped on his elbows over his plate, it seemed as though his eyes would close before his mouth would open.

His skin was scored by thorns and his shirt was in ribbons under the straps of his iron-sagged apron; but it was not by these marks that his twenty-odd hours showed: it was by his face. While yet his eyes were open and his wits still half awake, his face surrendered. The flesh relaxed into lines of stupor, a putty-formed, putty-colored mask of sleep.

Once he let himself be aroused. This was when, to an abstracted query as to Frank's whereabouts, Blossom told him Frank had been out with four others since dawn. He heaved clear of the table and opened his eyes at her, showing the red around the rims.

He spoke with the thick tongue of a drunkard. "If anybody but me lays hand on that stallion I'll kill him. I'll wring his neck."

Then he relapsed into his stupidity, and not even the arrival of the party bringing his brother's body seemed able to shake him so far clear of it again.

At first, when they had laid Frank on the floor where on the night before they had laid Jim, he seemed hardly to comprehend.

"What's wrong with Frank?"

"Some more of Jim's 'expiriment.' "

"Frank see him? He's scared, Frank is. Look at his face there."

"He's dead, Cam."

"Dead, you say? Frank dead? Dead of fright; is that it?"

Even when, rolling the body over they showed him what was what, he appeared incapable of comprehension, of amazement, of passion, or of any added grief. He looked at them all with a kind of befuddled protest. Returning to his chair and his place, he grumbled, "Le'me eat first, can't you? Can't you gi'me a little time to sleep?"

"Well, you wouldn't do much to-night anyway, I guess."

At White's words Blossom opened her mouth for the first time.

"No, nothing to-night, Cam. Cam! *Camden!* Say! Promise!"

"And then to-morrow, Cam, what we'll do is to get every last man in the valley, and we'll go at this right. We'll lay hand on that devil——"

Camden swallowed his mouthful of cold steak with difficulty. His obsession touched, he showed them the rims of his eyes again.

"You do and I'll wring your necks. The man that touches that animal before I do gets his neck wrang. That's all you need to remember."

"Yes, yes—no—that is——" Poor Blossom. "Yes, Mr. White, thanks; no, Cam's not going out to-night. . . . No, Cam, nobody's going to interfere—nor nothing. Don't you worry there. . . ."

Again poor Blossom! Disaster piled too swiftly on disaster; no discipline but instinct left. Caught in fire and flood and earthquake and not knowing what to come, and no creed but "save him who can!"—by hook or crook of wile or smile. With the valley of her life emptied out, and its emptiness repeopled monstrously and pressing down black on the roof under which (now that Frank was gone to the ice house too and the farmers back home) one brother was left of three— she would tread softly, she would talk or she would be dumb, as her sidelong glimpses of the awake-sleep man's face above the table told her was the instant's need; or if he would eat, she would magic out of nothing something, anything; or if he would sleep, he could sleep, so long as he slept in that house where she could know he was sleeping.

Only one thing. If she could touch him. If she could touch and cling. Lightning filled the windows. After a moment the thunder came avalanching down the pasture and brought up against the clapboards of the house. At this she was behind his chair. She put out a hand. She touched his shoulder. The shoulder was bare, the shirt ripped away; it was caked with sweat and with the blackening smears of scratches, but for all its exhaustion and dirt it was flesh alive—a living man to touch.

Camden blundered up. "What the hell!" He started off two steps and wheeled on her. "Why don't you get off to bed for Goll sake!"

"Yes, Cam, yes—right off, yes."

"Well, *I'm* going, I can tell you. For Goll sake, I need some sleep!"

"Yes, that's right, yes, Cam, good night, Cam—only—only you promise—promise you won't go out—nowheres."

"Go *out?* Not likely I won't! Not *likely!* Get along."

It took her no time to get along then—quick and quiet as a mouse.

Camden lingered to stand at one of the windows where the lightning came again, throwing the black barns and paddocks at him from the white sweep of the pastures crowned by woods.

As it had taken her no time to go, it took Blossom no time to undress and get in bed. When Camden was on his way to his room he heard her calling, "Cam! Just a second, Cam!"

In the dark outside her door he drew one hand down over his face, wiping off whatever might be there. Then he entered. "Yes? What?"

"Cam, set by me a minute, won't you? And Cam, oh Cam, hold my hand."

As he slouched down, his fist inclosing her fingers, thoughts awakened and ran and fastened on things. They fastened, tentatively at first, upon the farm. Jim gone. Frank gone. The smithy, the store, and the farm. The whole of Mill Crossing. The trinity. The three in one. . . .

"Tight, Cam, for pity's sake! Hold it tight!"

His eyes, falling to his fist, strayed up along the arm it held. The sleeve, rumpled near the shoulder, was trimmed with pretty lace. . . .

"Tighter, Cam!"

A box of apples. The memory hidden away in the cellar of his mind. Hidden away, clamped down in the dark, till the noxious vapors, the murderous vapors of its rotting had filled the shutup house he was. . . . A box of red apples for the apple-grower's girl . . . the girl who sniggered and ran away from him to laugh at him. . . .

And here, by the unfolding of a devious destiny, he sat in that girl's bedroom, holding that girl's hand. Jim who had got her, Frank who had wanted her lay side by side out there in the ice house under the lightning. While he, the "dumb one" —the last to be thought of with anything but amusement and the last to be feared—his big hot fist inclosing her imprecating hand now, and his eyes on the pretty lace at her shoulder. —He jumped up with a gulp and a clatter of iron.

"What the—," he flung her hand away. "What the— hell!" He swallowed. "Damn you, Blossie Beck!" He stared at her with repugnance and mortal fright. "Why, you—you —you——?"

He moderated his voice with an effort, wiping his brow, "Good night. You must excuse me, Blossie; I wasn't meaning —I mean—I hope you sleep good. *I* shall. . . . Good night!"

In his own brain was the one word, "Hurry!"

She lay and listened to his boots going along the hall and heard the closing of his door. She ought to have put out the lamp. But even with the shade drawn, the lightning around the edges of the window unnerved her; in the dark alone it would have been more than she could bear.

She lay so still she felt herself nearing exhaustion from the sustained rigidity of her limbs. Rain came and with the rain, wind. Around the eaves it neighed like wild stallions; down the chimneys it moaned like men.

Slipping out of bed and pulling on a bathrobe she ran from her room, barefooted, and along the hall to Camden's door.

"Cam!" she called. "Oh, Cam!" she begged. "Please, please!" And now he wouldn't answer her.

New lightning, diffused through all the sky by the blown rain, ran at her along the corridor. She pushed the door open.

The lamp was burning on the bureau but the room was empty and the bed untouched.

Taking the lamp she skittered down to the kitchen. No one there. . . .

"Hurry!"

Camden had reached the woods when the rain came. Lighting the lantern he had brought, he made his way on to the boundary fence. There, about a mile to the east of the path the others had taken that day, he pulled the rails down and tumbled the stones together in a pile. Then he proceeded another hundred yards, holding the lantern high and peering through the streaming crystals of the rain.

Blue Murder was there. Neither the chain nor the sapling had given way. The lantern and, better than the lantern, a globe of lightning, showed the tethered stallion glistening and quivering, his eyes all whites at the man's approach.

"Gentle, boy; steady, boy!" Talking all the while in the way he had with horses, Camden put a hand on the taut chain and bore with a gradually progressive weight, bringing the dark head nearer. "Steady, boy; gentle there, damn you; gentle!"

Was he afraid of horses? Who was it said he was afraid of horses?

The beast's head was against the man's chest, held there by an arm thrown over the bowed neck. As he smoothed the forehead and fingered the nose with false caresses, Camden's "horse talk" ran on— the cadence one thing, the words another.

"Steady, Goll damn you; you're going to get yours. Cheer up, cheer up, the worst is yet to come. Come now! Come easy! Come along!"

When he had unloosed the chain, he felt for and found with his free hand his hammer hidden behind the tree. Throwing the lantern into the brush, where it flared for an instant before dying, he led the stallion back as far as the break he had made in the fence. Taking a turn with the chain around the animal's nose, like an improvised hackamore, he swung from the stone pile to the slippery back. A moment's shying, a sliding caracole of amazement and distrust, a crushing of knees, a lash of the chain end and that was all there was to that. Blue Murder had been ridden before. . . .

In the smithy, chambered in the roaring of the falls and the swish and shock of the storm Camden sang as he pumped his bellows, filling the cave beneath the rafters with red. The air was nothing, the words were mumbo-jumbo, but they swelled his chest. His eyes, cast from time to time at his wheeling prisoner, had lost their look of helplessness and surly distraction.

Scared? He? No, no, no! Now that he wasn't any longer afraid of time, he wasn't afraid of anything on earth.

"Shy, you devil" He wagged his exalted head. "Whicker, you hellion! Whicker all you want to, stud horse! To-morrow they're going to get you, the numb fools! To-morrow they can have you. *I* got you *to-night!*"

He was more than other men; he was enormous. Fishing an iron shoe from that inseparable apron pocket of his, he thrust it into the coal and blew and blew. He tried it and it was burning red. He tried it again and it was searing white. Taking it out on the anvil he began to beat it, swinging his hammer one-handed, gigantic. So in the crimson light, ir-radiating iron sparks, he was at his greatest. Pounding, pounding. A man in the dark of night with a hammer about him can do wonders; with a horseshoe about him he can cover up a sin. And if the dark of night in a paddock won't hold it, then the dark of undergrowth on a mountain side will. . . .

Pounding, pounding; thinking, thinking, in a great halo of hot stars. Feeding his hungry, his insatiable muscles.

"Steady now, you blue bastard! Steady, boy!"

What he did not realize in his feverish exaltation was that his muscles were not insatiable. In the thirty-odd hours past they had had a feast spread before them and they had had their fill. . . . More than their fill.

As with the scorching iron in his tongs he approached the stallion, he had to step over the nail box he had stepped over five thousand times in the routine of every day.

A box of apples, eh? Apples to snigger at, eh? But whose girl are you now? . . . Scared, eh?

His foot was heavier of a sudden than it should have been. This five thousand and first time, by the drag of the tenth of an inch, the heel caught the lip of the nail box.

He tried to save himself from stumbling. At the same time, instinctively, he held the iron flame in his tongs away.

There was a scream out of a horse's throat; a whiff of hair and burnt flesh.

There was a lash of something in the red shadows. There was another sound and another wisp of stench. . . .

When, guided by the stallion's whinnying they found the smith next day they saw by the cant of his head that his neck was broken, and they perceived that he too had on him the mark of a shoe. It lay up one side of his throat and the broad of a cheek. It wasn't blue this time, however—it was red. It took them some instants in the sunshine pouring through the wide door to comprehend this phenomenon. It wasn't sunk in by a blow this time; it was burned in, a brand.

Darred called them to look at the stallion, chained behind the forge.

"Almighty God!" The words sounded funny in his mouth. They sounded the funnier in that they were the same ones the blundering smith had uttered when, staring uphill from his clever wreckage of the paddock fence he had seen the mares striking sparks from the stones where the stallion struck none. And he, of all men, a smith!

"Almighty God!" called Darred. "What you make of these here feet?"

One fore hoof was freshly pared for shoeing; the other three hoofs were as virgin as any yearling's on the plains. Blue Murder had never yet been shod . . . .

EDNA FERBER

(1887-   )

Edna Ferber's writing life has covered a period of more than forty years, and she has been active and successful in the novel, the short story and the drama. Most of her earlier works were about people and traditions of the Middle West, of which she herself is a product, but more recently she has written of other parts of the country as well—of New York and Texas, for instance. Her most frequent subject is that of the character whose inner strength grows to match the increasing difficulty of his (more often, her) life. Her stories reflect her admiration for people who are courageous and resourceful, who do not retreat before adversity but who see things through. Miss Ferber is not an innovator, and therefore she has not been widely imitated; but she has been immensely popular, and her best books, such as *So Big, Show Boat,* and *Cimarron,* have been very effective pictures of American Life. "Old Man Minick," one of her most popular short stories, has been successfully dramatized.

OLD MAN MINICK

HIS WIFE HAD ALWAYS SPOILED him outrageously. No doubt of that. Take, for example, the mere matter of the pillows. Old Man Minick slept high. That is, he thought he slept high. He liked two pillows on his side of the great, wide, old-fashioned cherry bed. He would sink into them with a vast grunting and sighing and puffing expressive of nerves and muscles relaxed and gratified. But in the morning there always was one pillow on the floor. He had thrown it there. Always, in the morning, there it lay, its plump white cheek turned reproachfully up at him from the side of the bed. Ma Minick knew this, naturally, after forty years of the cherry bed. But she never begrudged him that extra pillow. Each morning, when she arose, she picked it up on her way to shut the window. Each morning the bed was made up with two pillows on his side of it, as usual.

Then there was the window. Ma Minick liked it open wide. Old Man Minick, who rather prided himself on his modernism (he called it being up to date), was distrustful of the night air. In the folds of its sable mantle lurked a swarm of dread things—colds, clammy miasmas, fevers.

"Night air's just like any other air," Ma Minick would say, with some asperity. Ma Minick was no worm; and as modern as her husband. So when they went to bed the window would be open wide. They would lie there, the two old ones, talking comfortably about commonplace things. The kind of talk that goes on between a man and a woman who have lived together in wholesome peace (spiced with occasional wholesome bickerings) for more than forty years.

"Remind me to see Gerson tomorrow about that lock on the basement door. The paper's full of burglars."

"If I think of it." She never failed to.

"George and Nettie haven't been over in a week now."

"Oh, well, young folks. . . . Did you stop in and pay that Koritz the fifty cents for pressing your suit?"

"By golly, I forgot again! First thing in the morning."

A sniff. "Just smell the Yards." It was Chicago.

"Wind must be from the west."

Sleep came with reluctant feet, but they wooed her patiently. And presently she settled down between them and they slept lightly. Usually, sometime during the night, he awoke, slid cautiously and with infinite stealth from beneath the covers, and closed the wide-flung window to within a bare two inches of the sill. Almost invariably she heard him; but she was a wise old woman, a philosopher of parts. She knew better than to allow a window to shatter the peace of their marital felicity. As she lay there, smiling a little grimly in the dark and giving no sign of being awake, she thought, Oh, well, I guess a closed window won't kill me either.

Still, sometimes, just to punish him a little, and to prove that she was nobody's fool, she would wait until he had dropped off to sleep again and then she, too, would achieve a stealthy trip to the window and would raise it slowly, carefully, inch by inch.

"How did that window come to be open?" he would say in the morning, being a poor dissembler.

"Window? Why, it's just the way it was when we went to bed." And she would stoop to pick up the pillow that lay on the floor.

There was little or no talk of death between this comfortable, active, sound-appearing man of almost seventy and this plump, capable woman of sixty-six. But as always between husband and wife, it was understood wordlessly (and without reason) that Old Man Minick would go first. Not that either of them had the slightest intention of going. In fact, when it happened, they were planning to spend the winter in California and perhaps live there indefinitely if they liked it and didn't get too lonesome for George and Nettie, and the Chicago smoke, and Chicago noise, and Chicago smells and rush and dirt. Still, the solid sum paid yearly in insurance premiums showed clearly that he meant to leave her in comfort and security. Besides, the world is full of widows. Everyone sees that. But how many widowers? Few. Widows there are by the thousands; living alone, living in hotels, living with married daughters and sons-in-law or married sons and daughters-in-law. But of widowers in a like situation there are bewilderingly few. And why this should be no one knows.

So, then. The California trip never materialized. And the year that followed never was quite clear in Old Man Minick's dazed mind. In the first place, it was the year in which stocks tumbled and broke their backs. Gilt-edged securities showed themselves to be tinsel. Old Man Minick had retired from active business just one year before, meaning to live comfortably on the fruit of a half century's toil. He now saw that fruit rotting all about him. There was in it hardly enough nourishment to sustain them. Then came the day when Ma Minick went downtown to see Matthews about that pain right here and came home looking shriveled, talking shrilly about nothing, and evading Pa's eyes. Followed months that were just a jumble of agony, X-rays, hope, despair, morphia, nothingness.

After it was all over: "But I was going first," Old Man Minick said dazedly.

The old house on Ellis near Thirty-ninth was sold for what it would bring. George, who knew Chicago real estate if anyone did, said they might as well get what they could. Things would only go lower. You'll see. And nobody's going to have any money for years. Besides, look at the neighborhood!

Old Man Minick said George was right. He said everybody was right. You would hardly have recognized in this shrunken figure and wattled face the spruce and dressy old man whom Ma Minick used to spoil so delightfully. "You know best, George. You know best." He who used to stand up to George until Ma Minick was moved to say, "Now, Pa, you don't know everything."

After Matthews' bills, and the hospital, and the nurses and the medicines and the thousand and one things were paid, there was left exactly five hundred dollars a year.

"You're going to make your home with us, Father," George and Nettie said. Alma, too, said this would be the best. Alma, the married daughter, lived in Seattle. "Though you know Fred and I would be only too glad to have you."

Seattle! The ends of the earth. Oh, no. No! he protested, every fiber of his old frame clinging to the accustomed. Seattle, at seventy! He turned piteous eyes on his son, George, and his daughter-in-law, Nettie. "You're going to make your home with us, Father," they reassured him. He clung to them gratefully. After it was over Alma went home to her husband and their children.

So now he lived with George and Nettie in the five-room flat on South Park Avenue, just across from Washington Park. And there was no extra pillow on the floor.

Nettie hadn't said he couldn't have the extra pillow. He had told her he used two and she had given him two the first week. But every morning she had found a pillow on the floor.

"I thought you used two pillows, Father."

"I do."

"But there's always one on the floor when I make the bed in the morning. You always throw one on the floor. You only sleep on one pillow, really."

"I use two pillows."

But the second week there was one pillow. He tossed and turned a good deal there in his bedroom off the kitchen. But he got used to it in time. Not used to it, exactly, but—well——

The bedroom off the kitchen wasn't as menial as it sounds. It was really rather cozy. The five-room flat held living room, front bedroom, dining room, kitchen, and maid's room. The room off the kitchen was intended as a maid's room, but Nettie had no maid. George's business had suffered with the rest. George and Nettie had said, "I wish there was a front room for you, Father. You could have ours and we'd move back here, only this room's too small for twin beds and the dressing table and the chest of drawers." They had meant it— or meant to mean it.

"This is fine," Old Man Minick had said. "This is good enough for anybody." There were a narrow white enamel bed and a tiny dresser and a table. Nettie had made gay cretonne covers and spreads and put a little reading lamp on the table and arranged his things. Ma Minick's picture on the dresser with her mouth sort of pursed to make it look small. It wasn't a recent picture. Nettie and George had had it framed for him as a surprise. They had often urged her to have a picture taken, but she had dreaded it. Old Man Minick didn't think much of that photograph, though he never said so. He needed no photograph of Ma Minick. He had a dozen of them; a gallery of them; thousands of them. Lying on his one pillow, he could take them out and look at them one by one as they passed in review, smiling, serious, chiding, praising, there in the dark. He needed no picture on his dresser.

A handsome girl, Nettie, and a good girl. He thought of her

as a girl, though she was well past thirty. George and Nettie had married late. This was only the third year of their marriage. Alma, the daughter, had married young, but George had stayed on, unwed, in the old house on Ellis until he was thirty-six and all Ma Minick's friends' daughters had had a try at him in vain. The old people had urged him to marry, but it had been wonderful to have him around the house, just the same. Somebody young around the house. Not that George had stayed around very much. But when he was there you knew he was there. He whistled while dressing. He sang in the bath. He roared down the stairway, "Ma, where're my clean shirts?" The telephone rang for him. Ma Minick prepared special dishes for him. The servant girl said, "Oh, now, Mr. George, look what you've done! Gone and spilled the grease all over my clean kitchen floor!" and wiped it up adoringly while George laughed and gobbled his bit of food filched from pot or frying pan.

They had been a little surprised about Nettie. George was in the bond business and she worked for the same firm. A plump handsome eye-glassed woman with fine fresh coloring, a clear skin that Old Man Minick called appetizing, and a great coil of smooth dark hair. She wore plain tailored things and understood the bond business in a way that might have led you to think hers a masculine mind if she hadn't been so feminine, too, in her manner. Old Man Minick had liked her better than Ma Minick had.

Nettie had called him Pop and joked with him and almost flirted with him in a daughterly sort of way. He liked to squeeze her plump arm and pinch her soft cheek between thumb and forefinger. She would laugh up at him and pat his shoulder and that shoulder would straighten spryly and he would waggle his head doggishly.

"Look out there, George!" the others in the room would say. "Your dad'll cut you out. First thing you know you'll lose your girl, that's all."

Nettie would smile. Her teeth were white and strong and even. Old Man Minick would laugh and wink, immensely pleased and flattered. "We understand each other, don't we, Pop?" Nettie would say.

During the first years of their married life Nettie stayed home. She fussed happily about her little flat, gave parties, went to parties, played bridge. She seemed to love the ease, the relaxation, the small luxuries. She and George were very much in love. Before her marriage she had lived in a boardinghouse on Michigan Avenue. At mention of it now she puckered up her face. She did not attempt to conceal her fondness for these five rooms of hers, so neat, so quiet, so bright, so cozy. Overstuffed velvet in the living room, with silk lamp shades, and small tables holding books and magazines, and little boxes containing cigarettes or hard candies. Very modern. A gate-legged table in the dining room. Caramel-colored walnut in the bedroom, rich and dark and smooth. She loved it. An orderly woman. Everything in its place. Before eleven o'clock the little apartment was shining, spotless; cushions plumped, crumbs brushed, vegetables in cold water. The telephone. "Hello! . . . Oh, hello, Bess! . . . Oh, hours ago. . . . Not a thing. . . . Well, if George is willing. . . . I'll call him up and ask him. We haven't seen a show in two weeks. I'll call you back within the next half-hour. . . . No, I haven't done my marketing yet. . . . Yes, and have dinner downtown. Meet at seven."

Into this orderly, smooth-running mechanism was catapulted a bewildered old man. She no longer called him Pop. He never dreamed of squeezing the plump arm or pinching the smooth cheek. She called him Father. Sometimes George's father. Sometimes, when she was telephoning, there came to him: "George's father's living with us now, you know. I can't."

They were very kind to him, Nettie and George. "Now just you sit right down here, Father. What do you want to go poking off into your own room for?"

He remembered that in the last year Nettie had said something about going back to work. There wasn't enough to do around the house to keep her busy. She was sick of afternoon parties. Sew and eat, that's all, and gossip, or play bridge.

Besides, look at the money. Business was awful. The two old people had resented this idea as much as George had—more, in fact. They were scandalized.

"Young folks nowadays!" shaking their heads. "Young folks nowadays. What are they thinking of! In my day when you got married you had babies."

George and Nettie had had no babies. At first Nettie had said, "I'm so happy. I just want a chance to rest. I've been working since I was seventeen. I just want to rest, first." One year. Two years. Three. And now Pa Minick.

Ma Minick, in the old house on Ellis Avenue, had kept a loose sort of larder; not lavish, but plentiful. They both ate a great deal, as old people are likely to do. Old Man Minick, especially, had liked to nibble. A handful of raisins from the box on the shelf. A couple of nuts from the dish on the sideboard. A bit of candy, rolled beneath the tongue. At dinner (sometimes, toward the last, even at noontime) a plate of steaming soup, hot, revivifying. Plenty of this and plenty of that. "What's the matter, Jo? You're not eating." But he was, amply. Ma Minick had liked to see him eat too much. She was wrong, of course.

But at Nettie's things were different. Hers was a sufficient but stern ménage. So many mouths to feed; just so many lamb chops. Nettie knew about calories and vitamins and mysterious things like that, and talked about them. So many calories in this. So many calories in that. He never was quite clear in his mind about these things said to be lurking in his food. He had always thought of spinach as spinach, chops as chops. But to Nettie they were calories. They lunched together, these two. George was, of course, downtown. For herself Nettie would have one of those feminine pickup lunches; a dab of applesauce, a cup of tea, and a slice of cold toast left from breakfast. This she would eat while Old Man Minick guiltily supped up his cup of warmed-over broth, or his coddled egg. She always pressed upon him any bit of cold meat that was left from the night before, or any remnants of vegetable or spaghetti. Often there was quite a little fleet of saucers and sauce plates grouped about his main plate. Into these he dipped and swooped uncomfortably, and yet with a relish. Sometimes, when he had finished, he would look about, furtively.

"What'll you have, Father? Can I get you something?"

"Nothing, Nettie, nothing. I'm doing fine." She had finished the last of her wooden toast and was waiting for him, kindly.

Still, this balanced and scientific fare seemed to agree with him. As the winter went on he seemed actually to have regained most of his former hardiness and vigor. A handsome old boy he was, ruddy, hale, with the zest of a juicy old apple, slightly withered but still sappy. It should be mentioned that he had a dimple in his cheek which flashed unexpectedly when he smiled. It gave him a roguish—almost boyish—effect, most appealing to the beholder. Especially the female beholder. Much of his spoiling at the hands of Ma Minick had doubtless been due to this mere depression of the skin.

Spring was to bring a new and welcome source of enrichment into his life. But these first six months of his residence with George and Nettie were hard. No spoiling there. He missed being made much of. He got kindness, but he needed love. Then, too, he was rather a gabby old man. He liked to hold forth. In the old house on Ellis there had been visiting back and forth between men and women of his own age, and Ma's. At these gatherings he had waxed oratorical or argumentative, and they had heard him, some in agreement, some in disagreement, but always respectfully, whether he prated of real estate or social depravity, Prohibition or European exchange.

"Let me tell you, here and now, something's got to be done before you can get a country back on a sound financial basis. Why, take Russia alone, why . . ." Or: "Young people nowadays! They don't know what respect means. I tell you there's got to be a change and there will be, and it's the older generation that's got to bring it about. What do they know of hardship! What do they know about work—real work. Most of 'em's never done a real day's work in their life. All they think of is dancing and running around and drinking. Look at the way they dress! Look at . . ."

Ad lib.

"That's so," the others would agree. "I was saying only yesterday . . ."

Then, too, until a year or two before, he had taken active part in business. He had retired only at the urging of Ma and the children. They said he ought to rest and play and enjoy himself.

Now, as his strength and good spirits gradually returned he began to go downtown, mornings. He would dress, carefully, though a little shakily. He had always shaved himself and he kept this up. All in all, during the day, he occupied the bathroom literally for hours, and this annoyed Nettie to the point of frenzy, though she said nothing. He liked the white cheerfulness of the little tiled room. He puddled about in the water endlessly. Snorted and splashed and puffed and snuffled and blew. He was one of those audible washers who emerge dripping and whose ablutions are distributed impartially over ceiling, walls, and floor.

Nettie, at the closed door: "Father, are you all right?"

Splash! Prrf! "Yes. Sure. I'm all right."

"Well, I didn't know. You've been in there so long."

He was a neat old man, but there was likely to be a spot or so on his vest or his coat lapel, or his tie. Ma used to remove these, on or off him as the occasion demanded, rubbing carefully and scolding a little, making a chiding sound between tongue and teeth indicative of great impatience of his carelessness. He had rather enjoyed these sounds, and this rubbing and scratching on the cloth with the fingernail and a moistened rag. They indicated that someone cared. Cared about the way he looked. Had pride in him. Loved him. Nettie never removed spots. Though infrequently she said, "Father, just leave that suit out, will you? I'll send it to the cleaner's with George's. The man's coming tomorrow morning." He would look down at himself, hastily, and attack a spot here and there with a futile fingernail.

His morning toilette completed, he would make for the Fifty-first Street L. Seated in the train, he would assume an air of importance and testy haste; glance out of the window;

look at his watch. You got the impression of a handsome and well-preserved old gentleman on his way downtown to consummate a shrewd business deal. He had been familiar with Chicago's downtown for fifty years and he could remember when State Street was a tree-shaded cottage district. The noise and rush and clangour of the Loop had long been familiar to him. But now he seemed to find the downtown trip arduous, even hazardous. The roar of the elevated trains, the hoarse toots of the motor horns, the clang of the streetcars, the bedlam that is Chicago's downtown district bewildered him, frightened him almost. He would skip across the street like a harried hare, just missing a motor truck's nose and all unconscious of the stream of invective directed at him by its charioteer. "Heh! Whatcha! . . . Look!" Sometimes a policeman came to his aid, or attempted to, but he resented this proffered help.

"Say, look here, my lad," he would say to the tall, tired, and not at all burly policeman, "I've been coming downtown since long before you were born. You don't need to help me. I'm no jay from the country."

He visited the Stock Exchange. This depressed him. Stocks were lower than ever and still going down. His five hundred a year was safe, but the rest seemed doomed for his lifetime, at least. He would drop in at George's office. George's office was pleasantly filled with dapper, neat young men and (surprisingly enough) dapper, slim young women, seated at desks in the big light-flooded room. At one corner of each desk stood a polished metal placard bearing the name of the desk's occupant. Mr. Owens. Mr. Satterlee. Mr. James. Miss Rauch. Mr. Minick.

"Hello, Father," Mr. Minick would say, looking annoyed. "What's bringing you down?"

"Oh, nothing. Nothing. Just had a little business to tend to over at the Exchange. Thought I'd drop in. How's business?"

"Rotten."

"I should think it was!" Old Man Minick would agree. "I—should—think—it—was! Hm."

George wished he wouldn't. He couldn't have it, that's all.
Old Man Minick would stroll over to the desk marked Satterlee, or Owens, or James. These brisk young men would toss
an upward glance at him and concentrate again on the sheets
and files before them. Old Man Minick would stand, balancing
from heel to toe and blowing out his breath a little. He looked
a bit yellow and granulated and wavering, there in the cruel
morning light of the big plate-glass windows. Or perhaps it
was the contrast he presented with these slim, slick young
salesmen.

"Well, h'are you today, Mr.—uh—Satterlee? What's the
good word?"

Mr. Satterlee would not glance up this time. "I'm pretty
well. Can't complain."

"Good. Good."

"Anything I can do for you?"

"No-o-o. Not a thing. Just dropped in to see my son a
minute."

"I see." Not unkindly. Then, as Old Man Minick still stood
there, balancing, Mr. Satterlee would glance up again, frown-
ing a little. "Your son's desk is over there, I believe. Yes."

George and Nettie had a bedtime conference about these
visits and Nettie told him, gently, that the bond-house head
objected to friends and relatives dropping in. It was against
office rules. It had been so when she was employed there.
Strictly business. She herself had gone there only once since
her marriage.

Well, that was all right. Business was like that nowadays.
Rush and grab and no time for anything.

The winter was a hard one, with a record snowfall and in-
tense cold. He stayed indoors for days together. A woman of
his own age in like position could have occupied herself use-
fully and happily. She could have hemmed a sash curtain;
knitted or crocheted; tidied a room; taken a hand in the cooking or preparing of food; ripped an old gown; made over a
new one; indulged in an occasional afternoon festivity with
women of her own years. But for Old Man Minick there were

no small tasks. There was nothing he could do to make his place in the household justifiable. He wasn't even particularly good at those small jobs of hammering, or painting, or general "fixing." Nettie could drive a nail more swiftly, more surely than he. "Now, Father, don't you bother. I'll do it. Just you go and sit down. Isn't it time for your afternoon nap?"

He waxed a little surly. "Nap! I just got up. I don't want to sleep my life away."

George and Nettie frequently had guests in the evening. They played bridge, or poker, or talked.

"Come in, Father," George would say. "Come in. You all know Dad, don't you, folks?" He would sit down, uncertainly. At first he had attempted to expound, as had been his wont in the old house on Ellis. "I want to say, here and now, that this country's got to . . ." But they went on, heedless of him. They interrupted or refused, politely, to listen. So he sat in the room, yet no part of it. The young people's talk swirled and eddied all about him. He was utterly lost in it. Now and then Nettie or George would turn to him and with raised voice (he was not at all deaf and prided himself on it) would shout, "It's about this or that, Father. He was saying . . ."

When the group roared with laughter at a sally from one of them he would smile uncertainly but amiably, glancing from one to the other in complete ignorance of what had passed, but not resenting it. He took to sitting more and more in his kitchen bedroom, smoking a comforting pipe and reading and rereading the evening paper. During that winter he and Canary, the Negro washwoman, became quite good friends. She washed down in the basement once a week but came up to the kitchen for her massive lunch. A walrus-waisted black woman, with a rich, throaty voice, a rolling eye, and a kindly heart. He actually waited for her appearance above the laundry stairs.

"Weh, how's Mist' Minick today! Ah nev' did see a gennelman spry's you ah fo' yo' age. No, suh! nev' did."

At this rare praise he would straighten his shoulders and waggle his head. "I'm worth any ten of these young sprats today." Canary would throw back her head in a loud and companionable guffaw.

Nettie would appear at the kitchen swinging door. "Canary's having her lunch, Father. Don't you want to come into the front room with me? We'll have our lunch in another half-hour."

He followed her obediently enough. Nettie thought of him as a troublesome and rather pathetic child—a child who would never grow up. If she attributed any thoughts to that fine old head they were ambling thoughts, bordering, perhaps, on senility. Little did she know how expertly this old one surveyed her and how ruthlessly he passed judgment. She never suspected the thoughts that formed in that active brain.

He knew about women. He had married a woman. He had had children by her. He looked at this woman—his son's wife —moving about her little five-room flat. She had theories about children. He had heard her expound them. You didn't have them except under such and such circumstances. It wasn't fair otherwise. Plenty of money for their education. Well. He and his wife had had three children. Paul, the second, had died at thirteen. A blow, that had been. They had not always planned for the coming of the three, but they always had found a way, afterward. You managed, somehow, once the little wrinkled red ball had fought its way into the world. You managed. You managed. Look at George! Yet when he was born, thirty-nine years ago, Pa and Ma Minick had been hard put to it.

Sitting there, while Nettie dismissed him as negligible, he saw her clearly, grimly. He looked at her. She was plump, but not too short, with a generous width between the hips; a broad full bosom, but firm; round arms and quick slim legs; a fine sturdy throat. The curve between arm and breast made a graceful gracious line. . . . Working in a bond office . . . Working in a bond office . . . There was nothing in the Bible about working in a bond office. Here was a woman built for childbearing.

She thought him senile, negligible.

In March Nettie had in a sewing woman for a week. She had her two or three times a year. A hawk-faced woman of about forty-nine, with a blue-bottle figure and a rapacious eye. She sewed in the dining room and there was a pleasant hum of machine and snip of scissors and murmur of conversation and rustle of silky stuff; and hot, savory dishes for lunch. She and Old Man Minick became great friends. She even let him take out bastings. This when Nettie had gone out from two to four, between fittings.

He chuckled and waggled his head. "I expect to be paid regular assistant's wages for this," he said.

"I guess you don't need any wages, Mr. Minick," the woman said. "I guess you're pretty well fixed."

"Oh well, I can't complain." (Five hundred a year.)

"Complain! I should say not! If I was to complain it'd be different. Work all day to keep myself, and nobody to come home to at night."

"Widow, ma'am?"

"Since I was twenty. Work, work, that's all I've had. And lonesome! I suppose you don't know what lonesome is."

"Oh, don't I!" slipped from him. He had dropped the bastings.

The sewing woman flashed a look at him from the cold hard eye. "Well, maybe you do. I suppose living here like this, with sons and daughters, ain't so grand, for all your money. Now me, I've always managed to keep my own little place that I could call home to come back to. It's only two rooms, and nothing to rave about, but it's home. Evenings I just cook and fuss around. Nobody to fuss for, but I fuss, anyway. Cooking, that's what I love to do. Plenty of good food, that's what folks need to keep their strength up." Nettie's lunch that day had been rather scant.

She was there a week. In Nettie's absence, she talked against her. He protested, but weakly. Did she give him eggnogs? Milk? Hot toddy? Soup? Plenty of good, rich gravy and meat and puddings? Well! That's what folks needed when they weren't so young any more. Not that he looked old. My, no.

Spryer than many young boys, and handsomer than his own son, if she did say so.

He fed on it, hungrily. The third day she was flashing meaning glances at him across the luncheon table. The fourth she pressed his foot beneath the table. The fifth, during Nettie's afternoon absence, she got up, ostensibly to look for a bit of cloth which she needed for sewing, and, passing him, laid a caressing hand on his shoulder. Laid it there and pressed his shoulder ever so little. He looked up, startled. The glances across the luncheon had largely passed over his head; the foot beneath the table might have been an accident. But this— this was unmistakable. He stood up, a little shakily. She caught his hand. The hawklike face was close to his.

"You need somebody to love you," she said. "Somebody to do for you, and love you." The hawk face came nearer. He leaned a little toward it. But between it and his face was Ma Minick's face, plump, patient, quizzical. His head came back sharply. He threw the woman's hot hand from him.

"Woman!" he cried. "Jezebel!"

The front door slammed. Nettie. The woman flew to her sewing. Old Man Minick, shaking, went into his kitchen bedroom.

"Well," said Nettie, depositing her bundles on the dining-room table, "did you finish that faggoting? Why, you haven't done so very much, have you!"

"I ain't feeling so good," said the woman. "That lunch didn't agree with me."

"Why, it was a good plain lunch. I don't see——"

"Oh, it was plain enough, all right."

Next day she did not come to finish her work. Sick, she telephoned. Nettie called it an outrage. She finished the sewing herself, though she hated sewing. Pa Minick said nothing, but there was a light in his eye. Now and then he chuckled, to Nettie's infinite annoyance, though she said nothing.

"Wanted to marry me!" he said to himself, chuckling. "Wanted to marry me! The old rip!"

At the end of April, Pa Minick discovered Washington

Park, and the Club, and his whole life was from that day transformed.

He had taken advantage of the early spring sunshine to take a walk, at Nettie's suggestion.

"Why don't you go into the park, Father? It's really warm out. And the sun's lovely. Do you good."

He had put on his heaviest shirt, and a muffler, and George's old red sweater with the great white C on its front, emblem of George's athletic prowess at the University of Chicago; and over all, his greatcoat. He had taken warm mittens and his cane with the greyhound's-head handle, carved. So equipped, he had ambled uninterestedly over to the park across the way. And there he had found new life.

New life in old life. For the park was full of old men. Old men like himself, with greyhound's-head canes, and mufflers, and somebody's sweater worn beneath their greatcoats. They wore arctics, though the weather was fine. The skin of their hands and cheekbones was glazed and had a tight look, though it lay in fine little folds. There were splotches of brown on the backs of their hands, and on the temples and forehead. Their heavy gray or brown socks made comfortable pleats above their ankles. From that April morning until winter drew on, the park saw Old Man Minick daily. Not only daily, but by the day. Except for his meals, and a brief hour for his after-luncheon nap, he spent all his time there.

For in the park Old Man Minick and all the old men gathered there found a forum—a safety valve, a means of expression. It did not take him long to discover that the park was divided into two distinct sets of old men. There were the old men who lived with their married sons and daughters-in-law or married daughters and sons-in-law. Then there were the old men who lived in the Grant Home for Aged Gentlemen. You saw its fine red-brick façade through the trees at the edge of the park.

And the slogan of these first was:

"My son and my da'ter, they wouldn't want me to live in any public home. No, sirree! They want me right there with

them. In their own home. That's the kind of son and da'ter
I've got!"

The slogan of the second was:

"I wouldn't live with any son or daughter. Independent.
That's me. My own boss. Nobody to tell me what I can do and
what I can't. Treat you like a child. I'm my own boss. Pay
my own good money and get my keep for it!"

The first group, strangely enough, was likely to be spotted
of vest and a little frayed as to collar. You saw them going on
errands for their daughters-in-law. A loaf of bread. Spool of
white No. 100. They took their small grandchildren to the
duck pond, and between the two toddlers hand in hand—the
old and infirm and the infantile and infirm—it was hard to tell
which led which.

The second group was shiny as to shoes, spotless as to linen,
dapper as to clothes. They had no small errands. Theirs was a
magnificent leisure. And theirs was magnificent conversation.
The questions they discussed and settled there in the park—
these old men—were not international merely. They were
cosmic in scope.

The war? Peace? Disarmament? China? Mere conversational bubbles to be tossed in the air and disposed of in a burst
of foam. Strong meat for Old Man Minick, who had so long
been fed on pap. But he soon got used to it. Between four and
five in the afternoon, in a spot known as Under the Willows,
the meeting took the form of a club—an open forum. A certain
group made up of Socialists, freethinkers, parlor rebels, had
for years drifted there for talk. Old Man Minick learned high-
sounding phrases. "The Masters . . . democracy . . . toil of the
many for the good of the few . . . the ruling class . . . free
speech . . . the People. . . . "

The strong-minded ones held forth. The weaker ones drifted
about on the outskirts, sometimes clinging to the moist and
sticky paw of a round-eyed grandchild. Earlier in the day—at
eleven o'clock, say—the talk was not so general nor so inclu-
sive. The old men were likely to drift into groups of two or
three or four. They sat on sun-bathed benches, and their con-

versation was likely to be rather smutty at times, for all that they looked so mild and patriarchal and desiccated. They paid scant heed to the white-haired old women who, like themselves, were sunning in the park. They watched the young women switch by, with appreciative glances at their trim figures and slim ankles. The day of the short skirt was a grand time for them. They chuckled among themselves and made wicked comment. One saw only white-haired, placid, tremulous old men, but their minds still worked with belated masculinity. They were like naughty small boys talking behind the barn.

Old Man Minick early achieved a certain leadership in the common talk. He had always liked to hold forth. This last year had been one of almost unendurable bottling up. At first he had timidly sought the less assertive ones of his kind. Mild old men who sat in rockers in the pavilion, waiting for lunchtime. Their conversation irritated him. They remarked everything that passed before their eyes.

"There's a boat. Fella with a boat."

A silence. Then, heavily: "Yeh."

Five minutes.

"Look at those people lying on the grass. Shouldn't think it was warm enough for that. . . . Now they're getting up."

A group of equestrians passed along the bridle path on the opposite side of the lagoon. They made a frieze against the delicate spring greenery. The coats of the women were scarlet, vivid green, arresting.

"Riders."

"Yes."

"Good weather for riding."

A man was fishing near by. "Good weather for fishing."

"Yes."

"Wonder what time it is, anyway." From a pocket, deep-buried, came forth a great gold blob of a watch. "I've got one minute to eleven."

Old Man Minick dragged forth a heavy globe. "Mm. I've got eleven."

"Little fast, I guess."

Old Man Minick shook off this conversation impatiently. This wasn't conversation. This was oral death, though he did not put it thus. He joined the other men. They were discussing spiritualism. He listened, ventured an opinion, was heard respectfully and then combated mercilessly. He rose to the verbal fight, and won it.

"Let's see," said one of the old men. "You're not living at the Grant Home, are you?"

"No," Old Man Minick made reply, proudly. "I live with my son and his wife. They wouldn't have it any other way."

"Hm. Like to be independent myself."

"Lonesome, ain't it? Over there?"

"Lonesome! Say, Mr.—what'd you say your name was? Minick? Mine's Hughes—I never was lonesome in my life, 'cept for six months when I lived with my daughter and her husband and their five children. Yes, sir. That's what I call lonesome."

George and Nettie said, "It's doing you good, Father, being out in the air so much." His eyes were brighter, his figure was straighter, his color better. It was that day he had held forth so eloquently on the emigration question. He had to read a lot—papers and magazines and one thing and another—to keep up. He devoured all the books and pamphlets about bond issues and national finances brought home by George. In the park he was considered an authority on bonds and banking. He and a retired real-estate man named Mowry sometimes debated a single question for weeks. George and Nettie, relieved, thought he ambled to the park and spent senile hours with his drooling old friends discussing nothing amiably and witlessly. This while he was eating strong meat, drinking strong drink.

Summer sped. Was past. Autumn held a new dread for Old Man Minick. When winter came where should he go? Where should he go? Not back to the five-room flat all day, and the little back bedroom, and nothingness. In his mind there rang a childish old song they used to sing at school. A silly song:

Where do all the birdies go?
I know. I know.

But he didn't know. He was terror-stricken. October came and went. With the first of November the park became impossible, even at noon, and with two overcoats and the sweater. The first frost was a black frost for him. He scanned the heavens daily for rain or snow. There was a cigar store and billiard room on the corner across the boulevard and there he sometimes went, with a few of his park cronies, to stand behind the players' chairs and watch them at pinochle or rum. But this was a dull business. Besides, the Grant men never came there. They had card rooms of their own.

He turned away from this smoky little den on a drab November day, sick at heart. The winter. He tried to face it, and at what he saw he shrank and was afraid.

He reached the apartment and went around to the rear, dutifully. His rubbers were wet and muddy and Nettie's living-room carpet was a fashionable gray. The back door was unlocked. It was Canary's day downstairs, he remembered. He took off his rubbers in the kitchen and passed into the dining room. Voices. Nettie had company. Some friends, probably, for tea. He turned to go to his room, but stopped at hearing his own name. Father Minick. Father Minick. Nettie's voice.

"Of course, if it weren't for Father Minick I would have. But how can we as long as he lives with us? There isn't room. And we can't afford a bigger place now, with rents what they are. This way it wouldn't be fair to the child. We've talked it over, George and I. Don't you suppose? But not as long as Father Minick is with us. I don't mean we'd use the maid's room for a—for the—if we had a baby. But I'd have to have someone in to help, then, and we'd have to have that extra room."

He stood there in the dining room, quiet. Quiet. His body felt queerly remote and numb, but his mind was working frenziedly. Clearly, too, in spite of the frenzy. Death. That was the first thought. Death. It would be easy. But he didn't want to die. Strange, but he didn't want to die. He liked life. The park, the trees, the Club, the talk, the whole show. . . . Nettie was a good girl. . . . The old must make way for the young. They had the right to be born. . . . Maybe it was just another excuse. Almost four years married. Why not three years ago? . . . The right to live. The right to live. . . .

He turned, stealthily, stealthily, and went back into the kitchen, put on his rubbers, stole out into the darkening November afternoon.

In an hour he was back. He entered at the front door this time, ringing the bell. He had never had a key. As if he were a child, they would not trust him with one. Nettie's women friends were just leaving. In the air you smelled a mingling of perfume and tea and cakes and powder. He sniffed it, sensitively.

"How do you do, Mr. Minick!" they said. "How are you! Well, you certainly look it. And how do you manage these gloomy days?"

He smiled genially, taking off his greatcoat and revealing the red sweater with the big white C on it. "I manage. I manage." He puffed out his cheeks. "I'm busy moving."

"Moving!" Nettie's startled eyes flew to his, held them. "Moving, Father?"

"Old folks must make way for the young," he said gaily. "That's the law of life. Yes, sir! New ones. New ones."

Nettie's face was scarlet. "Father, what in the world——"

"I signed over at the Grant Home today. Move in next week." The women looked at her, smiling. Old Man Minick came over to her and patted her plump arm. Then he pinched her smooth cheek with a quizzical thumb and forefinger. Pinched it and shook it ever so little.

"I don't know what you mean," said Nettie, out of breath.

"Yes you do," said Old Man Minick, and while his tone was light and jesting there was in his old face something stern, something menacing. "Yes, you do."

When he entered the Grant Home a group of them was seated about the fireplace in the main hall. A neat, ruddy, septuagenarian circle. They greeted him casually, with delicacy of feeling, as if he were merely approaching them at their bench in the park.

"Say, Minick, look here. Mowry here says China ought to have been included in the four-power treaty. He says——"

Old Man Minick cleared his throat. "You take China, now," he said, "with her vast and practically, you might say, virgin resources, why——"

An apple-cheeked maid in a black dress and a white apron stopped before him. He paused.

"Housekeeper says for me to tell you your room's all ready, if you'd like to look at it now."

"Minute. Minute, my child." He waved her aside with the air of one who pays five hundred a year for independence and freedom. The girl turned to go. "Uh—young lady! Young lady!" She looked at him. "Tell the housekeeper two pillows, please. Two pillows on my bed. Be sure."

"Yes, sir. Two pillows. Yes, sir. I'll be sure."

PEARL BUCK

(1892-   )

Primarily a novelist, Pearl Buck has, however, written a
number of short stories, of which "The Old Demon," one
of her own favorites, is an excellent example. Although in
recent years she has written stories of American life, she is
best-known as an interpreter of life in China: the life of
the peasants, the personal relations between the Chinese and
the western settlers, the conflict between eastern tradition
and western innovation, the effects of revolution and natural
disaster. She has said that the country people, four-fifths
of the population, seem to her the source of China's strength;
and it is for this reason that she has written so much about
them. Her prose style, somewhat biblical in its simplicity,
is a highly appropriate medium for her revelations of the
lives and emotions of simple people. Among Pearl Buck's
best novels are *East Wind: West Wind, The Good Earth* and
Sons. In 1938 she was awarded the Nobel Prize in literature.

THE OLD DEMON

OLD MRS. WANG knew of course there was a war. Everybody had known for a long time that there was war
going on and that Japanese were killing Chinese. But
still it was not real and no more than hearsay since none of
the Wangs had been killed. The Village of Three Mile Wangs
on the flat banks of the Yellow River, which was old Mrs.
Wang's clan village, had never even seen a Japanese. This
was how they came to be talking about Japanese at all.

It was evening and early summer, and after her supper Mrs.
Wang had climbed the dike steps, as she did every day, to
see how high the river had risen. She was much more afraid
of the river than of the Japanese. She knew what the river

would do. And one by one the villagers had followed her up
the dike, and now they stood staring down at the malicious
yellow water, curling along like a lot of snakes, and biting at
the high dike banks.

"I never saw it as high as this so early," Mrs. Wang said.
She sat down on a bamboo stool that her grandson, Little Pig,
had brought for her, and spat into the water.

"It's worse than the Japanese, this old devil of a river,"
Little Pig said recklessly.

"Fool!" Mrs. Wang said quickly. "The river god will hear
you. Talk about something else."

So they had gone on talking about the Japanese. . . . How,
for instance, asked Wang, the baker, who was old Mrs. Wang's
nephew twice removed, would they know the Japanese when
they saw them?

Mrs. Wang at this point said positively, "You'll know them.
I once saw a foreigner. He was taller than the eaves of my
house and he had mud-colored hair and eyes the color of a
fish's eyes. Anyone who does not look like us—that is a
Japanese."

Everybody listened to her since she was the oldest woman
in the village and whatever she said settled something.

Then Little Pig spoke up in his disconcerting way. "You
can't see them, Grandmother. They hide up in the sky in airplanes."

Mrs. Wang did not answer immediately. Once she would
have said positively, "I shall not believe in an airplane until
I see it." But so many things had been true which she had
not believed—the Empress, for instance, whom she had not
believed dead, was dead. The Republic, again, she had not
believed in because she did not know what it was. She still
did not know, but they had said for a long time there had been
one. So now she merely stared quietly about the dike where
they all sat around her. It was very pleasant and cool, and
she felt nothing mattered if the river did not rise to flood.

"I don't believe in the Japanese," she said flatly.

They laughed at her a little, but no one spoke. Someone lit

her pipe—it was Little Pig's wife, who was her favorite, and she smoked it.

"Sing, Little Pig!" someone called.

So Little Pig began to sing an old song in a high quavering voice, and old Mrs. Wang listened and forgot the Japanese. The evening was beautiful, the sky so clear and still that the willows overhanging the dike were reflected even in the muddy water. Everything was at peace. The thirty-odd houses which made up the village straggled along beneath them. Nothing could break this peace. After all, the Japanese were only human beings.

"I doubt those airplanes," she said mildly to Little Pig when he stopped singing.

But without answering her, he went on to another song.

Year in and year out she had spent the summer evenings like this on the dike. The first time she was seventeen and a bride, and her husband had shouted to her to come out of the house and up the dike, and she had come, blushing and twisting her hands together to hide among the women while the men roared at her and made jokes about her. All the same, they had liked her. "A pretty piece of meat in your bowl," they had said to her husband. "Feet a trifle big," he had answered deprecatingly. But she could see he was pleased, and so gradually her shyness went away.

He, poor man, had been drowned in a flood when he was still young. And it had taken her years to get him prayed out of Buddhist purgatory. Finally she had grown tired of it, what with the child and the land all on her back, and so when the priest said coaxingly, "Another ten pieces of silver and he'll be out entirely," she asked, "What's he got in there yet?"

"Only his right hand," the priest said, encouraging her.

Well, then, her patience broke. Ten dollars! It would feed them for the winter. Besides, she had had to hire labor for her share of repairing the dike, too, so there would be no more floods.

"If it's only one hand, he can pull himself out," she said firmly.

She often wondered if he had, poor silly fellow. As like as not, she had often thought gloomily in the night, he was still lying there, waiting for her to do something about it. That was the sort of man he was. Well, some day, perhaps, when Little Pig's wife had had the first baby safely and she had a little extra, she might go back to finish him out of purgatory. There was no real hurry, though. . . .

"Grandmother, you must go in," Little Pig's wife's soft voice said. "There is a mist rising from the river now that the sun is gone."

"Yes, I suppose I must," old Mrs. Wang agreed. She gazed at the river a moment. That river—it was full of good and evil together. It would water the fields when it was curbed and checked, but then if an inch were allowed it, it crashed through like a roaring dragon. That was how her husband had been swept away—careless, he was, about his bit of the dike. He was always going to mend it, always going to pile more earth on top of it, and then in a night the river rose and broke through. He had run out of the house, and she had climbed on the roof with the child and had saved herself and it while he was drowned. Well, they had pushed the river back again behind its dikes, and it had stayed there this time. Every day she herself walked up and down the length of the dike for which the village was responsible and examined it. The men laughed and said, "If anything is wrong with the dikes, Granny will tell us."

It had never occurred to any of them to move the village away from the river. The Wangs had lived there for generations, and some had always escaped the floods and had fought the river more fiercely than ever afterward.

Little Pig suddenly stopped singing.

"The moon is coming up!" he cried. "That's not good. Airplanes come out on moonlight nights."

"Where do you learn all this about airplanes?" old Mrs. Wang exclaimed. "It is tiresome to me," she added, so severely that no one spoke. In this silence, leaning upon the arm of Little Pig's wife, she descended slowly the earthen steps which led down into the village, using her long pipe in the other hand as a walking stick. Behind her the villagers came down, one by one, to bed. No one moved before she did, but none stayed long after her.

And in her own bed at last, behind the blue cotton mosquito curtains which Little Pig's wife fastened securely, she fell peacefully asleep. She had lain awake a little while thinking about the Japanese and wondering why they wanted to fight. Only very coarse persons wanted wars. In her mind she saw large coarse persons. If they came one must wheedle them, she thought, invite them to drink tea, and explain to them, reasonably—only why should they come to a peaceful farming village . . . ?

So she was not in the least prepared for Little Pig's wife screaming at her that the Japanese had come. She sat up in bed muttering, "The tea bowls—the tea——"

"Grandmother, there's no time!" Little Pig's wife screamed. "They're here—they're here!"

"Where?" old Mrs. Wang cried, now awake.

"In the sky!" Little Pig's wife wailed.

They had all run out at that, into the clear early dawn, and gazed up. There, like wild geese flying in autumn, were great birdlike shapes.

"But what are they?" old Mrs. Wang cried.

And then, like a silver egg dropping, something drifted straight down and fell at the far end of the village in a field. A fountain of earth flew up, and they all ran to see it. There was a hole thirty feet across, as big as a pond. They were so astonished they could not speak, and then, before anyone could say anything, another and another egg began to fall and everybody was running, running . . .

Everybody, that is, but Mrs. Wang. When Little Pig's wife seized her hand to drag her along, old Mrs. Wang pulled away and sat down against the bank of the dike.

"I can't run," she remarked. "I haven't run in seventy years, since before my feet were bound. You go on. Where's Little

Pig?" She looked around. Little Pig was already gone. "Like his grandfather," she remarked, "always the first to run."

But Little Pig's wife would not leave her, not, that is, until old Mrs. Wang reminded her that it was her duty.

"If Little Pig is dead," she said, "then it is necessary that his son be born alive." And when the girl still hesitated, she struck at her gently with her pipe. "Go on—go on," she exclaimed.

So unwillingly, because now they could scarcely hear each other speak for the roar of the dipping planes, Little Pig's wife went on with the others.

By now, although only a few minutes had passed, the village was in ruins and the straw roofs and wooden beams were blazing. Everybody was gone. As they passed they had shrieked at old Mrs. Wang to come on, and she had called back pleasantly:

"I'm coming—I'm coming!"

But she did not go. She sat quite alone watching now what was an extraordinary spectacle. For soon other planes came, from where she did not know, but they attacked the first ones. The sun came up over the fields of ripening wheat, and in the clear summery air the planes wheeled and darted and spat at each other. When this was over, she thought, she would go back into the village and see if anything was left. Here and there a wall stood, supporting a roof. She could not see her own house from here. But she was not unused to war. Once bandits had looted their village, and houses had been burned then, too. Well, now it had happened again. Burning houses one could see often, but not this darting silvery shining battle in the air. She understood none of it—not what those things were, nor how they stayed up in the sky. She simply sat, growing hungry, and watching.

"I'd like to see one close," she said aloud. And at that moment, as though in answer, one of them pointed suddenly downward, and, wheeling and twisting as though it were wounded, it fell head down in a field which Little Pig had ploughed only yesterday for soybeans. And in an instant the sky was empty again, and there was only this wounded thing on the ground and herself.

She hoisted herself carefully from the earth. At her age she need be afraid of nothing. She could, she decided, go and see what it was. So, leaning on her bamboo pipe, she made her way slowly across the fields. Behind her in the sudden stillness two or three village dogs appeared and followed, creeping close to her in their terror. When they drew near to the fallen plane, they barked furiously. Then she hit them with her pipe.

"Be quiet," she scolded, "there's already been noise enough to split my ears!"

She tapped the airplane.

"Metal," she told the dogs. "Silver, doubtless," she added. Melted up, it would make them all rich.

She walked around it, examining it closely. What made it fly? It seemed dead. Nothing moved or made a sound within it. Then, coming to the side to which it tipped, she saw a young man in it, plumped into a heap in a little seat. The dogs growled, but she struck at them again and they fell back.

"Are you dead?" she inquired politely.

The young man moved a little at her voice, but did not speak. She drew nearer and peered into the hole in which he sat. His side was bleeding.

"Wounded!" she exclaimed. She took his wrist. It was warm, but inert, and when she let it go, it dropped against the side of the hole. She stared at him. He had black hair and a dark skin like a Chinese and still he did not look like a Chinese.

"He must be a Southerner," she thought. Well, the chief thing was, he was alive.

"You had better come out," she remarked. "I'll put some herb plaster on your side."

The young man muttered something dully.

"What did you say?" she asked. But he did not say it again.

"I am still quite strong," she decided after a moment. So she reached in and seized him about the waist and pulled him out slowly, panting a good deal. Fortunately he was rather a little fellow and very light. When she had him on the ground, he seemed to find his feet; and he stood shakily and clung to her, and she held him up.

"Now if you can walk to my house," she said, "I'll see if it is there."

Then he said something, quite clearly. She listened and could not understand a word of it. She pulled away from him and stared.

"What's that?" she asked.

He pointed at the dogs. They were standing growling, their ruffs up. Then he spoke again, and as he spoke he crumpled to the ground. The dogs fell on him, so that she had to beat them off with her hands.

"Get away!" she shouted. "Who told *you* to kill him?"

And then, when they had slunk back, she heaved him somehow onto her back, trembling, half carrying, half pulling him, she dragged him to the ruined village and laid him in the street while she went to find her house, taking the dogs with her.

Her house was quite gone. She found the place easily enough. This was where it should be, opposite the water gate into the dike. She had always watched that gate herself. Miraculously it was not injured now, nor was the dike broken. It would be easy enough to rebuild the house. Only, for the present, it was gone.

So she went back to the young man. He was lying as she had left him, propped against the dike, panting and very pale. He had opened his coat and he had a little bag from which he was taking out strips of cloth and a bottle of something. And again he spoke, and again she understood nothing. Then he made signs and she saw it was water he wanted, so she took up a broken pot from one of many blown about the street, and, going up the dike, she filled it with river water and brought it down again and washed his wound, and she tore off the strips he made from the rolls of bandaging. He knew how to put the cloth over the gaping wound and he made signs to her, and she followed these signs. All the time he was trying to tell her something, but she could understand nothing.

"You must be from the South, sir," she said. It was easy to see that he had education. He looked very clever. "I have heard your language is different from ours." She laughed a little to put him at his ease, but he only stared at her somberly with dull eyes. So she said brightly, "Now if I could find something for us to eat, it would be nice."

He did not answer. Indeed he lay back, panting still more heavily, and stared into space as though she had not spoken.

"You would be better with food," she went on. "And so would I," she added. She was beginning to feel unbearably hungry.

"It occurred to her that in Wang, the baker's shop, there might be some bread. Even if it were dusty with fallen mortar, it would still be bread. She would go and see. But before she went she moved the soldier a little so that he lay in the edge of shadow cast by a willow tree that grew in the bank of the dike. Then she went to the baker's shop. The dogs were gone.

The baker's shop was, like everything else, in ruins. No one was there. At first she saw nothing but the mass of crumpled earthen walls. But then she remembered that the oven was just inside the door, and the door frame still stood erect, supporting one end of the roof. She stood in this frame, and, running her hand in underneath the fallen roof inside, she felt the wooden cover of the iron caldron. Under this there might be steamed bread. She worked her arm delicately and carefully in. It took quite a long time, but, even so, clouds of lime and dust almost choked her. Nevertheless she was right. She squeezed her hand under the cover and felt the firm smooth skin of the big steamed bread rolls, and one by one she drew out four.

"It's hard to kill an old thing like me," she remarked cheerfully to no one, and she began to eat one of the rolls as she walked back. If she had a bit of garlic and a bowl of tea—but one couldn't have everything in these times.

It was at this moment that she heard voices. When she came in sight of the soldier, she saw surrounding him a crowd of other soldiers, who had apparently come from nowhere. They were staring down at the wounded soldier, whose eyes were now closed.

"Where did you get this Japanese, Old Mother?" they shouted at her.

"What Japanese?" she asked, coming to them.

"This one!" they shouted.

"Is he a Japanese?" she cried in the greatest astonishment. "But he looks like us—his eyes are black, his skin——"

"Japanese!" one of them shouted at her.

"Well," she said quietly, "he dropped out of the sky."

"Give me that bread!" another shouted.

"Take it," she said, "all except this one for him."

"A Japanese monkey eat good bread?" the soldier shouted.

"I suppose he is hungry also," old Mrs. Wang replied. She began to dislike these men. But then, she had always disliked soldiers.

"I wish you would go away," she said. "What are you doing here? Our village has always been peaceful."

"It certainly looks very peaceful now," one of the men said, grinning, "as peaceful as a grave. Do you know who did that, Old Mother? The Japanese!"

"I suppose so," she agreed. Then she asked, "Why? That's what I don't understand."

"Why? Because they want our land, that's why!"

"Our land!" she repeated. "Why, they can't have our land!"

"Never!" they shouted.

But all this time while they were talking and chewing bread they had divided among themselves, they were watching the eastern horizon.

"Why do you keep looking east?" old Mrs. Wang now asked.

"The Japanese are coming from there," the man replied who had taken the bread.

"Are you running away from them?" she asked, surprised.

"There are only a handful of us," he said apologetically. "We were left to guard a village—Pao An, in the county of ——"

"I know that village," old Mrs. Wang interrupted. "You

needn't tell me. I was a girl there. How is the old Pao who keeps the teashop in the main street? He's my brother."

"Everybody is dead there," the man replied. "The Japanese have taken it—a great army of men came with their foreign guns and tanks, so what could we do?"

"Of course, only run," she agreed. Nevertheless she felt dazed and sick. So he was dead, that one brother she had left! She was now the last of her father's family.

But the soldiers were straggling away again leaving her alone.

"They'll be coming, those little black dwarfs," they were saying. "We'd best go on."

Nevertheless, one lingered a moment, the one who had taken the bread, to stare down at the young wounded man, who lay with his eyes shut, not having moved at all.

"Is he dead?" he inquired. Then, before Mrs. Wang could answer, he pulled a short knife out of his belt. "Dead or not, I'll give him a punch or two with this——"

But old Mrs. Wang pushed his arm away.

"No, you won't" she said with authority. "If he is dead, then there is no use sending him into purgatory all in pieces. I am a good Buddhist myself."

The man laughed. "Oh well, he is dead," he answered; and then, seeing his comrades already at a distance, he ran after them.

A Japanese, was he? Old Mrs. Wang, left alone with this inert figure, looked at him tentatively. He was very young, she could see, now that his eyes were closed. His hand, limp in unconsciousness, looked like a boy's hand, unformed and still growing. She felt his wrist but could discern no pulse. She leaned over him and held to his lips the half of her roll which she had not eaten.

"Eat," she said very loudly and distinctly. "Bread!"

But there was no answer. Evidently he was dead. He must have died while she was getting the bread out of the oven.

There was nothing to do then but to finish the bread herself. And when that was done, she wondered if she ought not to

follow after Little Pig and his wife and all the villagers. The
sun was mounting and it was growing hot. If she were going,
she had better go. But first she would climb the dike and see
what the direction was. They had gone straight west, and as
far as eye could look westward was a great plain. She might
even see a good-sized crowd miles away. Anyway, she could
see the next village, and they might all be there.

So she climbed the dike slowly, getting very hot. There was
a slight breeze on top of the dike and it felt good. She was
shocked to see the river very near the top of the dike. Why,
it had risen in the last hour!

"You old demon!" she said severely. Let the river god hear
it if he liked. He was evil, that he was—so to threaten flood
when there had been all this other trouble.

She stooped and bathed her cheeks and her wrists. The
water was quite cold, as though with fresh rains somewhere.
Then she stood up and gazed around her. To the west there
was nothing except in the far distance the soldiers still half-
running, and beyond them the blur of the next village, which
stood on a long rise of ground. She had better set out for that
village. Doubtless Little Pig and his wife were there waiting
for her.

Just as she was about to climb down and start out, she saw
something on the eastern horizon. It was at first only an im-
mense cloud of dust. But, as she stared at it, very quickly it
became a lot of black dots and shining spots. Then she saw
what it was. It was a lot of men—an army. Instantly she
knew what army.

"That's the Japanese," she thought. Yes, above them were
the buzzing silver planes. They circled about, seeming to
search for someone.

"I don't know who you're looking for," she muttered, "unless
it's me and Little Pig and his wife. We're the only ones left.
You've already killed my brother Pao."

She had almost forgotten that Pao was dead. Now she remembered it acutely. He had such a nice shop—always clean,
and the tea good and the best meat dumplings to be had and

the price always the same. Pao was a good man. Besides, what about his wife and his seven children? Doubtless they were all killed, too. Now these Japanese were looking for her. It occurred to her that on the dike she could easily be seen. So she clambered hastily down.

It was when she was about halfway down that she thought of the water gate. This old river—it had been a curse to them since time began. Why should it not make up a little now for all the wickedness it had done? It was plotting wickedness again, trying to steal over its banks. Well, why not? She wavered a moment. It was a pity, of course, that the young dead Japanese would be swept into the flood. He was a nice-looking boy, and she had saved him from being stabbed. It was not quite the same as saving his life, of course, but still it was a little the same. If he had been alive, he would have been saved. She went over to him and tugged at him until he lay well near the top of the bank. Then she went down again.

She knew perfectly how to open the water gate. Any child knew how to open the sluice for crops. But she knew also how to swing open the whole gate. The question was, could she open it quickly enough to get out of the way?

"I'm only one old woman," she muttered. She hesitated a second more. Well, it would be a pity not to see what sort of a baby Little Pig's wife would have, but one could not see everything. She had seen a great deal in this life. There was an end to what one could see, anyway.

She glanced again to the east. There were the Japanese coming across the plain. They were a long clear line of black, dotted with thousands of glittering points. If she opened this gate, the impetuous water would roar toward them, rushing into the plains, rolling into a wide lake, drowning them, maybe. Certainly they could not keep on marching nearer and nearer to her and to Little Pig and his wife who were waiting for her. Well, Little Pig and his wife—they would wonder about her—but they would never dream of this. It would make a good story—she would have enjoyed telling it.

She turned resolutely to the gate. Well, some people fought

with airplanes and some with guns, but you could fight with a river, too, if it were a wicked one like this one. She wrenched out a huge wooden pin. It was slippery with silvery green moss. The rill of water burst into a strong jet. When she wrenched one more pin, the rest would give way themselves. She began pulling at it, and felt it slip a little from its hole.

"I might be able to get myself out of purgatory with this," she thought, "and maybe they'll let me have that old man of mine, too. What's a hand of his to all this? Then we'll——"

The pin slipped away suddenly, and the gate burst flat against her and knocked her breath away. She had only time to gasp, to the river:

"Come on, you old demon!"

Then she felt it seize her and lift her up to the sky. It was beneath her and around her. It rolled her joyfully hither and thither, and then, holding her close and enfolded, it went rushing against the enemy.

WILLIAM MARCH

(1894-   )

William Edward March Campbell has successfully combined two careers that would seem to most people to be irreconcilable. He has been a successful business man—he was for a number of years a high official with a large steamship company—and he has written novels and stories on a wide range of subjects. One of his principal topics has been World War I, in which he fought as a Marine and had experiences that provided him with material for *Company K*, perhaps his best-known novel. Like a number of other writers, he has had a rather scattered formal education—business school, some work in college, some courses in law school—very much augmented by work experience, travel and war. "Send in Your Answer," from his collection *Trial Balance*, is a good example of the satirical side of Mr. March's writing.

SEND IN YOUR ANSWER

A GONG with a plump, muffled sound struck four times on four separate notes, and "Heart Throbs of Our Day" was on the air. First, there were a few bars from Beethoven's Ninth Symphony to set the mood, to indicate to the frivolous that this was a program of earnestness and dignity; then, against the background of the receding music, a vibrant tenor voice said: "And now for Mr. Allen Underwood Paul, the well-known novelist, lecturer and radio personality, and his famous program, 'Heart Throbs of Our Day.' " He paused, and the theme, which had almost sunk to nothingness, flared up and died away once more.

"Yes," continued the tenor, "the makers of Minnits, the celebrated remedy compounded to cure headaches and the nausea which so often accompanies a headache, take pleasure at this time in presenting 'Heart Throbs of Our Day.' In a moment Allen Underwood Paul will speak to you personally, but first an important word from our special announcer, John Locksmith, regarding Minnits."

Instantly, a rich baritone voice with a faint hiss in it, said: "Friends, do you suffer from headaches and the nausea which so often accompanies a headache? Of course you do. We all do at times. But to you, the countless victims of a nagging, exhausting headache, we offer a message of hope. Why not go to your druggist at once and ask for Minnits by name? Say, 'I want Minnits! Minnits, please!' " He continued rapidly, pointing out that Minnits were compounded of rare ingredients, found hitherto in only the most expensive prescriptions. It was senseless to endure a headache when Minnits were easily obtainable, at all drug stores, in three sizes: the ten cent size, the twenty-five cent size, and the large, economical family size which sold for one dollar. He finished his plea with a recorded testimonial in the form of a drama:

CHILD: "Mummy, why don't you play with me anymore, like Shirley's Mummy plays with her? Why do you lie in a dark room with a wet towel around your head?"

MOTHER: "Mummy has a headache and the nausea which so often accompanies a headache, dear. Please go outside and play by yourself."

CHILD: "I think you should take Minnits, Mummy, like everybody else does; so I went to the corner drug store and bought a large, economical, family size box of that remarkable headache remedy. Now, you can take Minnits and be like Shirley's Mummy. Now, you can be bright and cheerful, and your old self again."

MOTHER: "Thank you, my darling. Of course I'll take Minnits, as you advise. It was stupid of me not to have had any in the house when my headache struck." (Sound effect of spoon against glass and of water being swallowed.)

CHILD: "Always remember, Minnits save the day!"

MOTHER (she is fully recovered—her old bright and cheerful

self again): "Yes, indeed! Minnits save the day! I won't forget it again!"

The commercial lasted exactly two minutes. When it had ended, Allen Underwood Paul himself spoke. His voice was clipped, brisk and very nearly British: "Friends, in this great city of ours, little, unnoticed dramas of little, unnoticed people daily unfold themselves before our eyes: dramas which we, in the hurry and bustle of life, are prone to pass over or to ignore. Now, as you know, 'Heart Throbs of Our Day' presents a true story of real life each week at this time for the makers of Minnits. This week I have chosen a story which I hope our great audience of Minnits users everywhere will find as intriguing as I did."

He paused significantly and then said: "A few months ago, as some of you will remember, there was an item in the papers regarding a certain man—a man whom I shall refer to on this program as Mr. George F. This gentleman was found dead in his modest apartment under suspicious circumstances, but after a proper investigation had been made, it was determined that death was due to natural causes. When pressed for the exact cause of death, the doctor who performed the autopsy said, 'In my opinion, this man died of grief: in other words, of that romantic ailment our grandfathers called a broken heart.'

"This, in itself, was enough to intrigue anyone's interest, but there was another factor in the case, a factor of equal fascination. You see, the dead man left a most remarkable message in his room, one which adds piquancy to our drama, and at the proper time you will hear that message read by John Locksmith. Then, at the conclusion of our story, it will be our purpose to ask you, the Great American Jury of Public Opinion, to determine why Mr. George F. wrote that intriguing message, and what, if anything, he meant by it. So, in order to help you form your opinion, we have summoned four people who knew Mr. George F. at different stages of his career. Listen carefully to their testimony. You will find it rewarding. . . . First, let us hear from a witness who knew Mr.

George F. during his formative years. Mr. Locksmith, the first witness, please!"

Mr. Locksmith's rich and hissing baritone rang out instantly: "Calling Mrs. Hattie M. Peterson! Will Mrs. Peterson take the stand?" Mrs. Peterson did so, and Mr. Paul began his examination without delay. "You are appearing on this broadcast as a special guest of the makers of Minnits, I understand. You reside in a City in the Midwest, do you not?"

"That's right. I live in Kansas City, Mis—"

Mr. Paul interrupted her. "Please! Please!" he cried out. You could not see him, but you knew from his voice that he had closed his eyes and had pressed his palms desperately against his temples. When he had recovered a little, he said with exasperated gravity: "No names of people, places or products are mentioned on this program, Madam! This is necessary through reasons of policy."

It was a rule, he said, which applied not only to Mrs. Peterson, but to the other witnesses as well. He asked if the matter were now clearly understood. The witnesses said that it was, and Mr. Paul replied patiently: "Thank you. Thank you for your cooperation." Then, turning back to his first witness, he continued: "I understand you grew up in the same town with Mr. George F. Am I correct in my assumption?"

Mrs. Peterson said, "George lived right across the street from us. I knew the whole family well. I saw them every day."

"Yes," said Mr. Paul. "Go on, please. Were they prosperous people? Were they well off? Were they poor?"

"I guess they were comfortably well off. George's father was Passenger Agent for one of the railroads and made a good salary. His mother gave singing lessons, but she did that free, as a service to others."

"Now, tell us something about the home life of George F. Were his parents happy together? What things interested them?"

"They took a prominent part in civic matters, like beautifying the parks and raising money for hospitals. George was their only child. Yes, sir. I'd say they were happy as a family."

Later, under Mr. Paul's prompting, she described Mr. F's appearance as a boy, the house he lived in, his character and his particular temperament. He had been called Socrates by his schoolmates, she said. That was because he was interested in deep subjects, and was such a reader. It was history and poetry and psychology that he read—subjects of that kind. Then, too, the whole family had a liking for music, and when Mr. F. senior had a vacation, they all went away somewhere to hear concerts. "I guess they all rode free," she said. "On railroad passes."

"From what you have said, Mrs. Peterson, I take it the boy was quite bright in his studies. Correct me, please, if I'm in error."

"I don't know whether he was especially bright, or just studious," said Mrs. Peterson. "Anyway, he did stand at the head of his class. He graduated first when he finished high school, too, and at the exercises he read an essay. It was entitled 'The Basic Nobility of Man,' and everybody kept applauding and bringing him back to bow. One of the papers published it the following Sunday, and people predicted that George would go far, with all that talent."

When she had finished, Mrs. Peterson stepped down from the witness box, disappointed, on the whole, with this, her initial experience on a national hookup. She had promised Mrs. Rosenberg and Mrs. McGovern, her closest friends back home, to mention their names over the air at least once, so that all those millions of listeners would know they existed; she had even promised her husband to work in a plug or so for his stationery and notions store. And she had done none of these things, for Mr. Paul, she felt, had thwarted her at every turn.

She was walking away, back to her original seat, when John Locksmith's voice rang out gaily: "Now, now, Mrs. Peterson! Surely you did not think we'd let such a charming lady escape so easily, did you? Here's a special gift for you: a generous-size guest-package of Minnits for your personal use." There was a burst of controlled applause from the audience. When it had lasted the precise number of seconds called for in the script, Mr. Locksmith stopped it and summoned the second witness, a Mr. Otto Wall.

Mr. Paul went to work at once, and the facts he desired to establish came rapidly to light: Mr. Wall resided in a City in the Southern Section of the United States, he said. He had met George F. during the First World War. They had both been attached to a field hospital as ambulance drivers, at that time. He had got to know George F. quite well.

"Just a moment," said Mr. Paul. "Let's try to fill in some of the gaps between the time Mrs. Peterson left him reading his essay and the time you knew him in France. Can you help out?"

"Yes, I think I can. George often talked about himself. I know his mother died right after he finished high school, and that fall he entered—well, a Famous Eastern University. He got his sheepskin in due time, but before he could go back for his Master's degree, his father died too, and there wasn't any money left. That was in 1917, the year war was declared, so George enlisted. He said he picked a non-combat unit because he couldn't reconcile killing others with his moral principles. Then, too, he thought that aiding the helpless and saving the wounded was a practical way of serving humanity in general. He told me these things one night in the dark near a town called Pont-a-Mousson."

Mr. Wall coughed nervously and then continued his story. People might be surprised to hear it, he thought, but George F. had made a fine record as a driver. In fact, he had become something of a legend with the combat troops, for he seemed to have neither regard for his comfort nor fear for his personal safety. As an example, the drivers weren't expected to go up to the line, but George had done that over and over. He was a big, powerfully built man, and you could often see him, only a little behind the advancing troops themselves, searching through the wheatfields or the underbrush for the wounded.

When he found them, he gave them first aid. If there were no stretcher-bearers to be had, he even carried them to safety on his back.

"How did the combat troops react to all this?"

"They thought he was a little cracked in the head, if you know what I mean. But everybody liked him, and everybody respected him, particularly after he was decorated for bravery before the regiment."

"You said a moment ago that George F. was considered a little—well, a little eccentric. Will you explain this a little?"

"He was always talking about justice, the common man and things like that. He maintained that the average man was naturally kind, unselfish and brave; that when he went wrong, it was only because his leaders had betrayed him or exploited his goodness. I guess his trouble was that he said aloud, before others, the things you expect to read in private, in a book."

"The men found his talk embarrassing, perhaps?"

"Some of them did. Most of them kidded him."

"Did he resent this joking at his expense?"

"He didn't even know they were making fun of him. George was always serious."

"I understand your association with George F. was continued in the United States, after the war was over. Will you tell us something of that period too?"

Mr. Wall explained that both he and George F. had gone to work for a Nationally Known Manufacturer of Plumbing Fixtures: Mr. Wall as a salesman, George in the accounting department. George had promptly fallen in love with one of the stenographers, a Miss Bernice Oliver.

"Please!" said Mr. Paul in a voice which was at once humorous and despairing. "No names on this program! Just use the lady's initials."

There was a moment's pause and then Mr. Wall continued: "And so George fell in love with this Miss B.O. and she seemed to like him, too—"

"Refer to the young lady as Miss O., please," said Mr. Paul coldly. "I think that will suffice."

"Well, anyway, they got married," said Mr. Wall, "and set up housekeeping; and that's about all I know. I got another job and left town about that time. I never saw George F. again."

"You mentioned earlier on the program that George F. was decorated for bravery. What decoration was that?"

"It was the Congressional Medal of Honor."

"But no such decoration turned up among the dead man's effects," said Mr. Paul in a surprised voice. "Do you know what became of that medal?"

"No, I don't."

Mr. Wall accepted his gift package of Minnits and stepped down, feeling that he had made an excellent impression. It was something, after all, to be brought all the way to New York, with all expenses paid, to appear on a broadcast as famous as "Heart Throbs of Our Day." One never knew what might result from such an appearance. Perhaps he, himself, would be sought out by the national advertisers and offered a position on the air. That would be wonderful, for Mr. Paul was said to earn more than one hundred thousand dollars annually.

Mr. Paul said: "In a short time you will hear from our third witness, who has an intriguing story to tell, but first, a friendly suggestion from John Locksmith regarding Minnits." Mr. Locksmith picked up his cue smoothly: To people of discrimination, Minnits represent the last word in headache relief, he said. Millions of happy, satisfied users daily attested its worth. He believed, frankly, that everyone should be told about Minnits, the wonder-remedy: that quick-acting, easy-dissolving headache remedy endorsed by medical men everywhere. His plea ended with another transcribed drama, the scene this time being the busy office of a big executive.

BIG EXECUTIVE (answering phone): "Cartright speaking. No I can't come, Chalmers. I have a headache, a terrible headache. Yes, I know we'll lose the Excelsior account as a result, but it can't be helped. That Acme crowd have licked us this time."

He hangs up the phone just as a hearty but respectful male

voice speaks at his elbow: "Beg pardon, Mr. Cartright, but I couldn't help overhearing your conversation, so I took the liberty of bringing you a Minnits. I'm never without them, for you can never tell when a headache will strike. Now, if you'll take one with this sip of water I have here for you, you'll soon agree that there's nothing like Minnits for quick-acting headache relief."

The big executive takes his Minnits with a grunt, a gurgle and a satisfied smacking of the lips. He is well instantly. He picks up the phone and says: "Get me Chalmers right away! ... Hello, Chalmers, this is Cartright again. I'll be right over. Hold that Excelsior crowd in line until I get there. I'll show them what a fight is, if that's what they're looking for! ... My headache? Oh, that's a thing of the past. You see, I took a Minnits, and Minnits save the day!"

He chuckles happily, hangs up the receiver and turns to his secretary, a Miss Forsythe. He says: "There's a quick-thinking man in our shipping department, an intelligent man with gumption enough to carry Minnits. See that he gets a raise of ten dollars a week at once."

The commercial was over at last, but there still remained a presentation ceremony to be worked through, for it appeared that the four million readers of *Loudspeaker*, the Magazine of Radio, had voted "Heart Throbs of Our Day" the most distinguished program on the air. The editors of *Loudspeaker*, obeying the verdict of their subscribers, took this opportunity to award a statuette commemorating the poll. Mr. Paul accepted for the makers of Minnits, promising *Loudspeaker* and its readers that "Heart Throbs of Our Day" would maintain the same uncompromising standard of refinement, the same stern level of good taste, that it had in the past.

Afterwards, the third witness was summoned, identified, and seated for examination. She was a Miss Elaine Marlowe, an actress. She had appeared in many dramatic successes in the past, she said, but at the moment she was recouping her energies between engagements. Some years ago, when she had been nothing but a child, she had worked for the same firm which had employed Mr. George F., so naturally she had got to know him. Her voice was low and dramatic, with many unexpected pauses. Listening, you could almost hear a coach whispering somewhere behind the soundness of her technique: "Timing! Always timing! Never forget that timing is the essence of good acting, Miss Marlowe!"

"Now, tell us of the remarkable theft which took place in the office, and the part which George F. played in it later," said Mr. Paul.

"Well," said Miss Marlowe huskily, "this large sum of money disappeared, and it looked as if Mr. George F. had taken it. He said that he had not, although he knew who the real thief was. Later the police questioned him too, but even then he wouldn't name the true criminal."

"Did he give a reason for such an eccentric attitude?"

"He said the real culprit must confess of his own accord, for the sake of his moral integrity; but nobody believed him, naturally, and so he was arrested and stood trial."

"Now, tell me, Miss Marlowe, did anybody come forward later and confess to the crime?"

Miss Marlowe seemed startled out of her dramatic pattern of controlled emotion for a moment. She laughed suddenly and her voice went an octave higher. "Don't be silly!" she said.

She went on to describe the trial and the sentence afterwards. George F. had served his term. He had come out without bitterness, as if what had happened to him was of little importance. His wife had divorced him by that time, and later he found it difficult to start his life over again. She went on and on, squeezing from the story the last drop of hysteria, tearing from it the final tatter of melodrama. When she paused for breath, Mr. Paul interrupted quickly:

"Did you believe in the innocence of George F., Miss Marlowe?"

"Yes, I did. I believed him with my heart, despite the evidence against him. You see I—I loved him."

She had rehearsed this scene over and over with her publicity manager, and they both hoped that the big Broadway producers would be listening to her performance. It was a marvelous opportunity to prove her ability, to establish her once more in the theater. It was an unexpected audition which had miraculously fallen into her lap just when her fortune was lowest, and she meant to make the most of it.

"Yes—I loved him," she repeated simply. "He was like an angel from another world! He was so good—so fine! Oh, I loved him so, Mr. Paul!" Her voice was husky, low and torn with emotion.

"Please," said Mr. Paul. "Please try to control yourself."

"But I loved him! Oh, I loved him so greatly, Mr. Paul!"

"Tell us something of his life after he left prison," said Mr. Paul; "something of his daily routine."

Miss Marlowe ignored him. "A short time ago you asked what became of his medal," she continued, "so I'll tell you now what became of it! He sold it to buy bread. He was hungry and friendless and abandoned by a world which had once honored him, you see. Oh, the terrible irony of such a situation! He had to sell his medal in order to have the bare necessities of life for a few days more. It was to a wealthy collector of military decorations that he sold it—a man who could not comprehend its value as a symbol of courage, patriotism and devotion to duty; a man who wanted it only to complete his collection."

She was sobbing now, and after a moment Mr. Paul spoke with a spurious gentleness: "I'm afraid you misunderstand the purpose of our investigation. Our program this week is concerned with the history of Mr. George F., not with your emotions."

Miss Marlowe, knowing that she had only a short time left, let herself go in earnest. "Where are you now, Greatheart?" she cried out. "Can you hear my voice, there beyond the stars? Can you feel my love mounting upward toward you. Come back to one who loves you, George! Come back to me! Back—"

"Mr. Locksmith, please assist the witness to her seat," said

Mr. Paul with cold exasperation. "I'm afraid she's too distraught to go on with her story."

"I loved him! I loved him!" said Miss Marlowe proudly. "I am not ashamed to confess my love." She was sobbing now without restraint, and she moved reluctantly from the microphone, her voice dying gradually away. The episode of the medal was something which neither she nor her manager had anticipated, but having turned up as it had, she felt that she had made the most of it. On the whole, she was pleased with the soundness of her performance, although there was one small thing which continued to bother her, for she kept wondering curiously which of her fellow-employees, remembered now so dimly, had really been Mr. George F. Mr. Locksmith assisted her to her chair and gave her a glass of water, but in the excitement he forgot to present her with her guest package of Minnits, which somehow seemed a pity.

The final witness, a man named Alfred Marks, took the stand quickly. He explained that there was a group of men who met in Central Park to play checkers, and that George F. had been one of them. That was about all he knew, he said, except that George had lived in a cheap apartment somewhere on the west side, near the river.

"Did he seem depressed when you first knew him, Mr. Marks?"

"No, sir. He was always cheerful. It was just like the other witnesses said: He talked a lot about the dignity and nobility of mankind—that sort of thing."

"How did he make a living—or do you know that?"

"He took orders for Christmas cards and calendars. He also made fancy boxes which he sold to decorators. He could have lived better than he did, I thought, but he was always giving away his money to people he considered less fortunate than himself."

Mr. Paul said: "Now, tell our great audience of Minnits users about the visit Mr. George F. paid you one night. Tell it as you told it to me last week, or as nearly as you can."

"Well, you see we got to know each other pretty well, and I

went over to his place a few times, and so one night I asked
him to my place. We played checkers awhile, and then I said
there was a program I wanted to hear, and so I turned on the
radio. It was one of those confession programs where people
tell their troubles and ask what to do, if you know what I
mean."

At that instant Mr. Paul broke one of his own inflexible
rules, for he said quickly: "The program was 'Tell Me Your
Troubles'—Dr. Christopher's program advertising Vimpep, the
whole wheat breakfast cereal, wasn't it?"

"That's right. It was."

"And how did George F. react to that particular program?"

"He reacted in a peculiar way, Mr. Paul, if you know what
I mean. At first he couldn't believe that real people would
shame themselves that way. So I told him they were real
people, all right, and asked where he'd been all these years,
but I didn't know at the time he'd been in prison. So then he
wanted to know why people were willing to do such a vulgar
thing, and I said I guessed it made them feel important to
have all that attention paid to them, or at least that's the way
I always sized it up, if you know what I mean."

"Did he say anything else you remember!"

"He said the whole thing was cheap and degrading, so I told
him he must be the only one who thought that, because the
program won the *Loudspeaker* popular poll—that was last
year, Mr. Paul—and people liked it well enough. Then he
wanted to know what purpose it served. I started laughing
about that time, but good-natured, like he was a little boy I
was talking to, and I said I didn't know what purpose it
served, but it seemed to be a very good way to sell a whole
wheat cereal. After that, he didn't speak for a time—just sat
there thinking, with a peculiar look in his face; but finally he
said: 'My life has been based on a false premise. Will you accept my apologies?' Then, a little later, he got his hat and
left."

Mr. Paul chuckled softly. When he spoke, you understood
why he had had no objection to having this particular pro-

gram identified plainly: "So Mr. George F. considered 'Tell Me Your Troubles' cheap and degrading, did he? Well, we mustn't tell Dr. Christopher that. He's a sensitive man, you know." He waited until the laughter of the studio audience had abated somewhat and then he continued: "Now, tell us, Mr. Marks, when you next saw George F."

Mr. Marks said: "I didn't see him again until a month or two later; then one day I happened to be in the neighborhood where he lived and I stopped by his place, thinking maybe he was sick, since he didn't come to the park to play checkers anymore; but I couldn't get an answer to my ring, so the janitor opened the door for me—and there he was, lying dead on a studio couch. The note was on the table, where the police found it later, and I guess that's about all I know."

After the witness was rewarded and dismissed, Mr. Paul said: "As Minnits users everywhere know, it is customary at this point for me to sum up the evidence. Now, I think I'm correct in saying that Mr. George F. was a man of good moral character, despite the cloud of suspicion which hung over his head regarding the theft. He was trustworthy, sober, unselfish and kind. He possessed strong altruistic traits and unusual courage; but he was also impractical, idealistic and lacking in common sense: In other words, a good but unworldly man— one badly handicapped for success in the great struggle of life." Then, pausing a little, he added solemnly: "And now we come to the message found on the dead man's table: the message which I promised Mr. Locksmith would read to you.— Mr. Locksmith, read the message, please!"

The Beethoven theme came up softly, subordinating itself to Mr. Locksmith's voice. "Man never had anything except dignity," he read slowly, "and now he has lost even that." He repeated the message for the dull, pausing a little between words, and when he had finished, Mr. Paul took over again.

"Friends," he began briskly, "you have heard the story of Mr. George F., and the message he left behind him. Now, we ask you, the Great American Jury of Public Opinion, to send in your answer explaining what, if anything, he meant by his cryptic words. Address your answer to Allen Underwood Paul in care of this station, but be sure to accompany it with a box top from a package of Minnits—preferably one from the large, economical family-size package. For the best and most original answer, the makers of Minnits will award a five hundred dollar war bond. So send in your answer at once. Who knows? You may be the lucky winner." He paused a second or two and then said, "And now a final friendly word from John Locksmith regarding Minnits."

Instantly there was the sound of trumpets blowing in triumph, and as they died away, John Locksmith's ripe, hissing voice said: "Friends, the sound you have just heard is the makers of Minnits blowing their own horn! And why shouldn't they? You see, we believe that when we have a product as wonderful as Minnits, the whole world should be told about it." He went on to discuss some of the great turning points in history. He said that one of them had occurred some years ago in a chemist's shop in Syracuse, New York, for it was on that day the first quick-acting, easy-dissolving, handy-packaged Minnits was carefully compounded from its rare ingredients. There was another little transcribed drama, this time concerning a girl who was left out of everything, since she was so often troubled with nagging, uncomfortable headaches. But one day a stranger on a bus told her about Minnits, and she had bought a package at once. Her life since that day was full and complete, for she was now invited everywhere and her telephone rang all day long.

Time was running short and in a few seconds "Heart Throbs of Our Day" must go off the air. Mr. Locksmith, realizing this, spoke his last message rapidly: "Friends," he said, "have you, at this very moment, a headache and the nausea which so often accompanies a headache? If you have, go at once to your drug store and ask for Minnits by name. Say, 'I want Minnits! Give me Minnits, please, for Minnits save the day!'"

F. SCOTT FITZGERALD

(1896-1940)

F. Scott Fitzgerald was the spokesman of the Jazz Age, the decade following World War I. His early books, *This Side of Paradise* and *The Beautiful and Damned,* were so popular that not only did they set the fashion for other stories of the younger generation, but they established a model which young people consciously imitated in their conversation and attitudes. The Depression of 1929 put an end to much of the irresponsible life that Fitzgerald wrote about, and difficulties in his own life gave him greater insight, so that a number of his stories written after 1930 are among his best, possessed of deeper penetration and more emotional complexity than much of his earlier work. "Babylon Revisited" is the story of a survivor of the reckless period of the 1920's, a man who has come to understand the nature of responsibility. Among Fitzgerald's best novels are *The Great Gatsby* and *Tender Is the Night.*

BABYLON REVISITED

AND WHERE'S MR. CAMPBELL?" Charlie asked.

"Gone to Switzerland. Mr. Campbell's a pretty sick man, Mr. Wales."

"I'm sorry to hear that. And George Hardt?" Charlie inquired.

"Back in America, gone to work."

"And where is the Snow Bird?"

"He was in here last week. Anyway, his friend, Mr. Schaeffer, is in Paris."

Two familiar names from the long list of a year and a half ago. Charlie scribbled an address in his notebook and tore out the page.

"If you see Mr. Schaeffer, give him this," he said. "It's my brother-in-law's address. I haven't settled on a hotel yet."

He was not really disappointed to find Paris was so empty. But the stillness in the Ritz bar was strange and portentous. It was not an American bar any more—he felt polite in it, and not as if he owned it. It had gone back into France. He felt the stillness from the moment he got out of the taxi and saw the doorman, usually in a frenzy of activity at this hour, gossiping with a *chasseur* by the servants' entrance.

Passing through the corridor, he heard only a single, bored voice in the once-clamorous women's room. When he turned into the bar he traveled the twenty feet of green carpet with his eyes fixed straight ahead by old habit; and then, with his foot firmly on the rail, he turned and surveyed the room, encountering only a single pair of eyes that fluttered up from a newspaper in the corner. Charlie asked for the head barman, Paul, who in the latter days of the bull market had come to work in his own custom-built car—disembarking, however, with due nicety at the nearest corner. But Paul was at his country house today and Alix giving him information.

"No, no more," Charlie said, "I'm going slow these days."

Alix congratulated him: "You were going pretty strong a couple of years ago."

"I'll stick to it all right," Charlie assured him. "I've stuck to it for over a year and a half now."

"How do you find conditions in America?"

"I haven't been to America for months. I'm in business in Prague, representing a couple of concerns there. They don't know about me down there."

Alix smiled.

"Remember the night of George Hardt's bachelor dinner here?" said Charlie. "By the way, what's become of Claude Fessenden?"

Alix lowered his voice confidentially: "He's in Paris, but he doesn't come here any more. Paul doesn't allow it. He ran up a bill of thirty thousand francs, charging all his drinks and his lunches, and usually his dinner, for more than a year. And when Paul finally told him he had to pay, he gave him a bad check."

Alix shook his head sadly.

"I don't understand it, such a dandy fellow. Now he's all bloated up——" He made a plump apple of his hands.

Charlie watched a group of strident queens installing themselves in a corner.

"Nothing affects them," he thought. "Stocks rise and fall, people loaf or work, but they go on forever." The place oppressed him. He called for the dice and shook with Alix for the drink.

"Here for long, Mr. Wales?"

"I'm here for four or five days to see my little girl."

"Oh-h! You have a little girl?"

Outside, the fire-red, gas-blue, ghost-green signs shone smokily through the tranquil rain. It was late afternoon and the streets were in movement; the *bistros* gleamed. At the corner of the Boulevard des Capucines he took a taxi. The Place de la Concorde moved by in pink majesty; they crossed the logical Seine, and Charlie felt the sudden provincial quality of the left bank.

Charlie directed his taxi to the Avenue de l'Opera, which was out of his way. But he wanted to see the blue hour spread over the magnificent façade, and imagine that the cab horns, playing endlessly the first few bars of *Le Plus que Lent*, were the trumpets of the Second Empire. They were closing the iron grill in front of Brentano's Book-store, and people were already at dinner behind the trim little bourgeois hedge of Duval's. He had never eaten at a really cheap restaurant in Paris. Five-course dinner, four francs fifty, eighteen cents, wine included. For some odd reason he wished that he had.

As they rolled on to the Left Bank and he felt its sudden provincialism, he thought, "I spoiled this city for myself. I didn't realize it, but the days came along one after another, and then two years were gone, and everything was gone, and I was gone."

He was thirty-five, and good to look at. The Irish mobility

of his face was sobered by a deep wrinkle between his eyes. As he rang his brother-in-law's bell in the Rue Palatine, the wrinkle deepened till it pulled down his brows; he felt a cramping sensation in his belly. From behind the maid who opened the door darted a lovely little girl of nine who shrieked "Daddy!" and flew up, struggling like a fish, into his arms. She pulled his head around by one ear and set her cheek against his.

"My old pie," he said.

"Oh, daddy, daddy, daddy, daddy, dads, dads, dads!"

She drew him into the salon, where the family waited, a boy and a girl his daughter's age, his sister-in-law and her husband. He greeted Marion with his voice pitched carefully to avoid feigned enthusiasm or dislike, but her response was more frankly tepid, though she minimized her expression of unalterable distrust by directing her regard toward his child. The two men clasped hands in a friendly way and Lincoln Peters rested his for a moment on Charlie's shoulder.

The room was warm and comfortably American. The three children moved intimately about, playing through the yellow oblongs that led to other rooms; the cheer of six o'clock spoke in the eager smacks of the fire and the sounds of French activity in the kitchen. But Charlie did not relax; his heart sat up rigidly in his body and he drew confidence from his daughter, who from time to time came close to him, holding in her arms the doll he had brought.

"Really extremely well," he declared in answer to Lincoln's question. "There's a lot of business there that isn't moving at all, but we're doing even better than ever. In fact, damn well. I'm bringing my sister over from America next month to keep house for me. My income last year was bigger than it was when I had money. You see, the Czechs——"

His boasting was for a specific purpose; but after a moment, seeing a faint restiveness in Lincoln's eye, he changed the subject:

"Those are fine children of yours, well brought up, good manners."

"We think Honoria's a great little girl too."

Marion Peters came back from the kitchen. She was a tall woman with worried eyes, who had once possessed a fresh American loveliness. Charlie had never been sensitive to it and was always surprised when people spoke of how pretty she had been. From the first there had been an instinctive antipathy between them.

"Well, how do you find Honoria?" she asked.

"Wonderful. I was astonished how much she's grown in ten months. All the children are looking well."

"We haven't had a doctor for a year. How do you like being back in Paris?"

"It seems very funny to see so few Americans around."

"I'm delighted," Marion said vehemently. "Now at least you can go into a store without their assuming you're a millionaire. We've suffered like everybody, but on the whole it's a good deal pleasanter."

"But it was nice while it lasted," Charlie said. "We were a sort of royalty, almost infallible, with a sort of magic around us. In the bar this afternoon"—he stumbled, seeing his mistake—"there wasn't a man I knew."

She looked at him keenly. "I should think you'd have had enough of bars."

"I only stayed a minute. I take one drink every afternoon, and no more."

"Don't you want a cocktail before dinner?" Lincoln asked.

"I take only one drink every afternoon, and I've had that."

"I hope you keep to it," said Marion.

Her dislike was evident in the coldness with which she spoke, but Charlie only smiled; he had larger plans. Her very aggressiveness gave him an advantage, and he knew enough to wait. He wanted them to initiate the discussion of what they knew had brought him to Paris.

At dinner he couldn't decide whether Honoria was most like him or her mother. Fortunate if she didn't combine the traits of both that had brought them to disaster. A great wave of protectiveness went over him. He thought he knew what to do for her. He believed in character; he wanted to jump back a whole generation and trust in character again as the eternally valuable element. Everything else wore out.

He left soon after dinner, but not to go home. He was curious to see Paris by night with clearer and more judicious eyes than those of other days. He bought a *strapontin* for the Casino and watched Josephine Baker go through her chocolate arabesques.

After an hour he left and strolled toward Montmartre, up the Rue Pigalle into the Place Blanche. The rain had stopped and there were a few people in evening clothes disembarking from taxis in front of cabarets, and *cocottes* prowling singly or in pairs, and many Negroes. He passed a lighted door from which issued music, and stopped with the sense of familiarity; it was Bricktop's, where he had parted with so many hours and so much money. A few doors farther on he found another ancient rendezvous and incautiously put his head inside. Immediately an eager orchestra burst into sound, a pair of professional dancers leaped to their feet and a maître d'hôtel swooped toward him, crying, "Crowd just arriving, sir!" But he withdrew quickly.

"You have to be damn drunk," he thought.

Zelli's was closed, the bleak and sinister cheap hotels surrounding it were dark; up in the Rue Blanche there was more light and a local, colloquial French crowd. The Poet's Cave had disappeared, but the two great mouths of the Café of Heaven and the Café of Hell still yawned—even devoured, as he watched, the meager contents of a tourist bus—a German, a Japanese, and an American couple who glanced at him with frightened eyes.

So much for the effort and ingenuity of Montmartre. All the catering to vice and waste was on an utterly childish scale, and he suddenly realized the meaning of the word "dissipate" —to dissipate into thin air; to make nothing out of something. In the little hours of the night every move from place to place was an enormous human jump, an increase of paying for the privilege of slower and slower motion.

He remembered thousand-franc notes given to an orchestra for playing a single number, hundred-franc notes tossed to a doorman for calling a cab.

But it hadn't been given for nothing.

It had been given, even the most wildly squandered sum, as an offering to destiny that he might not remember the things most worth remembering, the things that now he would always remember—his child taken from his control, his wife escaped to a grave in Vermont.

In the glare of a *brasserie* a woman spoke to him. He bought her some eggs and coffee, and then, eluding her encouraging stare, gave her a twenty-franc note and took a taxi to his hotel.

II

He woke upon a fine fall day—football weather. The depression of yesterday was gone and he liked the people on the streets. At noon he sat opposite Honoria at Le Grand Vatel, the only restaurant he could think of not reminiscent of champagne dinners and long luncheons that began at two and ended in a blurred and vague twilight.

"Now, how about vegetables? Oughtn't you to have some vegetables?"

"Well, yes."

"Here's *épinards* and *chou-fleur* and carrots and *haricots*."

"I'd like *chou-fleur*."

"Wouldn't you like to have two vegetables?"

"I usually only have one at lunch."

The waiter was pretending to be inordinately fond of children. *"Qu'elle est mignonne la petite! Elle parle exactement comme une Française."*

"How about dessert? Shall we wait and see?"

The waiter disappeared. Honoria looked at her father expectantly.

"What are we going to do?"

"First, we're going to that toy store in the Rue Saint-

Honoré and buy you anything you like. And then we're going to the vaudeville at the Empire."

She hesitated. "I like it about the vaudeville, but not the toy store."

"Why not?"

"Well, you brought me this doll." She had it with her. "And I've got lots of things. And we're not rich any more, are we?"

"We never were. But today you are to have anything you want."

"All right," she agreed resignedly.

When there had been her mother and a French nurse he had been inclined to be strict; now he extended himself, reached out for a new tolerance; he must be both parents to her and not shut any of her out of communication.

"I want to get to know you," he said gravely. "First let me introduce myself. My name is Charles J. Wales, of Prague."

"Oh, daddy!" her voice cracked with laughter.

"And who are you, please?" he persisted, and she accepted a rôle immediately: "Honoria Wales, Rue Palatine, Paris."

"Married or single?"

"No, not married. Single."

He indicated the doll. "But I see you have a child, madame."

Unwilling to disinherit it, she took it to her heart and thought quickly: "Yes, I've been married, but I'm not married now. My husband is dead."

He went on quickly, "And the child's name?"

"Simone. That's after my best friend at school."

"I'm very pleased that you're doing so well at school."

"I'm third this month," she boasted. "Elsie"—that was her cousin—"is only about eighteenth, and Richard is about at the bottom."

"You like Richard and Elsie, don't you?"

"Oh, yes, I like Richard quite well and I like her all right."

Cautiously and casually he asked: "And Aunt Marion and Uncle Lincoln—which do you like best?"

"Oh, Uncle Lincoln, I guess."

He was increasingly aware of her presence. As they came in, a murmur of ". . . adorable" followed them, and now the people at the next table bent all their silences upon her, staring as if she were something no more conscious than a flower.

"Why don't I live with you?" she asked suddenly. "Because mamma's dead?"

"You must stay here and learn more French. It would have been hard for daddy to take care of you so well."

"I don't really need much taking care of any more. I do everything for myself."

Going out of the restaurant, a man and a woman unexpectedly hailed him.

"Well, the old Wales!"

"Hello there, Lorraine. . . . Dunc."

Sudden ghosts out of the past: Duncan Schaeffer, a friend from college. Lorraine Quarrles, a lovely, pale blonde of thirty; one of a crowd who had helped them make months into days in the lavish times of three years ago.

"My husband couldn't come this year," she said, in answer to his question. "We're poor as hell. So he gave me two hundred a month and told me I could do my worst on that. . . . This your little girl?"

"What about coming back and sitting down?" Duncan asked.

"Can't do it." He was glad for an excuse. As always, he felt Lorraine's passionate, provocative attraction, but his own rhythm was different now.

"Well, how about dinner?" she asked.

"I'm not free. Give me your address and let me call you."

"Charlie, I believe you're sober," she said judicially. "I honestly believe he's sober, Dunc. Pinch him and see if he's sober."

Charlie indicated Honoria with his head. They both laughed.

"What's your address?" said Duncan skeptically.

He hesitated, unwilling to give the name of his hotel.

"I'm not settled yet. I'd better call you. We're going to see the vaudeville at the Empire."

"There! That's what I want to do," Lorraine said. "I want to see some clowns and acrobats and jugglers. That's just what we'll do, Dunc."

"We've got to do an errand first," said Charlie. "Perhaps we'll see you there."

"All right, you snob. . . . Good-by, beautiful little girl."

"Good-by."

Honoria bobbed politely.

Somehow, an unwelcome encounter. They liked him because he was functioning, because he was serious; they wanted to see him, because he was stronger than they were now, because they wanted to draw a certain sustenance from his strength.

At the Empire, Honoria proudly refused to sit upon her father's folded coat. She was already an individual with a code of her own, and Charlie was more and more absorbed by the desire of putting a little of himself into her before she crystallized utterly. It was hopeless to try to know her in so short a time.

Between the acts they came upon Duncan and Lorraine in the lobby where the band was playing.

"Have a drink?"

"All right, but not up at the bar. We'll take a table."

"The perfect father."

Listening abstractedly to Lorraine, Charlie watched Honoria's eyes leave their table, and he followed them wistfully about the room, wondering what they saw. He met her glance and she smiled.

"I liked that lemonade," she said.

What had she said? What had he expected? Going home in a taxi afterward, he pulled her over until her head rested against his chest.

"Darling, do you ever think about your mother?"

"Yes, sometimes," she answered vaguely.

"I don't want you to forget her. Have you got a picture of her?"

"Yes, I think so. Anyhow, Aunt Marion has. Why don't you want me to forget her?"

"She loved you very much."

"I loved her too."

They were silent for a moment.

"Daddy, I want to come and live with you," she said suddenly.

His heart leaped; he had wanted it to come like this.

"Aren't you perfectly happy?"

"Yes, but I love you better than anybody. And you love me better than anybody, don't you, now that mummy's dead?"

"Of course I do. But you won't always like me best, honey. You'll grow up and meet somebody your own age and go marry him and forget you ever had a daddy."

"Yes, that's true," she agreed tranquilly.

He didn't go in. He was coming back at nine o'clock and he wanted to keep himself fresh and new for the thing he must say then.

"When you're safe inside, just show yourself in that window."

"All right. Good-by, dads, dads, dads, dads."

He waited in the dark street until she appeared, all warm and glowing, in the window above and kissed her fingers out into the night.

III

They were waiting. Marion sat behind the coffee service in a dignified black dinner dress that just faintly suggested mourning. Lincoln was walking up and down with the animation of one who had already been talking. They were as anxious as he was to get into the question. He opened it almost immediately:

"I suppose you know what I want to see you about—why I really came to Paris."

Marion played with the black stars on her necklace and frowned.

"I'm awfully anxious to have a home," he continued. "And I'm awfully anxious to have Honoria in it. I appreciate your taking in Honoria for her mother's sake, but things have changed now"—he hesitated and then continued more forcibly —"changed radically with me, and I want to ask you to reconsider the matter. It would be silly for me to deny that about three years ago I was acting badly——"

Marion looked up at him with hard eyes.

"—but all that's over. As I told you, I haven't had more than a drink a day for over a year, and I take that drink deliberately, so that the idea of alcohol won't get too big in my imagination. You see the idea?"

"No," said Marion succinctly.

"It's a sort of stunt I set myself. It keeps the matter in proportion."

"I get you," said Lincoln. "You don't want to admit it's got any attraction for you."

"Something like that. Sometimes I forget and don't take it. But I try to take it. Anyhow, I couldn't afford to drink in my position. The people I represent are more than satisfied with what I've done, and I'm bringing my sister over from Burlington to keep house for me, and I want awfully to have Honoria too. You know that even when her mother and I weren't getting along well we never let anything that happened touch Honoria. I know she's fond of me and I know I'm able to take care of her and—well, there you are. How do you feel about it?"

He knew that now he would have to take a beating. It would last an hour or two hours, and it would be difficult, but if he modulated his inevitable resentment to the chastened attitude of the reformed sinner, he might win his point in the end.

Keep your temper, he told himself. You don't want to be justified. You want Honoria.

Lincoln spoke first: "We've been talking it over ever since we got your letter last month. We're happy to have Honoria here. She's a dear little thing, and we're glad to be able to help her, but of course that isn't the question——"

Marion interrupted suddenly. "How long are you going to stay sober, Charlie?" she asked.

"Permanently, I hope."

"How can anybody count on that?"

"You know I never did drink heavily until I gave up business and came over here with nothing to do. Then Helen and I began to run around with——"

"Please leave Helen out of it. I can't bear to hear you talk about her like that."

He stared at her grimly; he had never been certain how fond of each other the sisters were in life.

"My drinking only lasted about a year and a half—from the time we came over until I—collapsed."

"It was time enough."

"It was time enough," he agreed.

"My duty is entirely to Helen," she said. "I try to think what she would have wanted me to do. Frankly, from the night you did that terrible thing you haven't really existed for me. I can't help that. She was my sister."

"Yes."

"When she was dying she asked me to look out for Honoria. If you hadn't been in a sanitarium then, it might have helped matters."

He had no answer.

"I'll never in my life be able to forget the morning when Helen knocked at my door, soaked to the skin and shivering and said you'd locked her out."

Charlie gripped the sides of the chair. This was more difficult than he expected; he wanted to launch out into a long expostulation and explanation, but he only said: "The night I locked her out—" and she interrupted, "I don't feel up to going over that again."

After a moment's silence Lincoln said: "We're getting off the subject. You want Marion to set aside her legal guardianship and give you Honoria. I think the main point for her is whether she has confidence in you or not."

"I don't blame Marion," Charlie said slowly, "but I think she can have entire confidence in me. I had a good record up to three years ago. Of course, it's within human possibilities I might go wrong any time. But if we wait much longer I'll lose Honoria's childhood and my chance for a home." He shook his head, "I'll simply lose her, don't you see?"

"Yes, I see," said Lincoln.

"Why didn't you think of all this before?" Marion asked.

"I suppose I did, from time to time, but Helen and I were getting along badly. When I consented to the guardianship, I was flat on my back in a sanitarium and the market had cleaned me out. I knew I'd acted badly, and I thought if it would bring any peace to Helen, I'd agree to anything. But now it's different. I'm functioning, I'm behaving damn well, so far as——"

"Please don't swear at me," Marion said.

He looked at her, startled. With each remark the force of her dislike became more and more apparent. She had built up all her fear of life into one wall and faced it toward him. This trivial reproof was possibly the result of some trouble with the cook several hours before. Charlie became increasingly alarmed at leaving Honoria in this atmosphere of hostility against himself; sooner or later it would come out, in a word here, a shake of the head there, and some of that distrust would be irrevocably implanted in Honoria. But he pulled his temper down out of his face and shut it up inside him; he had won a point, for Lincoln realized the absurdity of Marion's remark and asked her lightly since when she had objected to the word "damn."

"Another thing," Charlie said: "I'm able to give her certain advantages now. I'm going to take a French governess to Prague with me. I've got a lease on a new apartment——"

He stopped, realizing that he was blundering. They couldn't be expected to accept with equanimity the fact that his income was again twice as large as their own.

"I suppose you can give her more luxuries than we can," said Marion. "When you were throwing away money we were living along watching every ten francs. . . . I suppose you'll start doing it again."

"Oh, no," he said. "I've learned. I worked hard for ten years, you know—until I got lucky in the market, like so many people. Terribly lucky. It won't happen again."

There was a long silence. All of them felt their nerves straining, and for the first time in a year Charlie wanted a drink. He was sure now that Lincoln Peters wanted him to have his child.

Marion shuddered suddenly; part of her saw that Charlie's feet were planted on the earth now, and her own maternal feeling recognized the naturalness of his desire; but she had lived for a long time with a prejudice—a prejudice founded on a curious disbelief in her sister's happiness, and which, in the shock of one terrible night, had turned to hatred for him. It had all happened at a point in her life where the discouragement of ill health and adverse circumstances made it necessary for her to believe in tangible villainy and a tangible villain.

"I can't help what I think!" she cried out suddenly. "How much you were responsible for Helen's death, I don't know. It's something you'll have to square with your own conscience."

An electric current of agony surged through him; for a moment he was almost on his feet, an unuttered sound echoing in his throat. He hung on to himself for a moment, another moment.

"Hold on there," said Lincoln uncomfortably. "I never thought you were responsible for that."

"Helen died of heart trouble," Charlie said dully.

"Yes, heart trouble." Marion spoke as if the phrase had another meaning for her.

Then, in the flatness that followed her outburst, she saw him plainly and she knew he had somehow arrived at control over the situation. Glancing at her husband, she found no help from him, and as abruptly as if it were a matter of no importance, she threw up the sponge.

"Do what you like!" she cried, springing up from her chair. "She's your child. I'm not the person to stand in your way. I think if it were my child I'd rather see her—" She managed to check herself. "You two decide it. I can't stand this. I'm sick. I'm going to bed."

She hurried from the room; after a moment Lincoln said:

"This has been a hard day for her. You know how strongly she feels—" His voice was almost apologetic: "When a woman gets an idea in her head."

"Of course."

"It's going to be all right. I think she sees now that you—can provide for the child, and so we can't very well stand in your way or Honoria's way."

"Thank you, Lincoln."

"I'd better go along and see how she is."

"I'm going."

He was still trembling when he reached the street, but a walk down the Rue Bonaparte to the *quais* set him up, and as he crossed the Seine, fresh and new by the *quai* lamps, he felt exultant. But back in his room he couldn't sleep. The image of Helen haunted him. Helen whom he had loved so until they had senselessly begun to abuse each other's love, tear it into shreds. On that terrible February night that Marion remembered so vividly, a slow quarrel had gone on for hours. There was a scene at the Florida, and then he attempted to take her home, and then she kissed young Webb at a table; after that there was what she had hysterically said. When he arrived home alone he turned the key in the lock in wild anger. How could he know she would arrive an hour later alone, that there would be a snowstorm in which she wandered about in slippers, too confused to find a taxi? Then the aftermath, her escaping pneumonia by a miracle, and all the attendant horror. They were "reconciled," but that was the beginning of the end, as Marion, who had seen with her own eyes and who imagined it to be one of many scenes from her sister's martyrdom, never forgot.

Going over it again brought Helen nearer, and in the white, soft light that steals upon half sleep near morning he found himself talking to her again. She said that he was perfectly right about Honoria and that she wanted Honoria to be with him. She said she was glad he was being good and doing better. She said a lot of other things—very friendly things—but she was in a swing in a white dress, and swinging faster and faster all the time, so that at the end he could not hear clearly all that she said.

IV

He woke up feeling happy. The door of the world was open again. He made plans, vistas, futures for Honoria and himself, but suddenly he grew sad, remembering all the plans he and Helen had made. She had not planned to die. The present was the thing—work to do and someone to love. But not to love too much, for he knew the injury that a father can do to a daughter or a mother to a son by attaching them too closely: afterward, out in the world, the child would seek in the marriage partner the same blind tenderness and, failing probably to find it, turn against love and life.

It was another bright, crisp day. He called Lincoln Peters at the bank where he worked and asked if he could count on taking Honoria when he left for Prague. Lincoln agreed that there was no reason for delay. One thing—the legal guardianship. Marion wanted to retain that a while longer. She was upset by the whole matter, and it would oil things if she felt that the situation was still in her control for another year. Charlie agreed, wanting only the tangible, visible child.

Then the question of a governess. Charles sat in a gloomy agency and talked to a cross Béarnaise and to a buxom Breton peasant, neither of whom he could have endured. There were others whom he would see tomorrow.

He lunched with Lincoln Peters at Griffons, trying to keep down his exultation.

"There's nothing quite like your own child," Lincoln said. "But you understand how Marion feels too."

"She's forgotten how hard I worked for seven years there," Charlie said. "She just remembers one night."

"There's another thing." Lincoln hesitated. "While you and

Helen were tearing around Europe throwing money away, we were just getting along. I didn't touch any of the prosperity because I never got ahead enough to carry anything but my insurance. I think Marion felt there was some kind of injustice in it—you not even working toward the end, and getting richer and richer."

"It went just as quick as it came," said Charlie.

"Yes, a lot of it stayed in the hands of *chasseurs* and saxophone players and maîtres d'hôtel—well, the big party's over now. I just said that to explain Marion's feeling about those crazy years. If you drop in about six o'clock tonight before Marion's too tired, we'll settle the details on the spot."

Back at his hotel, Charlie found a *pneumatique* that had been redirected from the Ritz bar where Charlie had left his address for the purpose of finding a certain man.

"DEAR CHARLIE: You were so strange when we saw you the other day that I wondered if I did something to offend you. If so, I'm not conscious of it. In fact, I have thought about you too much for the last year, and it's always been in the back of my mind that I might see you if I came over here. We *did* have such good times that crazy spring, like the night you and I stole the butcher's tricycle, and the time we tried to call on the president and you had the old derby rim and the wire cane. Everybody seems so old lately, but I don't feel old a bit. Couldn't we get together some time today for old time's sake? I've got a vile hang-over for the moment, but will be feeling better this afternoon and will look for you about five in the sweatshop at the Ritz.

"Always devotedly,

"LORRAINE."

His first feeling was one of awe that he had actually, in his mature years, stolen a tricycle and pedaled Lorraine all over the Étoile between the small hours and dawn. In retrospect it was a nightmare. Locking out Helen didn't fit in with any other act of his life, but the tricycle incident did—it was one of many. How many weeks or months of dissipation to arrive at that condition of utter irresponsibility?

He tried to picture how Lorraine had appeared to him then —very attractive; Helen was unhappy about it, though she said nothing. Yesterday, in the restaurant, Lorraine had seemed trite, blurred, worn away. He emphatically did not want to see her, and he was glad Alix had not given away his hotel address. It was a relief to think, instead, of Honoria, to think of Sundays spent with her and of saying good morning to her and of knowing she was there in his house at night, drawing her breath in the darkness.

At five he took a taxi and bought presents for all the Peters —a piquant cloth doll, a box of Roman soldiers, flowers for Marion, big linen handkerchiefs for Lincoln.

He saw, when he arrived in the apartment, that Marion had accepted the inevitable. She greeted him now as though he were a recalcitrant member of the family, rather than a menacing outsider. Honoria had been told she was going; Charlie was glad to see that her tact made her conceal her excessive happiness. Only on his lap did she whisper her delight and the question "When?" before she slipped away with the other children.

He and Marion were alone for a minute in the room, and on an impulse he spoke out boldly:

"Family quarrels are bitter things. They don't go according to any rules. They're not like aches or wounds; they're more like splits in the skin that won't heal because there's not enough material. I wish you and I could be on better terms."

"Some things are hard to forget," she answered. "It's a question of confidence." There was no answer to this and presently she asked, "When do you propose to take her?"

"As soon as I can get a governess. I hoped the day after tomorrow."

"That's impossible. I've got to get her things in shape. Not before Saturday."

He yielded. Coming back into the room, Lincoln offered him a drink.

"I'll take my daily whisky," he said.

It was warm here, it was a home, people together by a fire. The children felt very safe and important; the mother and father were serious, watchful. They had things to do for the children more important than his visit here. A spoonful of medicine was, after all, more important than the strained relations between Marion and himself. They were not dull people, but they were very much in the grip of life and circumstances. He wondered if he couldn't do something to get Lincoln out of his rut at the bank.

A long peal at the door-bell; the *bonne à tout faire* passed through and went down the corridor. The door opened upon another long ring, and then voices, and the three in the salon looked up expectantly; Richard moved to bring the corridor within his range of vision, and Marion rose. Then the maid came back along the corridor, closely followed by the voices, which developed under the light into Duncan Schaeffer and Lorraine Quarrles.

They were gay, they were hilarious, they were roaring with laughter. For a moment Charlie was astounded; unable to understand how they ferreted out the Peters' address.

"Ah-h-h!" Duncan wagged his finger roguishly at Charlie. "Ah-h-h!"

They both slid down another cascade of laughter. Anxious and at a loss, Charlie shook hands with them quickly and presented them to Lincoln and Marion. Marion nodded, scarcely speaking. She had drawn back a step toward the fire; her little girl stood beside her, and Marion put an arm about her shoulder.

With growing annoyance at the intrusion, Charlie waited for them to explain themselves. After some concentration Duncan said:

"We came to invite you out to dinner. Lorraine and I insist that all this shishi, cagy business 'bout your address got to stop."

Charlie came closer to them, as if to force them backward down the corridor.

"Sorry, but I can't. Tell me where you'll be and I'll phone you in half an hour."

This made no impression. Lorraine sat down suddenly on the side of a chair, and focusing her eyes on Richard, cried, "Oh, what a nice little boy! Come here, little boy." Richard glanced at his mother, but did not move. With a perceptible shrug of her shoulders, Lorraine turned back to Charlie:

"Come and dine. Sure your cousins won' mine. See you so sel'om. Or solemn."

"I can't," said Charlie sharply. "You two have dinner and I'll phone you."

Her voice became suddenly unpleasant. "All right, we'll go. But I remember once when you hammered on my door at four A.M. I was enough of a good sport to give you a drink. Come on, Dunc."

Still in slow motion, with blurred, angry faces, with uncertain feet, they retired along the corridor.

"Good night," Charlie said.

"Good night!" responded Lorraine emphatically.

When he went back into the salon Marion had not moved, only now her son was standing in the circle of her other arm. Lincoln was still swinging Honoria back and forth like a pendulum from side to side.

"What an outrage!" Charlie broke out. "What an absolute outrage!"

Neither of them answered. Charlie dropped into an armchair, picked up his drink, set it down again and said:

"People I haven't seen for two years having the colossal nerve——"

He broke off. Marion had made the sound "Oh!" in one swift, furious breath, turned her body from him with a jerk and left the room.

Lincoln set down Honoria carefully.

"You children go in and start your soup," he said, and when they obeyed, he said to Charlie:

"Marion's not well and she can't stand shocks. That kind of people make her really physically sick."

"I didn't tell them to come here. They wormed your name out of somebody. They deliberately——"

"Well, it's too bad. It doesn't help matters. Excuse me a minute."

Left alone, Charlie sat tense in his chair. In the next room he could hear the children eating, talking in monosyllables, already oblivious to the scene between their elders. He heard a murmur of conversation from a farther room and then the ticking bell of a telephone receiver picked up, and in a panic he moved to the other side of the room and out of earshot.

In a minute Lincoln came back. "Look here, Charlie. I think we'd better call off dinner for tonight. Marion's in bad shape."

"Is she angry with me?"

"Sort of," he said, almost roughly. "She's not strong and ——"

"You mean she's changed her mind about Honoria?"

"She's pretty bitter right now. I don't know. You phone me at the bank tomorrow."

"I wish you'd explain to her I never dreamed these people would come here. I'm just as sore as you are."

"I couldn't explain anything to her now."

Charlie got up. He took his coat and hat and started down the corridor. Then he opened the door of the dining room and said in a strange voice, "Good night, children."

Honoria rose and ran around the table to hug him.

"Good night, sweetheart," he said vaguely, and then trying to make his voice more tender, trying to conciliate something, "Good night, dear children."

V

Charlie went directly to the Ritz bar with the furious idea of finding Lorraine and Duncan, but they were not there, and he realized that in any case there was nothing he could do. He had not touched his drink at the Peters, and now he ordered a whisky-and-soda. Paul came over to say hello.

"It's a great change," he said sadly. "We do about half the business we did. So many fellows I hear about back in the States lost everything, maybe not in the first crash, but then in the second. Your friend George Hardt lost every cent, I hear. Are you back in the States?"

"No, I'm in business in Prague."

"I heard that you lost a lot in the crash."

"I did," and he added grimly, "but I lost everything I wanted in the boom."

"Selling short."

"Something like that."

Again the memory of those days swept over him like a nightmare—the people they had met travelling; then people who couldn't add a row of figures or speak a coherent sentence. The little man Helen had consented to dance with at the ship's party, who had insulted her ten feet from the table; the women and girls carried screaming with drinks or drugs out of public places——

—The men who locked their wives out in the snow, because the snow of twenty-nine wasn't real snow. If you didn't want it to be snow, you just paid some money.

He went to the phone and called the Peters' apartment; Lincoln answered.

"I called up because this thing is on my mind. Has Marion said anything definite?"

"Marion's sick," Lincoln answered shortly. "I know this thing isn't altogether your fault, but I can't have her go to pieces about it. I'm afraid we'll have to let it slide for six months; I can't take the chance of working her up to this state again."

"I see."

"I'm sorry, Charlie."

He went back to his table. His whisky glass was empty, but he shook his head when Alix looked at it questionably. There wasn't much he could do now except send Honoria some things; he would send her a lot of things tomorrow. He thought rather angrily that this was just money—he had given so many people money. . . .

"No, no more," he said to another waiter. "What do I owe you?"

He would come back some day; they couldn't make him pay forever. But he wanted his child, and nothing was much good now, beside that fact. He wasn't young any more, with a lot of nice thoughts and dreams to have by himself. He was absolutely sure Helen wouldn't have wanted him to be so alone.

ERNEST HEMINGWAY

(1899-   )

Hemingway is alone among major writers in the extent to which he has combined the active (boxing, fishing, hunting and war) and the writing lives. Disliking rhetorical writing and preferring the concrete symbol to the vague abstraction, and influenced by Stein, Turgenev, Anderson and Twain, among others, he has evolved the style that now bears his name: the style that is simple, direct, hard-hitting and precise, that employs no word its writer would not use in conversation, that deals in understatement and meaningful omission. "The dignity of movement of an iceberg," Hemingway has written (in *Death in the Afternoon*), "is due to only one-eighth of it being above water." The Hemingway style would be inadequate for intellectual analysis, but it is an admirable instrument for rendering the emotions that Hemingway deals in: love, despair, pride of battle, sexual appetite, the courage not to bow before hostile circumstances. Quite apart from the fact that he has been slavishly imitated, stylistically, by writers who were unable to write and who had nothing to say, Hemingway's influence in popularizing colloquial writing has been enormous. Some of his more important works are the novels *The Sun Also Rises*, *A Farewell to Arms*, *For Whom the Bell Tolls*, the novelette *The Old Man and the Sea*, and the short-story collections *In Our Time* and *Men Without Women* (from which "The Undefeated" is taken).

THE UNDEFEATED

MANUEL GARCIA climbed the stairs to Don Miguel Retana's office. He set down his suitcase and knocked on the door. There was no answer. Manuel, standing in the hallway, felt there was some one in the room. He felt it through the door.

"Retana," he said, listening.

There was no answer.

He's there, all right, Manuel thought.

"Retana," he said and banged the door.

"Who's there?" said some one in the office.

"Me, Manolo," Manuel said.

"What do you want?" asked the voice.

"I want to work," Manuel said.

Something in the door clicked several times and it swung open. Manuel went in, carrying his suitcase.

A little man sat behind a desk at the far side of the room. Over his head was a bull's head, stuffed by a Madrid taxidermist; on the walls were framed photographs and bull-fight posters.

The little man sat looking at Manuel.

"I thought they'd killed you," he said.

Manuel knocked with his knuckles on the desk. The little man sat looking at him across the desk.

"How many corridas you had this year?" Retana asked.

"One," he answered.

"Just that one?" the little man asked.

"That's all."

"I read about it in the papers," Retana said. He leaned back in the chair and looked at Manuel.

Manuel looked up at the stuffed bull. He had seen it often before. He felt a certain family interest in it. It had killed his brother, the promising one, about nine years ago. Manuel remembered the day. There was a brass plate on the oak shield the bull's head was mounted on. Manuel could not read it, but he imagined it was in memory of his brother. Well, he had been a good kid.

The plate said: "The Bull 'Mariposa' of the Duke of Veragua, which accepted 9 varas for 7 caballos, and caused the death of Antonio Garcia, Novillero, April 27, 1909."

Retana saw him looking at the stuffed bull's head.

"The lot the Duke sent me for Sunday will make a scandal," he said. "They're all bad in the legs. What do they say about them at the Café?"

"I don't know," Manuel said. "I just got in."

"Yes," Retana said. "You still have your bag."

He looked at Manuel, leaning back behind the big desk.

"Sit down," he said. "Take off your cap."

Manuel sat down; his cap off, his face was changed. He looked pale, and his coleta pinned forward on his head, so that it would not show under the cap, gave him a strange look.

"You don't look well," Retana said.

"I just got out of the hospital," Manuel said.

"I heard they'd cut your leg off," Retana said.

"No," said Manuel. "It got all right."

Retana leaned forward across the desk and pushed a wooden box of cigarettes toward Manuel.

"Have a cigarette," he said.

"Thanks."

Manuel lit it.

"Smoke?" he said, offering the match to Retana.

"No," Retana waved his hand, "I never smoke."

Retana watched him smoking.

"Why don't you get a job and go to work?" he said.

"I don't want to work," Manuel said. "I am a bull-fighter."

"There aren't any bull-fighters any more," Retana said.

"I'm a bull-fighter," Manuel said.

"Yes, while you're in there," Retana said.

Manuel laughed.

Retana sat, saying nothing and looking at Manuel.

"I'll put you in a nocturnal if you want," Retana offered.

"When?" Manuel asked.

"Tomorrow night."

"I don't like to substitute for anybody," Manuel said. That was the way they all got killed. That was the way Salvador got killed. He tapped with his knuckles on the table.

"It's all I've got," Retana said.

"Why don't you put me on next week?" Manuel suggested.

"You wouldn't draw," Retana said. "All they want is Litri and Rubito and La Torre. Those kids are good."

"They'd come to see me get it," Manuel said, hopefully.

"No, they wouldn't. They don't know who you are any more."

"I've got a lot of stuff," Manuel said.

"I'm offering to put you on tomorrow night," Retana said. "You can work with young Hernandez and kill two novillos after the Charlots."

"Whose novillos?" Manuel asked.

"I don't know. Whatever stuff they've got in the corrals. What the veterinaries won't pass in the daytime."

"I don't like to substitute," Manuel said.

"You can take it or leave it," Retana said. He leaned forward over the papers. He was no longer interested. The appeal that Manuel had made to him for a moment when he thought of the old days was gone. He would like to get him to substitute for Larita because he could get him cheaply. He could get others cheaply too. He would like to help him though. Still he had given him the chance. It was up to him.

"How much do I get?" Manuel asked. He was still playing with the idea of refusing. But he knew he could not refuse.

"Two hundred and fifty pesetas," Retana said. He had thought of five hundred, but when he opened his mouth it said two hundred and fifty.

"You pay Villalta seven thousand," Manuel said.

"You're not Villalta," Retana said.

"I know it," Manuel said.

"He draws it, Manolo," Retana said in explanation.

"Sure," said Manuel. He stood up. "Give me three hundred, Retana."

"All right," Retana agreed. He reached in the drawer for a paper.

"Can I have fifty now?" Manuel asked.

"Sure," said Retana. He took a fifty-peseta note out of his pocket-book and laid it, spread out flat, on the table.

Manuel picked it up and put it in his pocket.

"What about a cuadrilla?" he asked.

"There's the boys that always work for me nights," Retana said. "They're all right."

"How about picadors?" Manuel asked.

"They're not much," Retana admitted.

"I've got to have one good pic," Manuel said.

"Get him then," Retana said. "Go and get him."

"Not out of this," Manuel said. "I'm not paying for any cuadrilla out of sixty duros."

Retana said nothing but looked at Manuel across the big desk.

"You know I've got to have one good pic," Manuel said.

Retana said nothing but looked at Manuel from a long way off.

"It isn't right," Manuel said.

Retana was still considering him, leaning back in his chair, considering him from a long way away.

"There're the regular pics," he offered.

"I know," Manuel said. "I know your regular pics."

Retana did not smile. Manuel knew it was over.

"All I want is an even break," Manuel said reasoningly. "When I go out there I want to be able to call my shots on the bull. It only takes one good picador."

He was talking to a man who was no longer listening.

"If you want something extra," Retana said, "go and get it. There will be a regular cuadrilla out there. Bring as many of your own pics as you want. The charlotada is over by 10:30."

"All right," Manuel said. "If that's the way you feel about it."

"That's the way," Retana said.

"I'll see you tomorrow night," Manuel said.

"I'll be out there," Retana said.

Manuel picked up his suitcase and went out.

"Shut the door," Retana called.

Manuel looked back. Retana was sitting forward looking at some papers. Manuel pulled the door tight until it clicked.

He went down the stairs and out of the door into the hot brightness of the street. It was very hot in the street and the light on the white buildings was sudden and hard on his eyes. He walked down the shady side of the steep street toward the

Puerta del Sol. The shade felt solid and cool as running water. The heat came suddenly as he crossed the intersecting streets. Manuel saw no one he knew in all the people he passed.

Just before the Puerta del Sol he turned into a café.

It was quiet in the café. There were a few men sitting at tables against the wall. At one table four men played cards. Most of the men sat against the wall smoking, empty coffee-cups and liqueur-glasses before them on the tables. Manuel went through the long room to a small room in back. A man sat at a table in the corner asleep. Manuel sat down at one of the tables.

A waiter came in and stood beside Manuel's table.

"Have you seen Zurito?" Manuel asked him.

"He was in before lunch," the waiter answered. "He won't be back before five o'clock."

"Bring me some coffee and milk and a shot of the ordinary," Manuel said.

The waiter came back into the room carrying a tray with a big coffee-glass and a liqueur-glass on it. In his left hand he held a bottle of brandy. He swung these down to the table and a boy who had followed him poured coffee and milk into the glass from two shiny, spouted pots with long handles.

Manuel took off his cap and the waiter noticed his pigtail pinned forward on his head. He winked at the coffee-boy as he poured out the brandy into the little glass beside Manuel's coffee. The coffee-boy looked at Manuel's pale face curiously.

"You fighting here?" asked the waiter, corking up the bottle.

"Yes," Manuel said. "Tomorrow."

The waiter stood there, holding the bottle on one hip.

"You in the Charlie Chaplins?" he asked.

The coffee-boy looked away, embarrassed.

"No. In the ordinary."

"I thought they were going to have Chaves and Hernandez," the waiter said.

"No. Me and another."

"Who? Chaves or Hernandez?"

"Hernandez, I think."

"What's the matter with Chaves?"

"He got hurt."

"Where did you hear that?"

"Retana."

"Hey, Looie," the waiter called to the next room, "Chaves got cogida."

Manuel had taken the wrapper off the lumps of sugar and dropped them into his coffee. He stirred it and drank it down, sweet, hot, and warming in his empty stomach. He drank off the brandy.

"Give me another shot of that," he said to the waiter.

The waiter uncorked the bottle and poured the glass full, slopping another drink into the saucer. Another waiter had come up in front of the table. The coffee-boy was gone.

"Is Chaves hurt bad?" the second waiter asked Manuel.

"I don't know," Manuel said, "Retana didn't say."

"A hell of a lot he cares," the tall waiter said. Manuel had not seen him before. He must have just come up.

"If you stand in with Retana in this town, you're a made man," the tall waiter said. "If you aren't in with him, you might just as well go out and shoot yourself."

"You said it," the other waiter who had come in said. "You said it then."

"You're right I said it," said the tall waiter. "I know what I'm talking about when I talk about that bird."

"Look what he's done for Villalta," the first waiter said.

"And that ain't all," the tall waiter said. "Look what he's done for Marcial Lalanda. Look what he's done for Nacional."

"You said it, kid," agreed the short waiter.

Manuel looked at them, standing talking in front of his table. He had drunk his second brandy. They had forgotten about him. They were not interested in him.

"Look at that bunch of camels," the tall waiter went on. "Did you ever see this Nacional II?"

"I seen him last Sunday didn't I?" the original waiter said.

"He's a giraffe," the short waiter said.

"What did I tell you?" the tall waiter said. "Those are Retana's boys."

"Say, give me another shot of that," Manuel said. He had poured the brandy the waiter had slopped over in the saucer into his glass and drank it while they were talking.

The original waiter poured his glass full mechanically, and the three of them went out of the room talking.

In the far corner the man was still asleep, snoring slightly on the intaking breath, his head back against the wall.

Manuel drank his brandy. He felt sleepy himself. It was too hot to go out into the town. Besides there was nothing to do. He wanted to see Zurito. He would go to sleep while he waited. He kicked his suitcase under the table to be sure it was there. Perhaps it would be better to put it back under the seat, against the wall. He leaned down and shoved it under. Then he leaned forward on the table and went to sleep.

When he woke there was some one sitting across the table from him. It was a big man with a heavy brown face like an Indian. He had been sitting there some time. He had waved the waiter away and sat reading the paper and occasionally looking down at Manuel, asleep, his head on the table. He read the paper laboriously, forming the words with his lips as he read. When it tired him he looked at Manuel. He sat heavily in the chair, his black Cordoba hat tipped forward.

Manuel sat up and looked at him.

"Hello, Zurito," he said.

"Hello, kid," the big man said.

"I've been asleep." Manuel rubbed his forehead with the back of his fist.

"I thought maybe you were."

"How's everything?"

"Good. How is everything with you?"

"Not so good."

They were both silent. Zurito, the picador, looked at Manuel's white face. Manuel looked down at the picador's enormous hands folding the paper to put away in his pocket.

"I got a favor to ask you, Manos," Manuel said.

Manosduros was Zurito's nickname. He never heard it without thinking of his huge hands. He put them forward on the table self-consciously.

"Let's have a drink," he said.

"Sure," said Manuel.

The waiter came and went and came again. He went out of the room looking back at the two men at the table.

"What's the matter, Manolo?" Zurito set down his glass.

"Would you pic two bulls for me tomorrow night?" Manuel asked, looking up at Zurito across the table.

"No," said Zurito. "I'm not pic-ing."

Manuel looked down at his glass. He had expected that answer; now he had it. Well, he had it.

"I'm sorry, Manolo, but I'm not pic-ing." Zurito looked at his hands.

"That's all right," Manuel said.

"I'm too old," Zurito said.

"I just asked you," Manuel said.

"Is it the nocturnal tomorrow?"

"That's it. I figured if I had just one good pic, I could get away with it."

"How much are you getting?"

"Three hundred pesetas."

"I get more than that for pic-ing."

"I know," said Manuel. "I didn't have any right to ask you."

"What do you keep on doing it for?" Zurito asked. "Why don't you cut off your coleta, Manolo?"

"I don't know," Manuel said.

"You're pretty near as old as I am," Zurito said.

"I don't know," Manuel said. "I got to do it. If I can fix it so that I get an even break, that's all I want. I got to stick with it, Manos."

"No, you don't."

"Yes, I do. I've tried keeping away from it."

"I know how you feel. But it isn't right. You ought to get out and stay out."

"I can't do it. Besides, I've been going good lately."

Zurito looked at his face.

"You've been in the hospital."

"But I was going great when I got hurt."

Zurito said nothing. He tipped the cognac out of his saucer into his glass.

"The papers said they never saw a better faena," Manuel said.

Zurito looked at him.

"You know when I get going I'm good," Manuel said.

"You're too old," the picador said.

"No," said Manuel. "You're ten years older than I am."

"With me it's different."

"I'm not too old," Manuel said.

They sat silent, Manuel watching the picador's face.

"I was going great till I got hurt," Manuel offered.

"You ought to have seen me, Manos," Manuel said, reproachfully.

"I don't want to see you," Zurito said. "It makes me nervous."

"You haven't seen me lately."

"I've seen you plenty."

Zurito looked at Manuel, avoiding his eyes.

"You ought to quit it, Manolo."

"I can't," Manuel said. "I'm going good now, I tell you."

Zurito leaned forward, his hands on the table.

"Listen. I'll pic for you and if you don't go big tomorrow night, you'll quit. See? Will you do that?"

"Sure."

Zurito leaned back, relieved.

"You got to quit," he said. "No monkey business. You got to cut the coleta."

"I won't have to quit," Manuel said. "You watch me. I've got the stuff."

Zurito stood up. He felt tired from arguing.

"You got to quit," he said. "I'll cut your coleta myself."

"No, you won't," Manuel said. "You won't have a chance."

Zurito called the waiter.

"Come on," said Zurito. "Come on up to the house."

Manuel reached under the seat for his suitcase. He was happy. He knew Zurito would pic for him. He was the best picador living. It was all simple now.

"Come on up to the house and we'll eat," Zurito said.

Manuel stood in the patio de caballos waiting for the Charlie Chaplins to be over. Zurito stood beside him. Where they stood it was dark. The high door that led into the bull-ring was shut. Above them they heard a shout, then another shout of laughter. Then there was silence. Manuel liked the smell of the stables about the patio de caballos. It smelt good in the dark. There was another roar from the arena and then applause, prolonged applause, going on and on.

"You ever seen these fellows?" Zurito asked, big and looming beside Manuel in the dark.

"No," Manuel said.

"They're pretty funny," Zurito said. He smiled to himself in the dark.

The high, double, tight-fitting door into the bull-ring swung open and Manuel saw the ring in the hard light of the arc-lights, the plaza, dark all the way around, rising high; around the edge of the ring were running and bowing two men dressed like tramps, followed by a third in the uniform of a hotel bell-boy who stooped and picked up the hats and canes thrown down onto the sand and tossed them back up into the darkness.

The electric light went on in the patio.

"I'll climb onto one of those ponies while you collect the kids," Zurito said.

Behind them came the jingle of the mules, coming out to go into the arena and be hitched onto the dead bull.

The members of the cuadrilla, who had been watching the burlesque from the runway between the barrera and the seats, came walking back and stood in a group talking, under the electric light in the patio. A good-looking lad in a silver-and-orange suit came up to Manuel and smiled.

"I'm Hernandez," he said and put out his hand.

Manuel shook it.

"They're regular elephants we've got tonight," the boy said cheerfully.

"They're big ones with horns," Manuel agreed.

"You drew the worst lot," the boy said.

"That's all right," Manuel said. "The bigger they are, the more meat for the poor."

"Where did you get that one?" Hernandez grinned.

"That's an old one," Manuel said. "You line up your cuadrilla, so I can see what I've got."

"You've got some good kids," Hernandez said. He was very cheerful. He had been on twice before in nocturnals and was beginning to get a following in Madrid. He was happy the fight would start in a few minutes.

"Where are the pics?" Manuel asked.

"They're back in the corrals fighting about who gets the beautiful horses," Hernandez grinned.

The mules came through the gate in a rush, the whips snapping, bells jangling and the young bull ploughing a furrow of sand.

They formed up for the paseo as soon as the bull had gone through.

Manuel and Hernandez stood in front. The youths of the cuadrillas were behind, their heavy capes furled over their arms. In back, the four picadors, mounted, holding their steel-tipped push-poles erect in the half-dark of the corral.

"It's a wonder Retana wouldn't give us enough light to see the horses by," one picador said.

"He knows we'll be happier if we don't get too good a look at these skins," another pic answered.

"This thing I'm on barely keeps me off the ground," the first picador said.

"Well, they're horses."

"Sure, they're horses."

They talked, sitting their gaunt horses in the dark.

Zurito said nothing. He had the only steady horse of the lot. He had tried him, wheeling him in the corrals and he responded to the bit and the spurs. He had taken the bandage off his right eye and cut the strings where they had tied his ears tight shut at the base. He was a good, solid horse, solid on his legs. That was all he needed. He intended to ride him all through the corrida. He had already, since he had mounted, sitting in the half-dark in the big, quilted saddle, waiting for the paseo, pic-ed through the whole corrida in his mind. The other picadors went on talking on both sides of him. He did not hear them.

The two matadors stood together in front of their three peones, their capes furled over their left arms in the same fashion. Manuel was thinking about the three lads in back of him. They were all three Madrilenos, like Hernandez, boys about nineteen. One of them, a gypsy, serious, aloof, and dark-faced, he liked the look of. He turned.

"What's your name, kid?" he asked the gypsy.

"Fuentes," the gypsy said.

"That's a good name," Manuel said.

The gypsy smiled, showing his teeth.

"You take the bull and give him a little run when he comes out," Manuel said.

"All right," the gypsy said. His face was serious. He began to think about just what he would do.

"Here she goes," Manuel said to Hernandez.

"All right. We'll go."

Heads up, swinging with the music, their right arms swinging free, they stepped out, crossing the sanded arena under the arc-lights, the cuadrillas opening out behind, the picadors riding after, behind came the bull-ring servants and the jingling mules. The crowd applauded Hernandez as they marched across the arena. Arrogant, swinging, they looked straight ahead as they marched.

They bowed before the president, and the procession broke up into its component parts. The bull-fighters went over to the barrera and changed their heavy mantles for the light fighting capes. The mules went out. The picadors galloped jerkily around the ring, and two rode out the gate they had come in by. The servants swept the sand smooth.

Manuel drank a glass of water poured for him by one of

Retana's deputies, who was acting as his manager and sword-handler. Hernandez came over from speaking with his own manager.

"You got a good hand, kid," Manuel complimented him.

"They like me," Hernandez said happily.

"How did the paseo go?" Manuel asked Retana's man.

"Like a wedding," said the handler. "Fine. You came out like Joselito and Belmonte."

Zurito rode by, a bulky equestrian statue. He wheeled his horse and faced him toward the toril on the far side of the ring where the bull would come out. It was strange under the arc-light. He pic-ed in the hot afternoon sun for big money. He didn't like this arc-light business. He wished they would get started.

Manuel went up to him.

"Pic him, Manos," he said. "Cut him down to size for me."

"I'll pic him, kid," Zurito spat on the sand. "I'll make him jump out of the ring."

"Lean on him, Manos," Manuel said.

"I'll lean on him," Zurito said. "What's holding it up?"

"He's coming now," Manuel said.

Zurito sat there, his feet in the box-stirrups, his great legs in the buckskin-covered armor gripping the horse, the reins in his left hand, the long pic held in his right hand, his broad hat well down over his eyes to shade them from the lights, watching the distant door of the toril. His horse's ears quivered. Zurito patted him with his left hand.

The red door of the toril swung back and for a moment Zurito looked into the empty passageway far across the arena. Then the bull came out in a rush, skidding on his four legs as he came out under the lights, then charging in a gallop, moving softly in a fast gallop, silent except as he woofed through wide nostrils as he charged, glad to be free after the dark pen.

In the first row of seats, slightly bored, leaning forward to write on the cement wall in front of his knees, the substitute bull-fight critic of *El Heraldo* scribbled: "Campagnero, Negro, 42, came out at 90 miles an hour with plenty of gas————"

Manuel, leaning against the barrera, watching the bull, waved his hand and the gypsy ran out, trailing his cape. The bull, in full gallop, pivoted and charged the cape, his head down, his tail rising. The gypsy moved in a zigzag, and as he passed, the bull caught sight of him and abandoned the cape to charge the man. The gyp sprinted and vaulted the red fence of the barrera as the bull struck it with his horns. He tossed into it twice with his horns, banging into the wood blindly.

The critic of *El Heraldo* lit a cigarette and tossed the match at the bull, then wrote in his note-book, "large and with enough horns to satisfy the cash customers, Campagnero showed a tendency to cut into the terrain of the bull-fighters."

Manuel stepped out on the hard sand as the bull banged into the fence. Out of the corner of his eye he saw Zurito sitting the white horse close to the barrera, about a quarter of the way around the ring to the left. Manuel held the cape close in front of him, a fold in each hand, and shouted at the bull. "Huh! Huh!" The bull turned, seemed to brace against the fence as he charged in a scramble, driving into the cape as Manuel side-stepped, pivoted on his heels with the charge of the bull, and swung the cape just ahead of the horns. At the end of the swing he was facing the bull again and held the cape in the same position close in front of his body, and pivoted again as the bull recharged. Each time, as he swung, the crowd shouted.

Four times he swung with the bull, lifting the cape so it billowed full, and each time bringing the bull around to charge again. Then, at the end of the fifth swing, he held the cape against his hip and pivoted, so the cape swung out like a ballet dancer's skirt and wound the bull around himself like a belt, to step clear, leaving the bull facing Zurito on the white horse, come up and planted firm, the horse facing the bull, its ears forward, its lips nervous, Zurito, his hat over his eyes, leaning forward, the long pole sticking out before and behind in a sharp angle under his right arm, held half-way down, the tri-angular iron point facing the bull.

El Heraldo's second-string critic, drawing on his cigarette, his eyes on the bull, wrote: "the veteran Manolo designed a series of acceptable veronicas, ending in a very Belmontistic recorte that earned applause from the regulars, and we entered the tercio of the cavalry."

Zurito sat his horse, measuring the distance between the bull and the end of the pic. As he looked, the bull gathered himself together and charged, his eyes on the horse's chest. As he lowered his head to hook, Zurito sunk the point of the pic in the swelling hump of muscle above the bull's shoulder, leaned all his weight on the shaft, and with his left hand pulled the white horse into the air, front hoofs pawing, and swung him to the right as he pushed the bull under and through so the horns passed safely under the horse's belly and the horse came down, quivering, the bull's tail brushing his chest as he charged the cape Hernandez offered him.

Hernandez ran sideways, taking the bull out and away with the cape, toward the other picador. He fixed him with a swing of the cape, squarely facing the horse and rider, and stepped back. As the bull saw the horse he charged. The picador's lance slid along his back, and as the shock of the charge lifted the horse, the picador was already half-way out of the saddle, lifting his right leg clear as he missed with the lance and falling to the left side to keep the horse between him and the bull. The horse, lifted and gored, crashed over with the bull driving into him, the picador gave a shove with his boots against the horse and lay clear, waiting to be lifted and hauled away and put on his feet.

Manuel let the bull drive into the fallen horse; he was in no hurry, the picador was safe; besides, it did a picador like that good to worry. He'd stay on longer next time. Lousy pics! He looked across the sand at Zurito a little way out from the barrera, his horse rigid, waiting.

"Huh!" he called to the bull, "Tomar!" holding the cape in both hands so it would catch his eye. The bull detached himself from the horse and charged the cape, and Manuel, running sideways and holding the cape spread wide, stopped, swung on his heels, and brought the bull sharply around facing Zurito.

"Campagnero accepted a pair of varas for the death of one

rosinante, with Hernandez and Manolo at the quites," *El Heraldo's* critic wrote. "He pressed on the iron and clearly showed he was no horse-lover. The veteran Zurito resurrected some of his old stuff with the pike-pole, notably the suerte—"

"Olé! Olé!" the man sitting beside him shouted. The shout was lost in the roar of the crowd, and he slapped the critic on the back. The critic looked up to see Zurito, directly below him, leaning far out over his horse, the length of the pic rising in a sharp angle under his armpit, holding the pic almost by the point, bearing down with all his weight, holding the bull off, the bull pushing and driving to get at the horse, and Zurito, far out, on top of him, holding him, holding him, and slowly pivoting the horse against the pressure, so that at last he was clear. Zurito felt the moment when the horse was clear and the bull could come past, and relaxed the absolute steel lock of his resistance, and the triangular steel point of the pic ripped in the bull's hump of shoulder muscle as he tore loose to find Hernandez's cape before his muzzle. He charged blindly into the cape and the boy took him out into the open arena.

Zurito sat patting his horse and looking at the bull charging the cape that Hernandez swung for him out under the bright light while the crowd shouted.

"You see that one?" he said to Manuel.

"It was a wonder," Manuel said.

"I got him that time," Zurito said. "Look at him now."

At the conclusion of a closely turned pass of the cape the bull slid to his knees. He was up at once, but far out across the sand Manuel and Zurito saw the shine of the pumping flow of blood, smooth against the black of the bull's shoulder.

"I got him that time," Zurito said.

"He's a good bull," Manuel said.

"If they gave me another shot at him, I'd kill him," Zurito said.

"They'll change the thirds on us," Manuel said.

"Look at him now," Zurito said.

"I got to go over there," Manuel said, and started on a run for the other side of the ring, where the monos were leading a horse out by the bridle toward the bull, whacking him on the legs with rods and all, in a procession, trying to get him toward the bull, who stood, dropping his head, pawing, unable to make up his mind to charge.

Zurito, sitting his horse, walking him toward the scene, not missing any detail, scowled.

Finally the bull charged, the horse leaders ran for the barrera, the picador hit too far back, and the bull got under the horse, lifted him, threw him onto his back.

Zurito watched. The monos, in their red shirts, running out to drag the picador clear. The picador, now on his feet, swearing and flopping his arms. Manuel and Hernandez standing ready with their capes. And the bull, the great, black bull, with a horse on his back, hooves dangling, the bridle caught in the horns. Black bull with a horse on his back, staggering short-legged, then arching his neck and lifting, thrusting, charging to slide the horse off, horse sliding down. Then the bull into a lunging charge at the cape Manuel spread for him.

The bull was slower now, Manuel felt. He was bleeding badly. There was a sheen of blood all down his flank.

Manuel offered him the cape again. There he came, eyes open, ugly, watching the cape. Manuel stepped to the side and raised his arms, tightening the cape ahead of the bull for the veronica.

Now he was facing the bull. Yes, his head was going down a little. He was carrying it lower. That was Zurito.

Manuel flopped the cape; there he comes; he side-stepped and swung in another veronica. He's shooting awfully accurately, he thought. He's had enough fight, so he's watching now. He's hunting now. Got his eye on me. But I always give him the cape.

He shook the cape at the bull; there he comes; he side-stepped. Awful close that time. I don't want to work that close to him.

The edge of the cape was wet with blood where it had swept along the bull's back as he went by.

All right, here's the last one.

Manuel, facing the bull, having turned with him each charge, offered the cape with two hands. The bull looked at him. Eyes watching, horns straight forward, the bull looked at him, watching.

"Huh!" Manuel said, "Toro!" and leaning back, swung the cape forward. Here he comes. He side-stepped, swung the cape in back of him, and pivoted, so the bull followed a swirl of cape and then was left with nothing, fixed by the pass, dominated by the cape. Manuel swung the cape under his muzzle with one hand, to show the bull was fixed, and walked away.

There was no applause.

Manuel walked across the sand toward the barrera, while Zurito rode out of the ring. The trumpet had blown to change the act to the planting of the banderillos while Manuel had been working with the bull. He had not consciously noticed it. The monos were spreading canvas over the two dead horses and sprinkling sawdust around them.

Manuel came up to the barrera for a drink of water. Retana's man handed him the heavy porous jug.

Fuentes, the tall gypsy, was standing holding a pair of banderillos, holding them together, slim, red sticks, fish-hook points out. He looked at Manuel.

"Go on out there," Manuel said.

The gypsy trotted out. Manuel set down the jug and watched. He wiped his face with his handkerchief.

The critic of *El Heraldo* reached for the bottle of warm champagne that stood between his feet, took a drink, and finished his paragraph.

"—the aged Manolo rated no applause for a vulgar series of lances with the cape and we entered the third of the palings."

Alone in the center of the ring the bull stood, still fixed. Fuentes, tall, flat-backed, walking toward him arrogantly, his arms spread out, the two slim, red sticks, one in each hand, held by the fingers, points straight forward. Fuentes walked forward. Back of him and to one side was a peon with a cape. The bull looked at him and was no longer fixed.

His eyes watched Fuentes, now standing still. Now he leaned

back, calling to him. Fuentes twitched the two banderillos and the light on the steel points caught the bull's eye.

His tail went up and he charged.

He came straight, his eyes on the man. Fuentes stood still, leaning back, the banderillos pointing forward. As the bull lowered his head to hook, Fuentes leaned backward, his arms came together and rose, his two hands touching, the banderillos two descending red lines, and leaning forward drove the points into the bull's shoulder, leaning far in over the bull's horns and pivoting on the two upright sticks, his legs tight together, his body curving to one side to let the bull pass.

"Olé!" from the crowd.

The bull was hooking wildly, jumping like a trout, all four feet off the ground. The red shaft of the banderillos tossed as he jumped.

Manuel, standing at the barrera, noticed that he looked always to the right.

"Tell him to drop the next pair on the right," he said to the kid who started to run out to Fuentes with the new banderillos.

A heavy hand fell on his shoulder. It was Zurito.

"How do you feel, kid?" he asked.

Manuel was watching the bull.

Zurito leaned forward on the barrera, leaning the weight of his body on his arms. Manuel turned to him.

"You're going good," Zurito said.

Manuel shook his head. He had nothing to do now until the next third. The gypsy was very good with the banderillos. The bull would come to him in the next third in good shape. He was a good bull. It had all been easy up to now. The final stuff with the sword was all he worried over. He did not really worry. He did not even think about it. But standing there he had a heavy sense of apprehension. He looked out at the bull, planning his faena, his work with the red cloth that was to reduce the bull, to make him manageable.

The gypsy was walking out toward the bull again, walking heel-and-toe, insultingly, like a ballroom dancer, the red shafts of the banderillos twitching with his walk. The bull watched him, not fixed now, hunting him, but waiting to get close enough so he could be sure of getting him, getting the horns into him.

As Fuentes walked forward the bull charged. Fuentes ran across the quarter of a circle as the bull charged and, as he passed running backward, stopped, swung forward, rose on his toes, arm straight out, and sunk the banderillos straight down into the tight of the big shoulder muscles as the bull missed him.

The crowd were wild about it.

"That kid won't stay in this night stuff long," Retana's man said to Zurito.

"He's good," Zurito said.

"Watch him now."

They watched.

Fuentes was standing with his back against the barrera. Two of the cuadrilla were back of him, with their capes ready to flop over the fence to distract the bull.

The bull, with his tongue out, his barrel heaving, was watching the gypsy. He thought he had him now. Back against the red planks. Only a short charge away. The bull watched him.

The gypsy bent back, drew back his arms, the banderillos pointing at the bull. He called to the bull, stamped one foot. The bull was suspicious. He wanted the man. No more barbs in the shoulder.

Fuentes walked a little closer to the bull. Bent back. Called again. Somebody in the crowd shouted a warning.

"He's too damn close," Zurito said.

"Watch him," Retana's man said.

Leaning back, inciting the bull with the banderillos, Fuentes jumped, both feet off the ground. As he jumped the bull's tail rose and he charged. Fuentes came down on his toes, arms straight out, whole body arching forward, and drove the shafts straight down as he swung his body clear of the right horn.

The bull crashed into the barrera where the flopping capes had attracted his eye as he lost the man.

The gypsy came running along the barrera toward Manuel,

taking the applause of the crowd. His vest was ripped where he had not quite cleared the point of the horn. He was happy about it, showing it to the spectators. He made the tour of the ring. Zurito saw him go by, smiling, pointing at his vest. He smiled.

Somebody else was planting the last pair of banderillos. Nobody was paying any attention.

Retana's man tucked a baton inside the red cloth of a muleta, folded the cloth over it, and handed it over the barrera to Manuel. He reached in the leather sword-case, took out a sword, and holding it by its leather scabbard, reached it over the fence to Manuel. Manuel pulled the blade out by the red hilt and the scabbard fell limp.

He looked at Zurito. The big man saw he was sweating.

"Now you get him, kid," Zurito said.

Manuel nodded.

"He's in good shape," Zurito said.

"Just like you want him," Retana's man assured him.

Manuel nodded.

The trumpeter, up under the roof, blew for the final act, and Manuel walked across the arena toward where, up in the dark boxes, the president must be.

In the front row of seats the substitute bull-fight critic of *El Heraldo* took a long drink of the warm champagne. He had decided it was not worth while to write a running story and would write up the corrida back in the office. What the hell was it anyway? Only a nocturnal. If he missed anything he would get it out of the morning papers. He took another drink of the champagne. He had a date at Maxim's at twelve. Who were these bull-fighters anyway? Kids and bums. A bunch of bums. He put his pad of paper in his pocket and looked over toward Manuel, standing very much alone in the ring, gesturing with his hat in a salute toward a box he could not see high up in the dark plaza. Out in the ring the bull stood quiet, looking at nothing.

"I dedicate this bull to you, Mr. President, and to the public of Madrid, the most intelligent and generous of the world," was what Manuel was saying. It was a formula. He said it all. It was a little long for nocturnal use.

He bowed at the dark, straightened, tossed his hat over his shoulder, and, carrying the muleta in his left hand and the sword in his right, walked out toward the bull.

Manuel walked toward the bull. The bull looked at him; his eyes were quick. Manuel noticed the way the banderillos hung down on his left shoulder and the steady sheen of blood from Zurito's pic-ing. He noticed the way the bull's feet were. As he walked forward, holding the muleta in his left hand and the sword in his right, he watched the bull's feet. The bull could not charge without gathering his feet together. Now he stood square on them, dully.

Manuel walked toward him, watching his feet. This was all right. He could do this. He must work to get the bull's head down, so he could go in past the horns and kill him. He did not think about the sword, not about killing the bull. He thought about one thing at a time. The coming things oppressed him, though. Walking forward, watching the bull's feet, he saw successively his eyes, his wet muzzle, and the wide, forward-pointing spread of his horns. The bull had light circles about his eyes. His eyes watched Manuel. He felt he was going to get this little one with the white face.

Standing still now and spreading the red cloth of the muleta with the sword, pricking the point into the cloth so that the sword, now held in his left hand, spread the red flannel like the jib of a boat, Manuel noticed the points of the bull's horns. One of them was splintered from banging against the barrera. The other was sharp as a porcupine quill. Manuel noticed while spreading the muleta that the white base of the horn was stained red. While he noticed these things he did not lose sight of the bull's feet. The bull watched Manuel steadily.

He's on the defensive now, Manuel thought. He's reserving himself. I've got to bring him out of that and get his head down. Always get his head down. Zurito had his head down once, but he's come back. He'll bleed when I start him going and that will bring it down.

Holding the muleta, with the sword in his left hand widening it in front of him, he called to the bull.

The bull looked at him.

He leaned back insultingly and shook the wide-spread flannel.

The bull saw the muleta. It was a bright scarlet under the arc-light. The bull's legs tightened.

Here he comes. Whoosh! Manuel turned as the bull came and raised the muleta so that it passed over the bull's horns and swept down his broad back from head to tail. The bull had gone clean up in the air with the charge. Manuel had not moved.

At the end of the pass the bull turned like a cat coming around a corner and faced Manuel.

He was on the offensive again. His heaviness was gone. Manuel noted the fresh blood shining down the black shoulder and dripping down the bull's leg. He drew the sword out of the muleta and held it in his right hand. The muleta held low down in his left hand, leaning toward the left, he called to the bull. The bull's legs tightened, his eyes on the muleta. Here he comes, Manuel thought. Yuh!

He swung with the charge, sweeping the muleta ahead of the bull, his feet firm, the sword following a curve, a point of light under the arcs.

The bull recharged as the pase natural finished and Manuel raised the muleta for a pase de pecho. Firmly planted, the bull came by his chest under the raised muleta. Manuel leaned his head back to avoid the clattering banderillo shafts. The hot, black bull body touched his chest as it passed.

Too damn close, Manuel thought. Zurito, leaning on the barrera, spoke rapidly to the gypsy, who trotted out toward Manuel with a cape. Zurito pulled his hat down low and looked out across the arena at Manuel.

Manuel was facing the bull again, the muleta held low and to the left. The bull's head was down as he watched the muleta.

"If it was Belmonte doing that stuff, they'd go crazy," Retana's man said.

Zurito said nothing. He was watching Manuel out in the center of the arena.

"Where did the boss dig this fellow up?" Retana's man asked.

"Out of the hospital," Zurito said.

"That's where he's going damn quick," Retana's man said. Zurito turned on him.

"Knock on that," he said, pointing to the barrera.

"I was just kidding, man," Retana's man said.

"Knock on the wood."

Retana's man leaned forward and knocked three times on the barrera.

"Watch the faena," Zurito said.

Out in the center of the ring, under the lights, Manuel was kneeling, facing the bull, and as he raised the muleta in both hands the bull charged, tail up.

Manuel swung his body clear and, as the bull recharged, brought around the muleta in a half-circle that pulled the bull to his knees.

"Why, that one's a great bull-fighter," Retana's man said.

"No, he's not," said Zurito.

Manuel stood up and, the muleta in his left hand, the sword in his right, acknowledged the applause from the dark plaza.

The bull had humped himself up from his knees and stood waiting, his head hung low.

Zurito spoke to two of the other lads of the cuadrilla and they ran out to stand back of Manuel with their capes. There were four men back of him now. Hernandez had followed him since he first came out with the muleta. Fuentes stood watching, his cape held against his body, tall, in repose, watching lazy-eyed. Now the two came up. Hernandez motioned them to stand one at each side. Manuel stood alone, facing the bull.

Manuel waved back the men with the capes. Stepping back cautiously, they saw his face was white and sweating.

Didn't they know enough to keep back? Did they want to catch the bull's eye with the capes after he was fixed and ready? He had enough to worry about without that kind of thing.

The bull was standing, his four feet square, looking at the muleta. Manuel furled the muleta in his left hand. The bull's eyes watched it. His body was heavy on his feet. He carried his head low, but not too low.

Manuel lifted the muleta at him. The bull did not move. Only his eyes watched.

He's all lead, Manuel thought. He's all square. He's framed right. He'll take it.

He thought in bull-fight terms. Sometimes he had a thought and the particular piece of slang would not come into his mind and he could not realize the thought. His instincts and his knowledge worked automatically, and his brain worked slowly and in words. He knew all about bulls. He did not have to think about them. He just did the right thing. His eyes noted things and his body performed the necessary measures without thought. If he thought about it, he would be gone.

Now, facing the bull, he was conscious of many things at the same time. There were the horns, the one splintered, the other smoothly sharp, the need to profile himself toward the left horn, lance himself short and straight, lower the muleta so the bull would follow it, and, going in over the horns, put the sword all the way into a little spot about as big as a five-peseta piece straight in back of the neck, between the sharp pitch of the bull's shoulders. He must do all this and must then come out from between the horns. He was conscious he must do all this, but his only thought was in words: "Corto y derecho."

"Corto y derecho," he thought, furling the muleta. Short and straight. Corto y derecho, he drew the sword out of the muleta, profiled on the splintered left horn, dropped the muleta across his body, so his right hand with the sword on the level with his eye made the sign of the cross, and, rising on his toes, sighted along the dipping blade of the sword at the spot high up between the bull's shoulders.

Corto y derecho he launched himself on the bull.

There was a shock, and he felt himself go up in the air. He pushed on the sword as he went up and over, and it flew out of his hand. He hit the ground and the bull was on him. Manuel, lying on the ground, kicked at the bull's muzzle with his slippered feet. Kicking, kicking, the bull after him, missing him in his excitement, bumping him with his head, driving the horns into the sand. Kicking like a man keeping a ball in the air, Manuel kept the bull from getting a clean thrust at him.

Manuel felt the wind on his back from the capes flopping at the bull, and then the bull was gone, gone over him in a rush. Dark, as his belly went over. Not even stepped on.

Manuel stood up and picked up the muleta. Fuentes handed him the sword. It was bent where it had struck the shoulder-blade. Manuel straightened it on his knee and ran toward the bull, standing now beside one of the dead horses. As he ran, his jacket flopped where it had been ripped under his armpit.

"Get him out of there," Manuel shouted to the gypsy. The bull had smelled the blood of the dead horse and ripped into the canvas-cover with his horns. He charged Fuentes's cape, with the canvas hanging from his splintered horn, and the crowd laughed. Out in the ring, he tossed his head to rid himself of the canvas. Hernandez, running up from behind him, grabbed the end of the canvas and neatly lifted it off the horn.

The bull followed it in a half-charge and stopped still. He was on the defensive again. Manuel was walking toward him with the sword and muleta. Manuel swung the muleta before him. The bull would not charge.

Manuel profiled toward the bull, sighting along the dipping blade of the sword. The bull was motionless, seemingly dead on his feet, incapable of another charge.

Manuel rose to his toes, sighting along the steel, and charged.

Again there was the shock and he felt himself being borne back in a rush, to strike hard on the sand. There was no chance of kicking this time. The bull was on top of him. Manuel lay as though dead, his head on his arms, and the bull bumped him. Bumped his back, bumped his face in the sand. He felt the horn go into the sand between his folded arms. The bull hit him in the small of the back. His face drove into the sand. The horn drove through one of his sleeves and the bull ripped it off. Manuel was tossed clear and the bull followed the capes.

Manuel got up, found the sword and muleta, tried the point

of the sword with his thumb, and then ran toward the barrera
for a new sword.

Retana's man handed him the sword over the edge of the
barrera.

"Wipe off your face," he said.

Manuel, running again toward the bull, wiped his bloody
face with his handkerchief. He had not seen Zurito. Where was
Zurito?

The cuadrilla had stepped away from the bull and waited
with their capes. The bull stood, heavy and dull again after
the action.

Manuel walked toward him with the muleta. He stopped
and shook it. The bull did not respond. He passed it right and
left, left and right before bull's muzzle. The bull's eyes
watched it and turned with the swing, but he would not charge.
He was waiting for Manuel.

Manuel was worried. There was nothing to do but go in.
Corto y derecho. He profiled close to the bull, crossed the muleta in front of his body and charged. As he pushed in the
sword, he jerked his body to the left to clear the horn. The bull
passed him and the sword shot up in the air, twinkling under
the arc-lights, to fall red-hilted on the sand.

Manuel ran over and picked it up. It was bent and he
straightened it over his knee.

As he came running toward the bull, fixed again now, he
passed Hernandez standing with his cape.

"He's all bone," the boy said encouragingly.

Manuel nodded, wiping his face. He put the bloody handkerchief in his pocket.

There was the bull. He was close to the barrera now. Damn
him. Maybe he was all bone. Maybe there was not any place
for the sword to go in. The hell there wasn't! He'd show them.

He tried a pass with the muleta and the bull did not move.
Manuel chopped the muleta back and forth in front of the
bull. Nothing doing.

He furled the muleta, drew the sword out, profiled and drove
in on the bull. He felt the sword buckle as he shoved it in,
leaning his weight on it, and then it shot high in the air, end-

over-ending into the crowd. Manuel had jerked clear as the sword jumped.

The first cushions thrown down out of the dark missed him. Then one hit him in the face, his bloody face looking toward the crowd. They were coming down fast. Spotting the sand. Somebody threw an empty champagne-bottle from close range. It hit Manuel on the foot. He stood there watching the dark, where the things were coming from. Then something whished through the air and struck by him. Manuel leaned over and picked it up. It was his sword. He straightened it over his knee and gestured with it to the crowd.

"Thank you," he said. "Thank you."

Oh, the dirty bastards! Dirty bastards! Oh, the lousy, dirty bastards! He kicked into a cushion as he ran.

There was the bull. The same as ever. All right, you dirty, lousy bastard!

Manuel passed the muleta in front of the bull's black muzzle.

Nothing doing.

You won't! All right. He stepped close and jammed the sharp peak of the muleta into the bull's damp muzzle.

The bull was on him as he jumped back and as he tripped on a cushion he felt the horn go into him, into his side. He grabbed the horn with his two hands and rode backward, holding tight onto the place. The bull tossed him and he was clear. He lay still. It was all right. The bull was gone.

He got up coughing and feeling broken and gone. The dirty bastards!

"Give me the sword," he shouted. "Give me the stuff."

Fuentes came up with the muleta and the sword.

Hernandez put his arm around him.

"Go on to the infirmary, man," he said. "Don't be a damn fool."

"Get away from me," Manuel said. "Get to hell away from me."

He twisted free. Hernandez shrugged his shoulders. Manuel ran toward the bull.

There was the bull standing, firmly planted.

All right, you bastard! Manuel drew the sword out of the muleta, sighted with the same movement, and flung himself onto the bull. He felt the sword go in all the way. Right up to the guard. Four fingers and his thumb into the bull. The blood was hot on his knuckles, and he was on top of the bull.

The bull lurched with him as he lay on, and seemed to sink; then he was standing clear. He looked at the bull going down slowly over on his side, then suddenly four feet in the air.

Then he gestured at the crowd, his hand warm from the bull blood.

All right, you bastards! He wanted to say something, but he started to cough. It was hot and choking. He looked down for the muleta. He must go over and salute the president. President hell! He was sitting down looking at something. It was the bull. His four feet up. Thick tongue out. Things crawling around on his belly and under his legs. Crawling where the hair was thin. Dead bull. To hell with the bull! To hell with them all! He started to get to his feet and commenced to cough. He sat down again, coughing. Somebody came and pushed him up.

They carried him across the ring to the infirmary, running with him across the sand, standing blocked at the gate as the mules came in, then around under the dark passageway, men grunting as they took him up the stairway, and then laid him down.

The doctor and two men in white were waiting for him. They laid him out on the table. They were cutting away his shirt. Manuel felt tired. His whole chest felt scalding inside. He started to cough and they held something to his mouth. Everybody was very busy.

There was an electric light in his eyes. He shut his eyes.

He heard some one coming very heavily up the stairs. Then he did not hear it. Then he heard a noise far off. That was the crowd. Well, somebody would have to kill his other bull. They had cut away all his shirt. The doctor smiled at him. There was Retana.

"Hello, Retana!" Manuel said. He could not hear his voice.

Retana smiled at him and said something. Manuel could not hear it.

Zurito stood beside the table, bending over where his doctor was working. He was in his picador clothes, without his hat.

Zurito said something to him. Manuel could not hear it.

Zurito was speaking to Retana. One of the men in white smiled and handed Retana a pair of scissors. Retana gave them to Zurito. Zurito said something to Manuel. He could not hear it.

To hell with this operating-table. He'd been on plenty of operating-tables before. He was not going to die. There would be a priest if he was going to die.

Zurito was saying something to him. Holding up the scissors.

That was it. They were going to cut off his coleta. They were going to cut off his pigtail.

Manuel sat up on the operating-table. The doctor stepped back, angry. Some one grabbed him and held him.

"You couldn't do a thing like that, Manos," he said.

He heard suddenly, clearly, Zurito's voice.

"That's all right," Zurito said. "I won't do it. I was joking."

"I was going good," Manuel said. "I didn't have any luck. That was all."

Manuel lay back. They had put something over his face. It was all familiar. He inhaled deeply. He felt very tired. He was very, very tired. They took the thing away from his face.

"I was going good," Manuel said weakly. "I was going great."

Retana looked at Zurito and started for the door.

"I'll stay here with him," Zurito said.

Retana shrugged his shoulders.

Manuel opened his eyes and looked at Zurito.

"Wasn't I going good, Manos?" he asked, for confirmation.

"Sure," said Zurito. "You were going great."

The doctor's assistant put the cone over Manuel's face and he inhaled deeply. Zurito stood awkwardly, watching.

JOHN STEINBECK

(1902-   )

John Steinbeck, one of the principal names in contemporary American literature, started his professional writing career as a newspaper reporter. His too obvious sympathy for the underprivileged militated against his writing with the objectivity which becomes a newspaper reporter, and presently he was free to experiment with other occupations, among them bricklaying. He has lived most of his life in California, and it is about the people of that region that he has written his most important books: *Tortilla Flat* and *Cannery Row*, about the Mexican-American workers and idlers; *Of Mice and Men*, about the migrant ranch workers; and *The Grapes of Wrath*, about the farmers who went to work in California when, in the middle 1930's, their farms turned to dust from drought and lack of irrigation. Steinbeck's poetic rhythms, the depth of his social sympathies, and his warmth and humor make him especially congenial to many readers who find in Hemingway more manner than substance. His other fiction includes two collections of short stories, *The Long Valley*, from which "The Leader of the People" is taken, and *The Red Pony*.

THE LEADER OF THE PEOPLE

On Saturday afternoon Billy Buck, the ranch-hand, raked together the last of the old year's haystack and pitched small forkfuls over the wire fence to a few mildly interested cattle. High in the air small clouds like puffs of cannon smoke were driven eastward by the March wind. The wind could be heard whishing in the brush on the ridge crests, but no breath of it penetrated down into the ranch-cup.

The little boy, Jody, emerged from the house eating a thick piece of buttered bread. He saw Billy working on the last

172

of the haystack. Jody tramped down scuffing his shoes in a way he had been told was destructive to good shoe-leather. A flock of white pigeons flew out of the black cypress tree as Jody passed, and circled the tree and landed again. A half-grown tortoise-shell cat leaped from the bunkhouse porch, galloped on stiff legs across the road, whirled and galloped back again. Jody picked up a stone to help the game along, but he was too late, for the cat was under the porch before the stone could be discharged. He threw the stone into the cypress tree and started the white pigeons on another whirling flight.

Arriving at the used-up haystack, the boy leaned against the barbed wire fence. "Will that be all of it, do you think?" he asked.

The middle-aged ranch-hand stopped his careful raking and stuck his fork into the ground. He took off his black hat and smoothed down his hair. "Nothing left of it that isn't soggy from ground moisture," he said. He replaced his hat and rubbed his dry leathery hands together.

"Ought to be plenty mice," Jody suggested.

"Lousy with them," said Billy. "Just crawling with mice."

"Well, maybe, when you get all through, I could call the dogs and hunt the mice."

"Sure, I guess you could," said Billy Buck. He lifted a forkful of the damp ground-hay and threw it into the air. Instantly three mice leaped out and burrowed frantically under the hay again.

Jody sighed with satisfaction. Those plump, sleepy, arrogant mice were doomed. For eight months they had lived and multiplied in the haystack. They had been immune from cats, from traps, from poison and from Jody. They had grown smug in their security, overbearing and fat. Now the time of disaster had come; they would not survive another day.

Billy looked up at the top of the hills that surrounded the ranch. "Maybe you better ask your father before you do it," he suggested.

"Well, where is he? I'll ask him now."

"He rode up to the ridge ranch after dinner. He'll be back pretty soon."

Jody slumped against the fence post. "I don't think he'd care."

As Billy went back to his work he said ominously, "You'd better ask him anyway. You know how he is."

Jody did know. His father, Carl Tiflin, insisted upon giving permission for anything that was done on the ranch, whether it was important or not. Jody sagged farther against the post until he was sitting on the ground. He looked up at the little puffs of wind-driven cloud. "Is it like to rain, Billy?"

"It might. The wind's good for it, but not strong enough."

"Well, I hope it don't rain until after I kill those damn mice." He looked over his shoulder to see whether Billy had noticed the mature profanity. Billy worked on without comment.

Jody turned back and looked at the side-hill where the road from the outside world came down. The hill was washed with lean March sunshine. Silver thistles, blue lupins and a few poppies bloomed among the sage bushes. Halfway up the hill Jody could see Doubletree Mutt, the black dog, digging in a squirrel hole. He paddled for a while and then paused to kick bursts of dirt out between his hind legs, and he dug with an earnestness which belied the knowledge he must have had that no dog had ever caught a squirrel by digging in a hole.

Suddenly, while Jody watched, the black dog stiffened, and backed out of the hole and looked up the hill toward the cleft in the ridge where the road came through. Jody looked up too. For a moment Carl Tiflin on horseback stood out against the pale sky and then he moved down the road toward the house. He carried something white in his hand.

The boy started to his feet. "He's got a letter," Jody cried. He trotted away toward the ranch house, for a letter would probably be read aloud and he wanted to be there. He reached the house before his father did, and ran in. He heard Carl dismount from his creaking saddle and slap the horse on the side to send it to the barn where Billy would unsaddle it and turn it out.

Jody ran into the kitchen. "We got a letter!" he cried.

His mother looked up from a pan of beans. "Who has?"

"Father has. I saw it in his hand."

Carl strode into the kitchen then, and Jody's mother asked, "Who's the letter from, Carl?"

He frowned quickly. "How did you know there was a letter?"

She nodded her head in the boy's direction. "Big-Britches Jody told me."

Jody was embarrassed.

His father looked down at him contemptuously. "He is getting to be a Big-Britches," Carl said. "He's minding everybody's business but his own. Got his big nose into everything."

Mrs. Tiflin relented a little. "Well, he hasn't enough to keep him busy. Who's the letter from?"

Carl still frowned on Jody. "I'll keep him busy if he isn't careful." He held out a sealed letter. "I guess it's from your father."

Mrs. Tiflin took a hairpin from her head and slit open the flap. Her lips pursed judiciously. Jody saw her eyes snap back and forth over the lines. "He says," she translated, "he says he's going to drive out Saturday to stay for a little while. Why, this is Saturday. The letter must have been delayed." She looked at the postmark. "This was mailed day before yesterday. It should have been here yesterday." She looked up questioningly at her husband, and then her face darkened angrily. "Now what have you got that look on you for? He doesn't come often."

Carl turned his eyes away from her anger. He could be stern with her most of the time, but when occasionally her temper arose, he could not combat it.

"What's the matter with you?" she demanded again.

In his explanation there was a tone of apology Jody himself might have used. "It's just that he talks," Carl said lamely. "Just talks."

"Well, what of it? You talk yourself."

"Sure I do. But your father only talks about one thing."

"Indians!" Jody broke in excitedly. "Indians and crossing the plains!"

Carl turned fiercely on him. "You get out, Mr. Big-Britches! Go on, now! Get out!"

Jody went miserably out the back door and closed the screen with elaborate quietness. Under the kitchen window his shamed, downcast eyes fell upon a curiously shaped stone, a stone of such fascination that he squatted down and picked it up and turned it over in his hands.

The voices came clearly to him through the open kitchen window. "Jody's damn well right," he heard his father say. "Just Indians and crossing the plains. I've heard that story about how the horses got driven off about a thousand times. He just goes on and on, and he never changes a word in the things he tells."

When Mrs. Tiflin answered her tone was so changed that Jody, outside the window, looked up from his study of the stone. Her voice had become soft and explanatory. Jody knew how her face would have changed to match the tone. She said quietly, "Look at it this way, Carl. That was the big thing in my father's life. He led a wagon train clear across the plains to the coast, and when it was finished, his life was done. It was a big thing to do, but it didn't last long enough. Look!" she continued, "it's as though he was born to do that, and after he finished it, there wasn't anything more for him to do but think about it and talk about it. If there'd been any farther west to go, he'd have gone. He's told me so himself. But at last there was the ocean. He lives right by the ocean where he had to stop."

She had caught Carl, caught him and entangled him in her soft tone.

"I've seen him," he agreed quietly. "He goes down and stares off west over the ocean." His voice sharpened a little. "And then he goes up to the Horseshoe Club in Pacific Grove, and he tells people how the Indians drove off the horses."

She tried to catch him again. "Well, it's everything to him. You might be patient with him and pretend to listen."

Carl turned impatiently away. "Well, if it gets too bad, I can always go down to the bunkhouse and sit with Billy," he said irritably. He walked through the house and slammed the front door after him.

Jody ran to his chores. He dumped the grain to the chickens without chasing any of them. He gathered the eggs from the nests. He trotted into the house with the wood and interlaced it so carefully in the woodbox that two armloads seemed to fill it to overflowing.

His mother had finished the beans by now. She stirred up the fire and brushed off the stove-top with a turkey wing. Jody peered cautiously at her to see whether any rancor toward him remained. "Is he coming today?" Jody asked.

"That's what his letter said."

"Maybe I better walk up the road to meet him."

Mrs. Tiflin clanged the stove-lid shut. "That would be nice," she said. "He'd probably like to be met."

"I guess I'll just do it then."

Outside, Jody whistled shrilly to the dogs. "Come on up the hill," he commanded. The two dogs waved their tails and ran ahead. Along the roadside the sage had tender new tips. Jody tore off some pieces and rubbed them on his hands until the air was filled with the sharp wild smell. With a rush the dogs leaped from the road and yapped into the brush after a rabbit. That was the last Jody saw of them, for when they failed to catch the rabbit, they went back home.

Jody plodded on up the hill toward the ridge top. When he reached the little cleft where the road came through, the afternoon wind struck him and blew up his hair and ruffled his shirt. He looked down on the little hills and ridges below and then out at the huge green Salinas Valley. He could see the white town of Salinas far out in the flat and the flash of its windows under the waning sun. Directly below him, in an oak tree, a crow congress had convened. The tree was black with crows all cawing at once.

Then Jody's eyes followed the wagon road down from the ridge where he stood, and lost it behind a hill, and picked it up again on the other side. On that distant stretch he saw a cart slowly pulled by a bay horse. It disappeared behind the hill. Jody sat down on the ground and watched the place where the cart would reappear again. The wind sang on the hilltops and the puff-ball clouds hurried eastward.

Then the cart came into sight and stopped. A man dressed in black dismounted from the seat and walked to the horse's head. Although it was so far away, Jody knew he had unhooked the check-rein, for the horse's head dropped forward. The horse moved on, and the man walked slowly up the hill beside it. Jody gave a glad cry and ran down the road toward them. The squirrels bumped along off the road, and a roadrunner flirted its tail and raced over the edge of the hill and sailed out like a glider.

Jody tried to leap into the middle of his shadow at every step. A stone rolled under his foot and he went down. Around a little bend he raced, and there, a short distance ahead, were his grandfather and the cart. The boy dropped from his unseemly running and approached at a dignified walk.

The horse plodded stumble-footedly up the hill and the old man walked beside it. In the lowering sun their giant shadows flickered darkly behind them. The grandfather was dressed in a black broadcloth suit and he wore kid congress gaiters and a black tie on a short, hard collar. He carried his black slouch hat in his hand. His white beard was cropped close and his white eyebrows overhung his eyes like mustaches. The blue eyes were sternly merry. About the whole face and figure there was a granite dignity, so that every motion seemed an impossible thing. Once at rest, it seemed the old man would be stone, would never move again. His steps were slow and certain. Once made, no step could ever be retraced; once headed in a direction, the path would never bend nor the pace increase nor slow.

When Jody appeared around the bend, Grandfather waved his hat slowly in welcome, and he called, "Why, Jody! Come down to meet me, have you?"

Jody sidled near and turned and matched his step to the old man's step and stiffened his body and dragged his heels a little. "Yes, sir," he said. "We got your letter only today."

"Should have been here yesterday," said Grandfather. "It certainly should. How are all the folks?"

"They're fine, sir." He hesitated and then suggested shyly, "Would you like to come on a mouse hunt tomorrow, sir?"

"Mouse hunt, Jody?" Grandfather chuckled. "Have the people of this generation come down to hunting mice? They aren't very strong, the new people, but I hardly thought mice would be game for them."

"No, sir. It's just play. The haystack's gone. I'm going to drive out the mice to the dogs. And you can watch, or even beat the hay a little."

The stern, merry eyes turned down on him. "I see. You don't eat them, then. You haven't come to that yet."

Jody explained, "The dogs eat them, sir. It wouldn't be much like hunting Indians, I guess."

"No, not much—but then later, when the troops were hunting Indians and shooting children and burning teepees, it wasn't much different from your mouse hunt."

They topped the rise and started down into the ranch-cup, and they lost the sun from their shoulders. "You've grown," Grandfather said. "Nearly an inch, I should say."

"More," Jody boasted. "Where they mark me on the door, I'm up more than an inch since Thanksgiving even."

Grandfather's rich throaty voice said, "Maybe you're getting too much water and turning to pith and stalk. Wait until you head out, and then we'll see."

Jody looked quickly into the old man's face to see whether his feelings should be hurt, but there was no will to injure, no punishing nor putting-in-your-place light in the keen blue eyes. "We might kill a pig," Jody suggested.

"Oh, no! I couldn't let you do that. You're just humoring me. It isn't the time and you know it."

"You know Riley, the big boar, sir?"

"Yes, I remember Riley well."

"Well, Riley ate a hole into that same haystack, and it fell down on him and smothered him."

"Pigs do that when they can," said Grandfather.

"Riley was a nice pig, for a boar, sir. I rode him sometimes, and he didn't mind."

A door slammed at the house below them, and they saw Jody's mother standing on the porch waving her apron in welcome. And they saw Carl Tiflin walking up from the barn to be at the house for the arrival.

The sun had disappeared from the hills by now. The blue smoke from the house chimney hung in flat layers in the purpling ranch-cup. The puff-ball clouds, dropped by the falling wind, hung listlessly in the sky.

Billy Buck came out of the bunkhouse and flung a wash basin of soapy water on the ground. He had been shaving in mid-week, for Billy held Grandfather in reverence, and Grandfather said that Billy was one of the few men of the new generation who had not gone soft. Although Billy was in middle age, Grandfather considered him a boy. Now Billy was hurrying toward the house too.

When Jody and Grandfather arrived, the three were waiting for them in front of the yard gate.

Carl said, "Hello, sir. We've been looking for you."

Mrs. Tiflin kissed Grandfather on the side of his beard, and stood still while his big hand patted her shoulder. Billy shook hands solemnly grinning under his straw mustache. "I'll put up your horse," said Billy, and he led the rig away.

Grandfather watched him go, and then, turning back to the group, he said as he had said a hundred times before. "There's a good boy. I knew his father, old Mule-tail Buck. I never knew why they called him Mule-tail except he packed mules."

Mrs. Tiflin turned and led the way into the house. "How long are you going to stay, Father? Your letter didn't say."

"Well, I don't know. I thought I'd stay about two weeks. But I never stay as long as I think I'm going to."

In a short while they were sitting at the white oilcloth table eating their supper. The lamp with the tin reflector hung over the table. Outside the dining-room windows the big moths battered softly against the glass.

Grandfather cut his steak into tiny pieces and chewed slowly. "I'm hungry," he said. "Driving out here got my appetite up. It's like when we were crossing. We all got so hungry every night we could hardly wait to let the meat get done. I could eat about five pounds of buffalo meat every night."

"It's moving around does it," said Billy. "My father was a government packer. I helped him when I was a kid. Just the two of us could about clean up a deer's ham."

"I knew your father, Billy," said Grandfather. "A fine man he was. They called him Mule-tail Buck. I don't know why except he packed mules."

"That was it," Billy agreed. "He packed mules."

Grandfather put down his knife and fork and looked around the table. "I remember one time we ran out of meat—" His voice dropped to a curious low sing-song, dropped into a tonal groove the story had worn for itself. "There was no buffalo, no antelope, not even rabbits. The hunters couldn't even shoot a coyote. That was the time for the leader to be on the watch. I was the leader, and I kept my eyes open. Know why? Well, just the minute the people began to get hungry they'd start slaughtering the team oxen. Do you believe that? I've heard of parties that just ate up their draft cattle. Started from the middle and worked toward the ends. Finally they'd eat the lead pair, and then the wheelers. The leader of a party had to keep them from doing that."

In some manner a big moth got into the room and circled the hanging kerosene lamp. Billy got up and tried to clap it between his hands. Carl struck with a cupped palm and caught the moth and broke it. He walked to the window and dropped it out.

"As I was saying," Grandfather began again, but Carl interrupted him. "You'd better eat some more meat. All the rest of us are ready for our pudding."

Jody saw a flash of anger in his mother's eyes. Grandfather picked up his knife and fork. "I'm pretty hungry, all right," he said. "I'll tell you about that later."

When supper was over, when the family and Billy Buck sat in front of the fireplace in the other room, Jody anxiously watched Grandfather. He saw the signs he knew. The bearded head leaned forward; the eyes lost their sternness and looked wonderingly into the fire; the big lean fingers laced themselves on the black knees. "I wonder," he began, "I just wonder whether I ever told you how those thieving Piutes drove off thirty-five of our horses."

"I think you did," Carl interrupted. "Wasn't it just before you went up into the Tahoe country?"

Grandfather turned quickly toward his son-in-law. "That's right. I guess I must have told you that story."

"Lots of times," Carl said cruelly, and he avoided his wife's eyes. But he felt the angry eyes on him, and he said, " 'Course I'd like to hear it again."

Grandfather looked back at the fire. His fingers unlaced and laced again. Jody knew how he felt, how his insides were collapsed and empty. Hadn't Jody been called a Big-Britches that very afternoon? He arose to heroism and opened himself to the term Big-Britches again. "Tell about Indians," he said softly.

Grandfather's eyes grew stern again. "Boys always want to hear about Indians. It was a job for men, but boys want to hear about it. Well, let's see. Did I ever tell you how I wanted each wagon to carry a long iron plate?"

Everyone but Jody remained silent. Jody said. "No. You didn't."

"Well, when the Indians attacked, we always put the wagons in a circle and fought from between the wheels. I thought that if every wagon carried a long plate with rifle holes, the men could stand the plates on the outside of the wheels when the wagons were in the circle and they would be protected. It would save lives and that would make up for the extra weight of the iron. But of course the party wouldn't do it. No party had done it before and they couldn't see why they should go to the expense. They lived to regret it, too."

Jody looked at his mother, and knew from her expression

that she was not listening at all. Carl picked at a callus on his thumb and Billy Buck watched a spider crawling up the wall.

Grandfather's tone dropped into its narrative groove again. Jody knew in advance exactly what words would fall. The story droned on, speeded up for the attack, grew sad over the wounds, struck a dirge at the burials on the great plains. Jody sat quietly watching Grandfather. The stern blue eyes were detached. He looked as though he were not very interested in the story himself.

When it was finished, when the pause had been politely respected at the frontier of the story, Billy Buck stood up and stretched and hitched his trousers. "I guess I'll turn in," he said. Then he faced Grandfather. "I've got an old powder horn and a cap and ball pistol down to the bunkhouse. Did I ever show them to you?"

Grandfather nodded slowly. "Yes, I think you did, Billy. Reminds me of a pistol I had when I was leading the people across." Billy stood politely until the little story was done, and then he said, "Good night," and went out of the house.

Carl Tiflin tried to turn the conversation then. "How's the country between here and Monterey? I've heard it's pretty dry."

"It is dry," said Grandfather. "There's not a drop of water in the Laguna Seca. But it's a long pull from '87. The whole country was powder then, and in '61 I believe all the coyotes starved to death. We had fifteen inches of rain this year."

"Yes, but it all came too early. We could do with some now." Carl's eye fell on Jody. "Hadn't you better be getting to bed?"

Jody stood up obediently. "Can I kill the mice in the old haystack, sir?"

"Mice? Oh! Sure, kill them all off. Billy said there isn't any good hay left."

Jody exchanged a secret and satisfying look with Grandfather. "I'll kill every one tomorrow," he promised.

Jody lay in his bed and thought of the impossible world of Indians and buffaloes, a world that had ceased to be forever.

He wished he could have been living in the heroic time, but he knew he was not of heroic timber. No one living now, save possibly Billy Buck, was worthy to do the things that had been done. A race of giants had lived then, fearless men, men of a staunchness unknown in this day. Jody thought of the wide plains and of the wagons moving across like centipedes. He thought of Grandfather on a huge white horse, marshaling the people. Across his mind marched the great phantoms, and they marched off the earth and they were gone.

He came back to the ranch for a moment, then. He heard the dull rushing sound that space and silence make. He heard one of the dogs, out in the doghouse, scratching a flea and bumping his elbow against the floor with every stroke. Then the wind arose again and the black cypress groaned and Jody went to sleep.

He was up half an hour before the triangle sounded for breakfast. His mother was rattling the stove to make the flames roar when Jody went through the kitchen. "You're up early," she said. "Where are you going?"

"Out to get a good stick. We're going to kill the mice today."

"Who is 'we'?"

"Why, Grandfather and I."

"So you've got him in it. You always like to have someone in with you in case there's blame to share."

"I'll be right back," said Jody. "I just wanted to have a good stick ready for after breakfast."

He closed the screen door after him and went out into the cool blue morning. The birds were noisy in the dawn and the ranch cats came down from the hill like blunt snakes. They had been hunting gophers in the dark, and although the four cats were full of gopher meat, they sat in a semi-circle at the back door and mewed piteously for milk. Doubletree Mutt and Smasher moved sniffing along the edge of the brush, performing the duty with rigid ceremony, but when Jody whistled, their heads jerked up and their tails waved. They plunged down to him, wriggling their skins and yawning. Jody patted their heads seriously, and moved on to the weathered scrap pile. He selected an old broom handle and a short piece of inch-square scrap wood. From his pocket he took a shoelace and tied the ends of the sticks loosely together to make a flail. He whistled his new weapon through the air and struck the ground experimentally, while the dogs leaped aside and whined with apprehension.

Jody turned and started down past the house toward the old haystack ground to look over the field of slaughter, but Billy Buck, sitting patiently on the back steps, called to him, "You better come back. It's only a couple of minutes till breakfast."

Jody changed his course and moved toward the house. He leaned his flail against the steps. "That's to drive the mice out," he said. "I'll bet they're fat. I'll bet they don't know what's going to happen to them today."

"No, nor you either," Billy remarked philosophically, "nor me, nor anyone."

Jody was staggered by this thought. He knew it was true. His imagination twitched away from the mouse hunt. Then his mother came out on the back porch and struck the triangle, and all thoughts fell in a heap.

Grandfather hadn't appeared at the table when they sat down. Billy nodded at his empty chair. "He's all right? He isn't sick?"

"He takes a long time to dress," said Mrs. Tiflin. "He combs his whiskers and rubs up his shoes and brushes his clothes."

Carl scattered sugar on his mush. "A man that's led a wagon train across the plains has got to be pretty careful how he dresses."

Mrs. Tiflin turned to him. "Don't do that, Carl! Please don't!" There was more of threat than of request in her tone. And the threat irritated Carl.

"Well, how many times do I have to listen to the story of the iron plates, and the thirty-five horses? That time's done. Why can't he forget it, now it's done?" He grew angrier while he talked, and his voice rose. "Why does he have to tell them over and over? He came across the plains. All right! Now it's finished. Nobody wants to hear about it over and over."

The door into the kitchen closed softly. The four at the table sat frozen. Carl laid his mush spoon on the table and touched his chin with his fingers.

Then the kitchen door opened and Grandfather walked in. His mouth smiled tightly and his eyes were squinted. "Good morning," he said, and he sat down and looked at his mush dish.

Carl could not leave it there. "Did—did you hear what I said?"

Grandfather jerked a little nod.

"I don't know what got into me, sir. I didn't mean it. I was just being funny."

Jody glanced in shame at his mother, and he saw that she was looking at Carl, and that she wasn't breathing. It was an awful thing that he was doing. He was tearing himself to pieces to talk like that. It was a terrible thing to him to retract a word, but to retract it in shame was infinitely worse.

Grandfather looked sidewise. "I'm trying to get right side up," he said gently. "I'm not being mad. I don't mind what you said, but it might be true, and I would mind that."

"It isn't true," said Carl. "I'm not feeling well this morning. I'm sorry I said it."

"Don't be sorry, Carl. An old man doesn't see things sometimes. Maybe you're right. The crossing is finished. Maybe it should be forgotten, now it's done."

Carl got up from the table. "I've had enough to eat. I'm going to work. Take your time, Billy!" He walked quickly out of the dining-room. Billy gulped the rest of his food and followed soon after. But Jody could not leave his chair.

"Won't you tell any more stories?" Jody asked.

"Why, sure I'll tell them, but only when—I'm sure people want to hear them."

"I like to hear them, sir."

"Oh! Of course you do, but you're a little boy. It was a job for men, but only little boys like to hear about it."

Jody got up from his place. "I'll wait outside for you, sir. I've got a good stick for those mice."

He waited by the gate until the old man came out on the porch. "Let's go down and kill the mice now," Jody called.

"I think I'll just sit in the sun, Jody. You go kill the mice."

"You can use my stick if you like."

"No, I'll just sit here a while."

Jody turned disconsolately away, and walked down toward the old haystack. He tried to whip up his enthusiasm with thoughts of the fat juicy mice. He beat the ground with his flail. The dogs coaxed and whined about him, but he could not go. Back at the house he could see Grandfather sitting on the porch, looking small and thin and black.

Jody gave up and went to sit on the steps at the old man's feet.

"Back already? Did you kill the mice?"

"No sir. I'll kill them some other day."

The morning flies buzzed close to the ground and the ants dashed about in front of the steps. The heavy smell of sage slipped down the hill. The porch boards grew warm in the sunshine.

Jody hardly knew when Grandfather started to talk. "I shouldn't stay here, feeling the way I do." He examined his strong old hands. "I feel as though the crossing wasn't worth doing." His eyes moved up the side-hill and stopped on a motionless hawk perched on a dead limb. "I tell those old stories, but they're not what I want to tell. I only know how I want people to feel when I tell them.

"It wasn't Indians that were important, nor adventures, nor even getting out here. It was a whole bunch of people made into one big crawling beast. And I was the head. It was westering and westering. Every man wanted something for himself, but the big beast that was all of them wanted only westering. I was the leader, but if I hadn't been there, someone else would have been the head. The thing had to have a head.

"Under the little bushes the shadows were black at white noonday. When we saw the mountains at last, we cried—all of us. But it wasn't getting here that mattered, it was movement and westering.

"We carried life out here and set it down the way those ants carry eggs. And I was the leader. The westering was as big as God, and the slow steps that made the movement piled up and piled up until the continent was crossed.

"Then we came down to the sea, and it was done." He stopped and wiped his eyes until the rims were red. "That's what I should be telling instead of stories."

When Jody spoke, Grandfather started and looked down at him. "Maybe I could lead the people some day," Jody said.

The old man smiled. "There's no place to go. There's the ocean to stop you. There's a line of old men along the shore hating the ocean because it stopped them."

"In boats I might, sir."

"No place to go, Jody. Every place is taken. But that's not the worst—no, not the worst. Westering has died out of the people. Westering isn't a hunger any more. It's all done. Your father is right. It is finished." He laced his fingers on his knee and looked at them.

Jody felt very sad. "If you'd like a glass of lemonade I could make it for you."

Grandfather was about to refuse, and then he saw Jody's face. "That would be nice," he said. "Yes, it would be nice to drink a lemonade."

Jody ran into the kitchen where his mother was wiping the last of the breakfast dishes. "Can I have a lemon to make a lemonade for Grandfather?"

His mother mimicked—"And another lemon to make a lemonade for you."

"No, ma'am. I don't want one."

"Jody! You're sick!" Then she stopped suddenly. "Take a lemon out of the cooler," she said softly. "Here, I'll reach the squeezer down to you."

THYRA SAMTER WINSLOW

(1903-   )

Thyra Samter Winslow writes chiefly about obscure people who (as in "City Folks") lead the most ordinary of lives. No one, to be sure, is insignificant to himself. If Miss Winslow's characters were unconcerned about their situations—didn't care how much money they had, where they could afford to live, how well or badly they married, what people thought of them—then it would be impossible to find them interesting. But they do care intensely, and the reader finds himself involved in their preoccupation with themselver even though he suspects that in life he would not find them the most stimulating of company. These characters if treated by a naturalistic writer could be extremely boring, but Miss Winslow has a keen eye for the particularizing detail, and a fine sense of selection. She has another quality which is noticeable in her longer stories, such as "Orphant Annie" and "A Cycle of Manhattan," and that is the ability to handle in rapid synopsis events which occur over a long period of time, and to do this without losing her unity of effect.

CITY FOLKS

I

JOE and Mattie Harper lived in Harlem. They lived in a four-room apartment in the second of a row of brown, unattractive-looking apartment buildings—six of them just alike—in One Hundred and Thirty-second Street.

They lived in Apartment 52, which means the fifth floor, and there was no elevator. But the rent was reasonable, fifty dollars, and both Joe and Mattie said they didn't mind a "walk-up" at all—you get used to it after a while, and Mattie knew it kept her hips down. Then, too, by going to the fifth floor, you get a much better view, though why a view of the building across the street—another brown barracks of exactly the same age and design—is desirable, only Joe and Mattie and other similarly situated folks know. The air was cleaner, though, on the fifth floor—they felt that any one would know that.

One Hundred and Thirty-second Street, Harlem, lacked all outstanding features. If the street signs had suddenly disappeared, there would have been nothing to identify it, to pin it to—a bleak street, without trees, a fairly clean street, decent and neat looking (after the garbage man had passed and the tins had disappeared), wide enough to lack misery, narrow enough to lack grandeur.

We are about to have two meals with Joe and Mattie—the most important meals of their day, for Joe's lunch was usually a sandwich and a glass of milk at the Automat, or beans or a beef stew in the lunch room across from his office; Mattie's a glass of soda and a sandwich or a dish of ice cream, if she were down-town—it is a shame about the new price of sodas —a scramble of left overs from last night's dinner, if she spent the day at home.

Breakfast:

The alarm clock had buzzed at six-thirty, as it always did. It was a good alarm clock and had cost $1.48 at Liggett's, two years before.

Mattie's little dog, who slept in the front hall, had heard the alarm and scrambled into their bedroom with his usual yip of pleasure—he was rather deaf, but he could make out sounds as definite as the ringing of a bell and he listened for the alarm each morning. He was a nice fellow, a white poodle, overly fat, with red-rimmed eyes. If you didn't molest him nor try to pet him nor step on him, he wouldn't snap or try to bite you. Mattie and Joe were quite fond of him and took him for walks in Central Park on Sundays or around Harlem in the evenings. His name had, in turn, been, stylishly, Snowball, Snoodles and Snookums and had at last reached Ikkle Floppit, all of which he answered to with stolid indifference.

Joe had heard the alarm, had jumped up and turned it off, and had waked Mattie, who slept more soundly. Ikkle Floppit had jumped, wheezily, upon the bed and licked all visible portions of Mattie's face. Mattie, then, had given up trying to doze again and had stroked the dog's uneven coat with a fond hand.

Toilets followed, rapid plunges into the dwarf-sized white tub with its rather insecure shower attachment—Joe talking while he shaved, about the office, the man who worked with him, his boss who didn't appreciate him, the weather that was still too warm for comfort, their friends, the Taylors, who they both agreed were too stuck up for words since Taylor had got his new job.

"His people aren't anything at all," Mattie had said, "awfully ordinary—and the way they do put on airs, you'd think they amounted to something. Why, my cousin Mabel knew his sister in Perryville, where they used to live, and she said they weren't anything at all there. And now, how they do go on with a maid and a car. They've never even taken us for a ride in their old car and they can hold their breath until I'd step into it. It beats all—"

And Joe, his face twisted for the razor's path beyond the possibilities of conversation, had grunted assent.

Now Mattie had completed the simple breakfast, six pieces of toast, buttered unevenly and a bit burned on the edges, as always, a halved orange for each of them, some coffee and some bought preserves with a slight strawberry-like flavour. She and Joe faced each other over the almost clean tablecloth —it had been clean on Sunday and this was just Tuesday morning.

The dining-room was small, lighted vaguely with two court windows. Even now, at seven-thirty, the electric light had been turned on in the red and green glass electrolier.

Mattie knew the electrolier was out of fashion, she would have preferred a more modern "inverted bowl," but this one was included with the apartment, so there seemed nothing to do about it. She would also have preferred mahogany to the fumed oak dining-room set, bought eight years before—she had bought the mahogany tea wagon with her last year's Christmas money from Joe, looking forward to the time when they could buy a whole new mahogany set.

Mattie was not at all a bad-looking breakfast companion, seated there in her half-clean pink gingham bungalow apron—she wore these aprons constantly in the house to save her other clothes. She was a slender, brown-haired woman of about thirty, with clear brown eyes, a nose that turned slightly upward, a mouth inclined to be a little large, rather uneven but white teeth—indefinite features, a pleasant, usual, hard-to-place face.

And Joe, across from her, was equally pleasing, with a straight nose and rather a weak chin, dark hair starting to recede just a little at thirty-three, sloping shoulders inclined a bit to the roundness of the office man.

"What's in the paper, Joe?" asked Mattie, already nibbling toast.

Joe, deep in the morning *World*, threw out interesting items —the progress of a murder trial, news of an airplane flight.

They talked about little things, a friend Joe had passed on the street the day before, the choice of a show for Friday or Saturday night—they tried to attend the theatre once each week, during the winter.

The door bell rang, three short rings. Ikkle Floppit gave three asthmatic yips. Mattie threw down her napkin, sprang to her feet.

"I'll go," she said, as she usually said it, "you go on eating or you'll be late again. I bet it's nothing but a bill, anyhow."

She returned in a moment with a thick letter in her hand.

"From your mother, Joe," she said.

She knew the printed address in the corner of the envelope, "The Banner Store, General Merchandise, E. J. Harper, Prop., Burton Center, Missouri," the neat, old-fashioned handwriting, the post-mark.

Mattie and Joe had come from Burton Center, Mattie eight years and Joe nine years before. They had grown up together in Burton Center, one of the jolly crowd who attended the

High School, went to Friday night dances, later were graduated into the older crowd, which meant a few more dances, went to the Opera House when a show came to town, had happy love affairs.

Joe and Mattie became engaged three years after Joe left High School, which was the year after Mattie graduated. Joe went to work at the Banner Store, under his father. But youth and ambition knew not Burton Center, so, a little later, Joe had come to New York in search of fortune.

He had not obeyed the usual law of fiction and forgotten Mattie, nor had Mattie changed while she waited. No, though Joe found neither fame nor fortune, he did get an office job that looked as if it might support two in comfort, if Mattie and Joe were the two concerned, took a vacation, went back to Burton Center, found Mattie even more alluring and dimpled and giggling than he had remembered her—how much prettier Burton Center girls looked than those in New York! —and they were married.

Eight years, then, of New York, of subway rides, of the weekly theatre, the weekly restaurant dinner, of apartment hunting about every second October, of infrequent clothes buying, of occasional calls on stray acquaintances, of little quarrels and little peace-makings, weekly letters from home— little lives going on—

Joe tore open the letter.

"Gee, it's a thick one," he said.

Then:

"Well, I guess they are all well or ma wouldn't have written so much. Listen, Mattie."

Joe read the letter, a folksy letter—Mrs. Harper, senior, was well and so was "your father," as all mothers speak of their husbands to their children, in letters. She had seen Millie's mother a few days before and she was looking well and hoping to see them soon in Burton Center. The youngest Rosemond girl was engaged to a Mr. Secor from St. Louis, who was in the lumber business.

Then there followed, long and unparagraphed, something

that made Joe and Mattie look at each other, hard and seriously, across the table. For Joe's mother had written something that they had always thought might be suggested to them but they had never discussed, even with each other:

"Your father isn't as well as he once was, nor as young, you know, and, though you need not worry about him, he is eating and sleeping fine, even in hot weather, I think it would be better if you and Mattie came here to live. You could step right into the store and take charge of things as soon as you wanted to. It is not a big store as you know, but your father has always made a nice living from it and Burton Center is growing right along. The Millers have put up some new bungalows out on Crescent Hill, you'd be surprised to see how it has grown up out there, all of the young people are moving out there and with the new Thirteenth Street car line it is very convenient. The cottages are all taken but two, both white with green blinds and room back of them for garages and we could get you one of them if you wanted us to. The George Hendricks are living there and Mr. and Mrs. Tucker and the Williams boy, Phillip, I think that's his name, you used to go with. The new country club isn't far from there and you could play tennis after work, which would be good for you. I wish you could make up your mind at once, so you could get here before long or your father will have to get a man to help him, for he really ought to have more time to himself and take a nap after dinner, now that the season's trade is starting. Talk this over with Mattie and let us know as soon as you can. I hope you are keeping well in this changeable weather. Your father sends love to both and so do I.

"Affectionately, your Mother."

Mattie and Joe looked at each other, looked and looked and forgot their toast and coffee. But they saw each other not at all. Nor did they visualize One Hundred and Thirty-second Street, New York, drab and bare, nor even Fifth Avenue nor Broadway.

They saw a little town, with rows of old trees along its

quiet streets, little white houses on little squares of green, each house with its hedge or its garden or its hammocked lawn, peace, and the smell of growing things after a rain—

"What say, Mattie?" asked Joe. "Sound pretty good? Of course, you've always said you loved New York and I don't want to persuade you against your will. Perhaps you wouldn't care to move—still, Burton Center, we've got some good friends there—it'd be sort of fun, seeing the old crowd, belong to a country club, tennis, things like that, even managing the business. But, of course, if you wouldn't want to leave the city—"

Mattie, mentally, had far outdistanced him.

She clapped her hands, pleasantly excited.

"Joe can't you just see that little house—I bet it's awfully cute. Last summer, when we were out in the country, I certainly did envy people living in little houses—I get so tired of New York, sometimes. But I never wanted to say anything, knowing how much you liked it here. But that little house— we could sell all of our furniture except the tea wagon and the table in the living-room and my new dressing-table—it really would be cheaper to buy new things than to pay for shipping. And we could find out how many windows there are and I could get some new cretonne here—sort of set the styles in Burton Center. It sure would be funny, living back there and knowing everybody. Here I never see a soul I know in weeks, or talk to anybody. Honest, sometimes I get just hungry for—for people. The trouble is, we haven't really got anything here."

"I know," Joe nodded. "New York's all right for some people—if you've got money. It's a great city all right, but we don't get anything out of it. I get so sick of being squeezed into subways night and morning—hardly standing room all the way home—and no place to go Sundays or evenings but a movie or a show or to see people who live miles away and don't care anything about you anyhow and who you see about twice a year. Burton Center will look awfully good—folks take an interest in you there."

"You bet they do."

"And it isn't as if I've failed here. I haven't. I'm due for another raise pretty soon—but we aren't putting anything aside, getting any place. It isn't as if we were terribly poor. You look awfully well in your clothes on the street, but we are always having to skimp and do without things—we never have the best of anything, always cheap seats at shows or cheap meals in second-class restaurants, a cheap street to live on—it gets on a person's nerves."

"Why, I didn't know you felt that way, Joe. I thought you liked New York. Why, it makes me so jealous, going down Fifth Avenue, seeing all those people in limousines, not a bit better nor better looking than I am, all dressed up, lolling back so—so superior, with nasty little dogs not near so nice as Floppit—and with chauffeurs and everything. Why, in Burton Center we'd be somebody, as good as any one. We could fix up that house awfully nice—and have a little garden and all that. But you said you hated the Banner Store so—now don't go and make up your mind—"

"You needn't worry about me. The Banner Store is all right—I think differently about things than I did years ago. I thought the city was just going to fall apart in my hand—but I found someone else got here first. I'm not complaining, you know. It isn't that I've failed—why, in Burton Center they'll look at us as a success, we'll be city folks, don't you see. They know I haven't failed. I didn't come sneaking back the year I left, the way Ray Wulberg did. No, sir, when folks came to New York to visit, we showed them a good time, took 'em to restaurants and shows—they think we got along fine here—that we're all right—"

"You bet they do, Joe. But I just can hardly wait to see that cottage—and everybody. I bet Crescent Hill is awfully pretty. To-night, you write to your mother—don't make it too sudden, you know, or too anxious—for you know how she is— she means fine, but she'll like to spread the news about us coming back. You just say that, under the circumstances, as long as your father is getting old and needs you, you feel it's your duty to go there and as soon as you can arrange your affairs and resign your position and train one of your assistants so that he can take care of your work—"

"You leave that to me. I can fix that part up all right."

The buzzer of the dumb-waiter zinged into their talk.

"Joe, there's the janitor, It's late. You'd better hurry. You know the call-down you got last week for being late."

Mattie and Joe arose simultaneously, Joe grabbed his paper, folded it conveniently, hurried to the door, Mattie after him.

"Going down-town to-day?" he asked.

"Thought I would, when I get the house straightened up. I want to look at a new waist. My good one is starting to tear at the back."

"All right. I'll be home early, about six-thirty—won't have to stay over-time. In a few months, I'll be my own boss, no hurrying off in the morning or rushing home in subways— we'll fix that letter up to-night."

He brushed off his mouth with his hand and gave Mattie the usual and rather hearty good-bye kiss and, closing the door behind him, Joe and Mattie parted for the day with visions of little houses nestling in green gardens uppermost in their minds.

II

Dinner:

Dinner times with the Harpers varied slightly according to the way Mattie had spent the afternoon, the amount of work at Joe's office and where the Harpers were dining. They usually dined at home, but, once a week, usually Saturday, when they followed the feast with a visit to the theatre, they ate at one of the table d'hote restaurants some place within ten blocks of Broadway and Forty-second Street.

They thought themselves quite cosmopolitan because they had been to Italian, Greek, French, Chinese, Russian and Armenian restaurants, choosing in each the dish prepared for the curious—and eating it according to American table customs as they practised them.

This particular Tuesday they were dining at home.

Joe reached the apartment exactly at six-thirty, the trip home taking nearly an hour. Joe had been watching the clock for the last twenty minutes of his business day so as to escape at the first possible opportunity.

Mattie, in the kitchen, heard his key in the lock and hurried to greet him. They kissed quite as fondly as they had in the morning, Floppit gave a little yip of welcome and received a pat on the head in reply.

Dinner was nearly ready, Mattie informed Joe, table set and all.

Joe hurried with his ablutions and reached the dining-room, accompanied by his newspaper, the *Journal* this time, at a quarter of seven. He divided the paper so that Mattie might have the last page, where are shown the strips of comics—he had read them hanging to a strap in the subway. Then he helped Mattie to bring in the hot dishes from the kitchen.

There was a small platter of five chops, fried quite brown, two for each one of them and one—to be cut into bits later—for Ikkle Floppit. Mattie always fried chops or steaks the days she went down-town, and sometimes other days besides.

There were potatoes, in their jackets to save her the trouble of peeling them, a dish of canned corn. There was a neat square of butter, too, and some thinly sliced bread on a silver-plated bread plate—a last year's Christmas present from one of Mattie's aunts—and a small dish of highly-spiced pickles.

Besides this, on the new tea wagon stood two pieces of bakery pastry, of a peculiarly yellow colour that had aimed at but far surpassed the result of eggs in the batter.

They sat down. Joe served the chops, Mattie the potatoes and corn. Mattie had put on her bungalow apron as soon as she returned home—so as to save her suit from the spots and wear incidental to dinner-getting. Joe looked just as he had in the morning, plus a small amount of beard and minus his coat and vest.

Yet, as the morning's conversation had been spontaneous and enthusiastic and happy, this evening's meal had a curious cloud of restraint over it.

"Good dinner," said Joe, after his first mouthful.

"Yes, it does taste good," agreed Mattie.

"Go down-town?"

"Uh-huh, I went down about eleven. Just got home an hour ago. I looked at the waists, but didn't get any—they seemed awfully high. I may go down and get one to-morrow or Thursday. Any news in the paper?"

"Not much doing," Joe rustled his own sheets.

He never really read at dinner but he liked to have the paper near him.

"Look at Floppit, Joe. Isn't he cute, standing up that way? I've just got to give him a bite. It won't make him too fat, not what I give him. Come here, Missus' lamb."

Silence, then, save for the sound of knife against plate, a curious silence, a silence of avoidance. Then meaningless sentences, bits about anything, a struggle to appear happy, indifferent.

Joe, then,

"See any one down-town you know? Where'd you have lunch? Thought maybe you'd call up and have lunch with me."

"I did think of it, but I didn't come down your way. I stopped at Loft's and had chocolate cake and a cherry sundae. No—I didn't see any one I knew—exactly. . . . Anything happen at the office?"

"Well, nothing much. We got that Detroit order."

"Did you, Joe? I'm sure glad of that."

A silence. Then, Joe, suddenly, enthusiastically, as if some barrier had broken, as if he could no longer stay repressed, upon the path he had set for himself.

"Say, Mattie, guess what happened this afternoon! You know Ferguson, the fellow who used to be in our office, whose brother is in the show business? Well, he came in and gave me a couple of seats to see 'Squaring the Triangle' for Friday night. They say it's a good show and in for a long run, but they want to keep the house filled while the show is new, till it gets a start."

"Did he, honestly? Say, that's great, isn't it? Where are they, downstairs?"

"Sure. You don't think he'd give away balcony seats, or at least offer them to me, do you? Remember, he gave us some last Spring. That makes three times this year we've been to shows on passes. Pretty good, eh, Mattie?"

"Well, I guess yes. We're some people, knowing relatives of managers. I tell you, I think—"

A pause, then.

Mattie's face lost its sudden smile and resumed its sadness of the earlier part of the meal.

"What's the matter?" asked Joe.

"Nothing the matter with me."

"Something else happened, too," Joe went on, enthusiastically, "at noon, I'd just left Childs'—and guess who I passed on the street?"

"Some one we know?"

"We don't know him exactly."

"Oh, I can't guess. Tell me."

"I know you can't—well, it was—William Gibbs McAdoo! Honest to goodness—McAdoo. It sure seemed funny. There he was, walking down the street, just like I've seen him in the movies half a dozen times. It sure gives you a thrill, seeing people like that."

Why the mention of William G. McAdoo should bring tears to the eyes of a woman who had never met him may be inexplicable to some. But tears came into the eyes of Mattie Harper. She wiped her eyes on the corner of her bungalow apron, sniffed a little, came over to Joe, put her arms around him.

"I just—just can't stand it," she sobbed. "I've been worrying and worrying. Your seeing McAdoo seems the strangest thing, after what happened to me."

"What was it, Mattie?"

Quite kindly and understandingly, Joe pushed his chair back from the table, gathered his wife on his knee.

"What was it, honey? Come tell Joe."

"It wasn't anything—anything to cry about. I—don't know what's the matter with me. It—it was in Lord & Taylor's, this afternoon. I was looking at gloves—and I looked up—and there, right beside me, not two feet away, stood Billie Burke. Honestly! I know it was her. She looked exactly like her pictures—and I saw her in 'The Runaway' years ago, and not long ago in the movies. Yes, sir, Billie Burke. Joe, she's simply beautiful."

"Well, well, think of seeing Billie Burke!"

"And Joe, when I saw her, the awfulest feeling came over me. I tried not to tell you about it—after the letter this morning. I'd been thinking about Burton Center—but seeing Billie Burke just knocked it all out. Joe, you know I love you and want to do what you want—but, I—I just can't move to Burton Center—unless you've got your heart set on it. I'd go then, of course—any place. But I don't want to be—buried alive in that little town. Imagine those people—never seeing or doing anything—no new shows or famous people—nor any kind of life. And here I went down-town and saw Billie Burke and you—"

Joe's pats became even fonder. He smoothed her hair with his too-pale hand.

"There, there, don't cry. It's all right. Nobody's asking or expecting you to go to Burton Center. Funny thing, that. I had the same feeling. First, passing McAdoo—and then those theatre tickets. I guess there's something about New York that gets you. They've got to forget that stuff about Burton Center, I can tell you that."

Mattie jumped off Joe's lap, took the used dishes from the table, put on the pastry and sat down in her own place, across from Joe.

"This is good," said Joe, taking a bite; "where'd you get it?"

"At that little new French pastry shop we passed the night the black dog tried to bite Floppit."

"Oh, yes, looked nice and clean in there."

They ate their pastry slowly. Mattie dried her eyes. Joe spoke to her:

"Say, Mattie, don't worry for a minute more about that Burton Center stuff. After eight years of living in the city, seeing famous people, living right in the center of things—didn't we see all the warships and airplanes nearly every day? They can't expect us to live in a rube place like Burton Center. We're used to more, that's all there is to it."

"I know," said Mattie, "I'd just die if I couldn't walk down Fifth Avenue and see what people wore. It's just weighed on me, terribly. I just saw us on the train going out there, and living in an awful little house without hot water or steam heat —and seeing Billie Burke just—"

The 'phone burred into the conversation.

Mattie answered it, as usual, assuming a nonchalant, society air.

"Yes, this is the Harpers' apartment. Yes, this is Mrs. Harper speaking. Who? Oh, Mrs. Taylor. How do you do. I haven't heard your voice in ages. We're fine, thank you. . . . No, I don't know much news. A friend of Mr. Harper's, a brother of Ferguson, the theatrical producer, invited us to see 'Squaring the Triangle' as his guests on Friday. They say it's a wonderful show. We saw 'The Tattle-tale' last Saturday. Yes, we liked it a great deal. . . . Saturday afternoon? Wait and I'll ask Mr. Harper if he has an engagement."

Hand over telephone mouthpiece, then:

"Want to go riding with the Taylors in their new car Saturday afternoon and stop at some road-house for supper?"

Resuming the polite conversational tone of the telephone:

"Yes, thank you, Mr. Harper and I will be delighted to go. Awfully nice of you. At four? Fine. By the way, did I tell you I saw Billie Burke to-day? I did. She looked simply beautiful, not a day older than she looked last year. Wonderful hair, hasn't she? And Mr. Harper passed William G. McAdoo on the street. Yes, New York is a wonderful city. You did? Isn't that nice! All right, we'll be ready on Saturday—don't bother coming up, just honk for us, that's what all our friends do. Thanks so much, good-bye."

Mattie sat down at the table again.

"Well," she said, "it's time they asked us—they'll take us now and be through for a year. Still, we may have a nice time. But—what we were talking about—you sure you are in earnest about Burton Center?"

"You bet I am. The folks at home had the wrong dope, that's all. Why, I've got my position here, too important to give up at any one's beck and call. Didn't the boss congratulate me to-day on the way I wrote those Detroit letters? I bet I get a raise in another three months."

They folded their napkins into their silver-plated napkin-rings, rose from the table, walked together into the living-room, stood looking out into the drab bleakness of One Hundred and Thirty-second Street, across to the factory-like, monotonous row of apartment houses opposite, where innumerable lights twinkled from other little caves, where other little families lived, humdrum, unmarked, inconsequential, grey. And from the minds of Mattie and Joe faded the visions of little white houses and cool, green lanes.

They remembered, instead, the city, their city—Mattie had seen a moving picture taken, once, from a Fifth Avenue bus—three years ago Joe had been introduced to—actually taken the hand of—William Jennings Bryan—they had both seen James Montgomery Flagg draw a picture for the Liberty Loan on the Public Library steps—a woman in a store had pointed out Lady Duff Gordon to Mattie—they had seen, on the street, a man who looked exactly like Charles M. Schwab—it might easily have been. . . .

"I'll write that letter right away and have it over with," said Joe, "I won't hurt ma's feelings—she and Dad mean all right. Living in Burton Center all their lives we can't expect them to understand things. It's ridiculous, of course. I don't know what came over us for a minute this morning. Of course we've got the crowded subways, here, and it costs a lot to live and—and all that. You can't expect a place to be perfect. But—New Yorkers like us couldn't stand that dead Burton Center stuff for five minutes. Why, we're, we're—city folks!"

JEROME WEIDMAN

(1913-   )

Jerome Weidman, a native New Yorker, has written principally of the city streets and the people thereon. He has remarked that he has never seen a sunset or a mountain top that could match in interest the spectacle of Fourteenth Street on a late afternoon. Early in life Mr. Weidman decided that he wanted to be a writer, and he pursued his aim with the same nondigressive singleness of purpose with which he now writes his stories. He learned what he could about writing from other people, notably Somerset Maugham, but he himself was his own principal teacher. He even learned shorthand so that he could, while pretending to take notes from his professors' lectures, actually write stories during his law classes at New York University. He writes an excellent colloquial English, and his stories of the meannesses of double-dealing people are thoroughly readable, as are his treatments of human inconsistencies or, in "The Tuxedos," consistencies. Among his best books are the novel *I Can Get It for You Wholesale* and the short-story collection *The Horse That Could Whistle Dixie*.

THE TUXEDOS

EVER SINCE THE TIME, some ten years ago, when I worked for Mr. Brunschweig on Canal Street, I have been peculiarly sensitive to the half-hour of the day that comes between five-thirty and six o'clock in the late afternoon. Mr. Brunschweig was an excellent boss, as bosses go, except for one lamentable defect: he was a minute-pincher. He carried two large pocket watches and spent a good part of each day comparing them with each other and with the huge Seth Thomas on the wall. I am certain that he was a little terrified by the inexorableness of time and that his sensitivity to it was a direct result of the way he earned his living. Mr. Brunschweig rented tuxedos.

The tuxedo-renting business, as I knew it, was distinguished by two cardinal rules. First, the suits had to be made of the toughest and heaviest materials available. And second, it was necessary to deliver them as close to the moment of wearing as possible and even more imperative to pick them up as soon after they were taken off as the wearer would permit. Mr. Brunschweig's timing in this respect was so good and I was so nimble as a delivery boy that while many of his customers cursed him roundly for having delayed them in getting to a wedding, not one of them could say with honesty that he had worn a Brunschweig tuxedo to more than one affair for the price of a single renting.

My relations with Mr. Brunschweig were amicable if somewhat exhausting, but every day, as the hands of the clock crept around to half-past five, a definite tension would come into the atmosphere. My quitting time was six o'clock. As a general rule, Mr. Brunschweig arranged deliveries in such fashion that the last one carried me up to, or past, that hour. We had an understanding to the effect that if I took out a delivery at any time after five-thirty and could not get to my destination until six o'clock or a few minutes before, I did not have to return to the Canal Street store that night and was at liberty to go directly home. However, the possibility of his only employee departing for home five or ten minutes ahead of quitting time was so disturbing to Mr. Brunschweig that very often he would detain me in the store before I went on my final delivery, talking about the weather or discussing the baseball scores, just to make sure that I could not possibly complete delivery before six o'clock.

Strangely enough, I did not resent these obvious subterfuges, because I sensed that Mr. Brunschweig was a little ashamed of them. What I did resent was that unconsciously I was being forced into practices I didn't approve of to combat him.

For instance, I would instinctively stall on any delivery after five-fifteen to make certain that I would not get back to the store in time to make another delivery before quitting. Or I would rush through a four-o'clock delivery to make sure that there would be ample time for still another one before six o'clock. In either case it was very unsettling, and scarcely a day went by that I didn't have a struggle with my conscience or the clock.

There were times, of course, when my energy overcame my caution. One day, in an industrious mood, I returned from an uptown delivery at twenty minutes to six. It had been a long trip and I could have stretched it for another twenty minutes with ease, but I had temporarily forgotten Mr. Brunschweig's vice and I did not realize my mistake until I came into the store. He was boxing an unusually large order, and I could tell from his cheery greeting that this one would carry me well past six o'clock. I was about to dismiss the occurrence as simply another occasion on which I had been outmaneuvered by Mr. Brunschweig when I saw that he had stacked six boxes, one on top of the other.

"Is that *one* delivery?" I asked in amazement.

The average delivery weighed well over ten pounds and consisted of a tuxedo, a shirt, a tie, studs, and a pair of patent-leather pumps, packed neatly into a heavy cardboard box. Two or three of these boxes were a load. Six of them were an incredible amount.

"Yeah," he said cheerfully. "Italian wedding. It all goes to one family. I'll give you a help to the subway."

I should have been grateful to him for this offer, I suppose, since it was an unusual move, but all I could think of was the prospect of juggling sixty pounds of tuxedos through the subway in the rush hour.

"Where's it going?" I asked.

"Brooklyn," he said. "It's just over the bridge. Won't take you long."

The boxes weighed so much I could scarcely raise them from the floor.

"Here," he said. "You take the hats. I'll take the suits till we get to the train."

I hadn't even thought about top hats. They were not very heavy, but they were the most perishable items in Mr. Brunschweig's stock and consequently were always packed with great care in individual boxes.

"We gotta hurry," Mr. Brunschweig said, handing me a slip of paper with an address on it. "It's the bride's family and I promised them early. Name is Lasquadro."

He took the lashed tuxedo boxes and I took the pile of hatboxes, tied one on top of another so that they resembled a small steamship funnel. In the street we paused for a moment while he locked the store and then we started off down Canal Street to the subway station.

The only satisfactory recollection I have of that evening is the brief memory of Mr. Brunschweig tottering along in front of me under the weight of six boxes of tuxedos and accessories. The rest was a nightmare. I remember being on the subway platform, between my two huge bundles, trying to get into train after train. I had to let seven or eight go by before I could wedge my way into one of them. Then I remember standing, perspiring and exhausted, outside the subway station in Brooklyn, looking at the two bundles and realizing that I could carry them no further. It had grown quite dark and I began to be worried, too, about being late with the delivery. Finally I worked out a plan. I dragged the tuxedos along the ground for a short distance, then went back for the hats, dragged them up to the tuxedos, and then repeated the process. It was an effective method but an extremely slow one. Though the address Mr. Brunschweig had given me was only three blocks from the Brooklyn subway station, it was almost twenty minutes later that I stopped, breathless, in front of the correct house number.

The street was deserted and dark; the house was a two-story brownstone affair and only the basement windows showed lights from behind drawn shades. As I wiped the perspiration from my face and tried to think of an excuse for being so late, I heard noises coming from the basement. Figures kept passing the windows quickly and the sounds of scuffling and angry voices reached me clearly. I was frightened and spent another precious minute trying to puzzle out a way of leaving my bundles without having to face the people inside the house.

Then, in a burst of nervous courage, I tumbled the bulky bundles down the steps that led to the basement door and knocked gently. There was no answer. The angry noises inside continued, and I knocked again. Still no answer. Then I discovered a push button on the wall beside the door, jabbed at it hastily, and a bell pealed shrilly somewhere inside the house. At once the door was pulled open and a small young man in shirt sleeves, with a tight, dark, scowling face, shot his head out and glared at me.

"What the hella *you* want?" he demanded harshly.

"The—the tuxedos," I said awkwardly. "I brought the tuxedos." The young man turned his head and yelled at someone in the room behind him. "He brought the tuxedos! You hear that? He brought the tuxedos!"

He laughed unpleasantly and a man's voice replied from inside the room, "Tell him he knows what he can do with them!"

The young man in front of me reached for the door and started to slam it shut. The thought that I might have to drag those two bundles back to Canal Street that night was enough to make me forget my fright. I braced my shoulder against the door and held it open.

"I have to leave these here," I said quickly. "I have to—I have to get the receipt signed."

The little dark face glared at me and the hand on the door drew back threateningly. "Aah," he started to say, and then stopped. "O. K., O. K., come on. Bring 'em in and beat it." He dragged the bundles in and the door swung shut behind me. As I began to fumble in my pocket for the receipt book, I stole a scared look at the scene in the room. It was a large, shabbily furnished living room, with a new radio in one corner, a huge potted rubber plant in another, and embroidered mottoes on the wall. A pretty, dark-haired girl in a white wedding gown was sitting at a table in the middle of the room. Five men, all in vests and shirt sleeves and all looking as if they must be brothers of the young man who had opened the door for me, were standing over her. One of the men held the girl and was twisting her arm behind her, and she was sobbing violently. A tiny old woman, with white hair in a knot at the back of her head and wearing a black alpaca apron, hovered on the outskirts of the group around the table, jabbering shrilly in Italian. The young man who had let me in joined his brothers. Nobody paid any attention to me.

"Come on," one of the men said, leaning over the girl. "What's his address? Give us that address!"

The girl shook her head and the man who was holding her arm gave it another twist. She screamed and dropped her head forward. Another man pushed his face down close to hers.

"Come on!" he yelled. "Give it to us. We're doing this for the family, ain't we? What's his address?"

The girl shook her head again; the little old lady chattered away. One of the brothers reached over and slapped the girl's face.

"Where was he when he called up?" he said. "Come on, tell us. We ain't gonna hurt him. We'll just murder the louse, that's all. Where was he?"

She didn't answer.

"Come on, you damn fool," the man who held her arm said. "Talk! You want him to go spreading it to the whole world he walked out on you an hour before the wedding?" He shook her angrily. "Where was he when he called up? Where does he live? We'll fix him so he won't talk. What's his address?"

The girl did not answer. He started to shake her again, then he saw me standing near the door. "Get that guy out of here," he said. The brother who had let me in came across the room in three steps and grabbed my shoulder. "Come on, kid," he said. "Beat it!"

I lifted my receipt book in front of his face. "The receipt," I said. "I must get my receipt signed. I can't leave the——"

He snatched the book from me and fumbled in his vest pocket for a pencil. He couldn't find one. I held my own out to him and he scribbled his name in my receipt book.

"O.K., kid," he said sharply. "Outside!" and he shoved the receipt book and pencil at me. I took them and started toward the door. Suddenly the little old lady grabbed my arm and pulled me back.

"What the hellsa matter?" the young man asked angrily.

She gestured violently toward me and poured a stream of Italian at him.

"All right, all right," he said, and reached into his pocket, pulled out a coin and tossed the tip to me. I caught it and turned toward the door again.

"Thanks," I said quickly. But before I could open the door the old lady was on me. She clawed at my hand until I opened it so she could see the coin. It was a quarter. She swung around to the young man and clutched his coat.

"What the hellsa matter now?" he cried. "I gave him the tip, didn't I?"

Again she started talking in Italian, pointing at the bundle of tuxedos and tapping off the boxes with her finger—one, two, three, four, five, six. She waved six fingers in his face and yelled at him. He bit his lip, dug into his pocket again, and slapped some more coins into my palm. At once the little old lady seized my hand again. Now there were two quarters, a dime, and a nickel in it. She counted them quickly, snatched up the nickel, and counted again. Sixty cents remained. Another glance at the tuxedos and another glance at the two quarters and dime in my hand. Six tuxedos. Sixty cents. She nodded sharply to herself. Now it was all right.

"Give us that address!" shouted one of the brothers. There was the sound of a slap and the girl screamed again. "Where was he when he called up?"

The little old lady pulled open the door, pushed me out roughly, and slammed it shut behind me.

The American Heritage Series

The Library of Liberal Arts